AN EGYPTIAN TALE: AMULETS OF PRINCESS AMUN-RA VOLUME 2

VERANICE BERRY

First edition
Edited by: Kristin Campbell & Pace Michele
Cover Artist: Mauricio Marquez
Formatter: eDesk Services

For Uncle Ray and Uncle Erick

CONTENTS

"Behold, I am bringing punishment upon Pharaoh and Egypt and HER GODS and her Kings, upon Pharaoh and those who trust him."

— - JEREMIAH 46:25

1

A TALE

The man has been traveling for many days. His home in the south was destroyed. He remembers he was working in the crop fields then fell into a slumber. A deep slumber. He does not know for how long. When he came to, he rushed home quickly and, to his relief, his family was there. But not his wife. His two sons and two daughters were awakening from the deep sleep. The village was in a state of mourning. It seems all the women and most of the daughters were missing. His wife usually took their daughters to the meetings in the mountains. He is grateful she did not this time.

The men searched, but there was no sign of the women. His heart is heavy. He cannot care for the children alone.

Afraid, he packed up his family and headed to Upper Egypt. He would seek sanctuary from the earth god, the pharaoh, and visit *Gnue*, the temple of the gods. He would pray for help and answers to his beloved wife's whereabouts.

They hike through the hot deserts, finding what they need near the Nile to keep them going. A cow will appear every so often to give milk to the children. The traveler is so thankful, for he knows Hathor, the patron of mothers, is blessing him.

He reaches Upper Egypt in one piece. The Asirians are gracious. There is also a new being in the area, but all the same, they treat him like family. They take him and the children in and help him find work immediately.

The traveler is astonished to find that Horus is no longer Pharaoh and that he has even missed the period of Isis' ruling.

How long was he asleep? Not only were there no gods walking with man, but there is also a human Pharaoh in power. The traveler is a humble man who loves his children more than anything, but there is something itching at him. A new emotion he has never felt before. And he lets it consume him.

2

ZARHMEL

Zarhmel stands on the south tower of the palace that overlooks the entrance grounds. The sun is setting, and the air has a chill to it, in more than one way.

Everything is a mess. His brother showed up, and his cursed army caused mayhem. Statues were knocked over and the royal's village had fires set.

He watches as his men whip the new beings to hurriedly clean the mess that was made. There are bodies being collected for the pyre built near the Nile. His most trusted vizier has not been found dead, nor alive. King Kadir is in the morgue, unconscious, knocked cold by his own son.

He hears a loud crash somewhere behind the palace. He assumes it is Izzi's statue. He commanded that it be pulled down immediately, having demanded right away for Izzi's ties to the kingdom to be erased. She is his enemy, which makes her the enemy of all Egypt.

His defenses weak, he barely has enough men to cover the front to prevent another intrusion. Therefore, he needs to send word to his surrounding villages for help.

With a final sweep over the grounds, he walks back inside,

heading straight to the east end and down a dark corridor. He goes through a trap door and emerges into a brilliantly lit chamber.

Nephthila sits on a stool, not looking up at Zarhmel from the piece of debris that she is painting on. There is a long silence. Neither wants to start.

Zarhmel walks around the room, taking note that he has never known his wife to paint. She has always tended to the earth.

"And the earth is shifting," she says.

Zarhmel turns to his queen, who still has not glanced at him. "You were dead in my arms. I watched you take your final breath. Izzi-Ra is something evil, and my brother is back to take the crown. Look at me!"

His menacing tone does not startle Nephthila. She simply continues to paint.

Zarhmel storms over to her and slaps the brush and paint from her hands, also pushing the slab of rock that she was painting on out of the way. It cracks in half. That is when he gazes down to see that she was panting herself and a baby covered in a blanket. He kneels before her, their eyes level with one another.

She can smell the heat rising from him, feel the anger boiling within him.

"Are you going to lock me down here forever, Pharaoh?"

"You were dead. Lifeless. Obissi was going to start the process, call Anubis to hold your *Ka* until the ritual. Then you wake up and ... What are you?"

She rubs his face, and he close his eyes, wooed by the delicate touch of his queen's hands. He snaps himself out of it and grabs her shoulders.

"Answer me now, Nephi." He never raised his voice at her before.

"I am not like Izzi-Ra. No being, human, or god is like Izzi-Ra. But you have always known, Zarhmel. You have always feared her, felt her strength, her power, which is truly the only power you have ever witnessed. True, she is not your child, because we did not affaire at that time. She is not Drahzil's, either, if that is what you think."

"Tell me everything *now*," he demands.

4

Nephthila closes her eyes and groans a little. Then she sighs and glares at Zarhmel sternly in the face. "I will tell you when the night eats away at the moon, with the ultimate symbol in the sky. It will be time. But, for now, My Pharaoh, what are you to do with me?" She pulls his grip from her shoulders and stands.

He felt the strength in her little arm and flinches. What is she?

"My maids and I will return to my chamber above. You have more pressing matters this hour to attend to."

He is about to remind her that she is not going anywhere when a horn sounds in the distance.

"Do not leave this room. Your pharaoh commands you," he says sternly.

"I will be where I want to be—with my maidens. No one knows I was wounded last night except you and your priest." She brushes past him and leaves the room.

Zarhmel fumes, but he cannot deal with his queen now. The security horn is sounding, which means there is trouble.

As Zarhmel reaches the grounds, his best men rush to his side.

"Pharaoh, the intruders are back. We do not have the manpower to take them," a guard says. He is young, his locks hanging loosely around his round face, and he has a bandaged arm. All the men appear fearful.

Zarhmel reaches the gates, seeing a ball of fire flying overhead and flames on the path, heading toward him. He pulls his pole, his men following his lead.

"Put that away, brother. We are not here to fight."

Zarhmel turns around toward the voice that spoke behind him and his men. He becomes angry that his men did not hear Drahzil behind them. He could have killed them all!

The men around Zarhmel begin to recognize Drahzil. A couple want to kneel before their rightful pharaoh, yet Zarhmel gives them a menacing expression.

"We are not here to fight. We mussst build an alliance."

The guard with the bandaged arm steps forward. "Drahzil? Is that you? Is it really you?"

"Little brother ... Etepp," Eban says, stepping from behind Drahzil.

The guard, Etepp, backs up as he takes in Eban's features, confusion, disbelief, and recognition setting in. Then Etepp rushes into Eban's arms, the two embracing.

Drahzil smiles. "I am here to bring honor back into Asir, to reunite families."

Zarhmel swells with anxiety. Drahzil should not have shown himself. His men stare, wondering what happened to him, how is he still alive, and this may complicate things since he is the rightful pharaoh.

"Open the gatesss, Zarhmel," Drahzil tells him. "I have a surprise for you."

Thoughts and actions quickly race about Zarhmel's mind, but one shuts down the other. They do not have the manpower, and it looks like some of his men will now even switch sides. He must remain in control.

He signals for his men in the tower to open the golden gates, and the fiery camels and creatures come inside.

"Ssstand aside, brother."

Zarhmel and his men move aside as the riders pass, and then people, all huddled together, are forced through the gate. Women, children, boys, men herded inside by the creatures.

Zarhmel grabs a tall, muscled male and pulls him toward him. "Who are you?" he demands.

The boy stands tall and proud, no fear on his face. "My name is Annut Kuja. I am a warrior from the Pakhet tribe."

Zarhmel almost chokes. He watches the people milling in then glances back to the boy who is astonishingly not afraid.

"You captured the Pakhet tribe?"

Drahzil is about to answer when Annut cuts him off. "They did not fight us like men." Annut looks Drahzil up and down. "Guess he really isn't a man, though, is he?"

Drahzil starts toward Annut, but Zarhmel holds up his hand to stop him.

"Did you know a woman in the village by the name of Adallah?"

Annut snorts. "The pretty lady with the scrawny nephew she had to raise."

Drahzil and Zarhmel exchange looks. Drahzil wants to kill him, but Zarhmel sees this as an opportunity. Besides, he likes the boy.

"Yujihme, take this boy to the north end. Do not let him out of your sight."

A guard takes Annut by the arm and leads him away.

Zarhmel steps out of listening range, Drahzil reluctantly following.

"You and your men will not stay on the palace grounds. You will consult with me on everything."

"Oh, no royal women?"

"You will not touch my people. The new beings are fair game. Do not harm them too much. They need to work. You wounded my queen. You will stay away from her."

Drahzil smiles at Zarhmel, revealing those nasty, yellow teeth. "So Nephi lives and is unharmed. You keep her out of my way. And your daughter?"

Zarhmel chooses his words wisely, not trusting his brother with information. "We cannot just go attacking her without a plan. We need to understand what she is and what she possesses. Anyone who was closely associated with her will be rounded up and questioned."

"I saw them both today. Fought the boy. They have goddesses at their call. I saw Isis, Hathor, and your goddesses with them. Your daughter has an amulet—Khepri's beetle. Adallah was at her side. The children took down Anubis. They have power beyond anything we imagined," Drahzil finishes.

Zarhmel tries to make no expression, not wanting his thoughts to betray him, especially the fact that their sisters are alive. At least one of them.

He always loved his sisters. They had a good relationship. He does not understand why his sisters are involved. However, his sister has the boy and Izzi's trust. He must get to her.

Izzi-Ra is ... and then his queen ...

Drahzil knows more about Nephi than him. That was his queen first.

He is about to express his concerns, but then he decides to ask something else.

"These amulets ... that is our common goal?"

They stare each other right in the eyes, neither one trusting the other. Both want this power for themselves.

"For now, yesss."

Zarhmel turns, walking back to his palace, his mind racing, and then he turns to his brother, who is watching him go. "You tried to kill me last night, and all my people. Why have you changed your mind now?"

Drahzil sucks in a deep breath. "I have my reasonsss for needing your help, just as you have yoursss for letting us in."

Drahzil is about to say more when they hear a noise behind some brush. Zarhmel draws his pole, and Drahzil ignites a ball in his hands. They round the bush, ready to attack, when they see a man crumpled in a heap.

"You should be dead!" Drahzil exclaims to the man he had dragged to the Underworld and left there for dead.

"Jabari, are you okay?" Zarhmel bends down next to the man, checking his pulse. There is a shallow heartbeat.

Zarhmel lifts the man over his shoulders, telling his brother, "I must get him help. We will talk later. And stay out of trouble, please." Zarhmel slouches away, carrying the man and leaving his brother to ponder his next plans that no doubt will cause trouble.

Anubis let the man live for a reason, and it is not in the advantage of Drahzil.

3

THE GODS

I sis is in her time and space. She sits in a garden, with the *ka* of the Nile flowing before her. The trees are fruitful, the grass is a green that the earth will never see, the moon and the sun are both in the distance together, and the sky is the perfect peach. Glowing golden butterflies flutter around her. She picks one randomly and puts it into the Nile. It burns bright then disappears.

"I always found your way of answering prayers very interesting," comes from behind her.

She does not bother to look. She simply plucks another golden butterfly and puts it in the Nile.

The gods have many ways of answering their followers' prayers. Isis uses butterflies. Every time someone specifically prays to her, a butterfly appears right in this garden. She grants the wish, and the person will find their answer near the Nile as a butterfly will flutter past them on earth. Her humans never have to worry, because they know the Nile will provide, and they know their goddess will answer.

"Amun-Re, the great Egi god. The creation god of men and women. You have jeopardized us all," she says as she stands to face him.

He does not appear moved or remorseful.

Mankind began to destroy the beautiful land and life that he gave them before he created the amulets.

"Why did you create them?" she asks.

"Come here, child." Re's expressions and emotions are nowhere to be found on his face.

Isis remains where she is, not sure if she should.

"You want to know. It is time you knew the whole story. But remember, we all walked the earth as humans, and we have retained those personalities and qualities. Tell the truth to those you must."

She thinks for a few moments, deciding she cannot wait any longer. Then Isis runs right into Amun-Re's body, and they swallow one another in a burst of golden light and disappear.

Through the thick grass, down a gold-lit corridor, and into a dimly lit chamber, other gods and goddesses stand at a long table, discussing the events that occurred at the mountain.

Amun-Re glides into the room and goes straight for Meretseger, who stands. Re gently grabs her hands, caressing them in his. No emotion on either face, but within them both are two souls embracing and becoming one again, sharing one another.

Hathor glances around. "Where is Isis?"

"She is where she is," Re responds, eyes still for Meretseger.

Thoth cocks his head at the god, pulling at the gods' sources, as he has the power to do so. No one notices, of course, because they are all preoccupied with the news of earth children with great light.

Montu's and Anubis's chairs have been placed in the corner with Osiris's chair.

"They are a threat to our existence." Wadjet bangs a fist on the table, talking directly to Amun-Re. Her sister is at her side, awaiting an answer.

"Meretseger, good to have you back. I am sorry there was nothing I could do," Amun says to her finally.

Meretseger nods in understanding.

"They wounded Anpu! They can hurt us," Sekret's response is full of fire.

The gods are in disarray.

Meretseger and Amun turn to face the group.

"We should talk in private," Amun tells Thoth before he waves his hand, and the room turns upside down. The chattering from others is now silenced.

He gazes down into the table to see below him. On the other side, Nekhbet and Wadjet are still yelling at him, while Thoth stands quietly. Then Re glances up, in the space he is in, and sees Maat, Thoth, Meretseger, Shu, and Hathor in their chairs. On the other side of the table, the five gods attempt to calm the others.

"Much better. Maat, good to see you," he says.

The goddess nods to him. Her skin is like the night's sky, with actual twinkling stars down her arms. She has a single feather upright from her crown and two long braids that hang past her shoulders. She wears a one strap, blue silk dress. Maat wears no makeup. In fact, she looks sort of simple today, but they all know that is for now. Maat can be dramatic in her appearances.

"What has happened? I was stuck in my mountain for countless Ahkets. I have a human girl who I am to believe is at fault, and another human girl with light who saved me. Pure, golden light. She is not tethered, not a deity, and a boy with *clou*," Meretseger says to the small council.

"Hathor." Amun nods.

The disk between Hathor's horns begins to spin. She pulls it from her head and lets it float to the center of the table. The others on the other side of the table disappear to not distract from the disk. It spins and expands, and then they see the amulets.

Meretseger leans in to see them better. "That was in my mountain. Only the child seemed to be able to touch it. It burned Isis. Why?" she asks the room.

"The amulets are of the blood and flesh of Amun in his human form. He created them. They are somehow connected to the existence of the children. The men on the Venji were cursed by the amulets. He and his army can only break the curse if he gains possession of them, or so that is what the human believes," Hathor tells her.

"Thoth, make sense of this for me." Meretseger turns to the god.

A book is to the side of him, hieroglyphics being etched on the pages in gold ink. The book closes, and Thoth waves it into nonexistence.

"I have always known the boy was not a deity or tethered. His light is pure purple. Only one god has that kind of light. We know what the children are. There is no doubt about it. The question is: what path will you all take? It has already been recorded. I cannot change the true outcome, but there are many ways to get there," Thoth tells the room.

Maat nods in agreement.

"Why!" Meretseger roars, upset and for good reason, considering she was trapped in a mountain with over five hundred slain women and children for many moons.

"Come to me, my love; let me show you rather than tell," Amun says to her.

Thoth nods to her, and Maat shrugs.

Meretseger pulsates green with flecks of golden light around her. Her snakes come from her neck, and her head shrinks. One snake absorbs her entire body then coils around the other snake. The lonesome snake then slithers quickly to Amun, up his leg and around his middle, squeezing him.

"Hathor, go to her; see what she knows and where the others are. Maat, go to the Underworld, to your other kingdom. We will need eyes on Anubis and Montu. I have a feeling Osiris will rise soon and take his rightful place. Shu, you know what to do. Make sure she is there and that they do not release her," Amun orders, his midsection becoming tighter from the snake.

"You want me to go see her?" Shu asks with a hint of fear.

"You are the only god who can go without setting off the goddess and her people," Amun tells him.

There is a break, and Amun falls into nothing but a heap of robes.

"Not to fear, Shu. I will accompany you to Murku Isle, but I will be ahead of you in time," Thoth tells Shu.

"What is it you are not telling us Thoth?" Maat asks the god as a golden beam of light shoots down around him.

"All will choose a separate path, but no matter what the journey may be on those endeavors, we are set to meet at the completion as one." He disappears.

4

IZZI-RA

We ride on the outskirts of the desert heading west. These camels seem to not need water or ever get tired. They are swift in the sand and comfortable to ride.

We spot a small valley and stay to the outskirts, not sure if there is a nearby village or not. Neenho goes up in his *clou* and checks out the area. He gives us the all-clear, and then we make camp.

According to Chike, we cannot just walk into her home village. We need to hike up the mountain and scouts will see us coming.

I sit off under a tree alone. I do not want to talk, too tired. The mountain was the scariest place I have ever gone. What a birthday.

Chike and Adallah cook over a fire. Assim took down a wild animal, getting meat for us. The twins were able to get water from a stream, as there is no leg of the Nile here. I see Kade sitting alone in the distance. He has not really said too much since we left the disastrous mountain. I guess I will try to be nice.

I walk over and sit with him. "Are you thanking the gods for the blissful marriage we are enjoying?"

He gazes at me, right in my face.

I did not laugh or smile. I was not making a joke.

"Want to talk?" I watch every emotion cross his face.

He moves his mouth, but nothing comes out. Then he closes his eyes and just takes deep breaths.

"I do not have answers for you Kade. I am sorry. I never wanted to marry you and drag you into anything. I did not know this would be my life today. Your father, I am sorry you had to fight him."

"I did not have to fight him. I *chose* to defend you. All in an instant ... We have the best ... I did not even think. He did not think. We took our weapons to one another." Kade bows his head and sniffles. His tears fall slowly, splashing onto the dead leaves under him. I watch as a tear rolls off the leaf and into the dirt, sucked into the soil.

I stare at him, his bowed head, and I want to comfort him. I want to ...

Then I think of my father and how I wanted to kill him. How my mother is now dead, and I have no time to mourn what is now a gaping hole. I cannot comfort him when I cannot make myself feel better.

"I organized a beautiful outing for you to take place today ... for your birthday. It was going to be a special day. More pampering than you get on a regular basis. And then we would ride to Shiza, where the seamstress would make you all new clothing. Whatever colors you liked." He laughs, picking at the ground.

I am at a loss for words, imagining my birthday today. How my mother would have had a breakfast prepared out in the gardens, like every birthday. How Beni and Jita would have been there to wake me and tease me about my new husband. How him surprising me would have made me blush, and I would have made sure Heleka saw it all.

My entire world has changed, and I cannot stop it.

I caused Kade all the pain he feels now. And, as much as I want to be selfish, I cannot. So, I take his hand, holding one of his large, soft hands in mine. Then I lean back against the tree and close my eyes. We sit there for I do not even know how long, and I keep my eyes shut, not allowing a tear to escape.

Without looking, I know Assim is watching me.

5

NEENHOKANO

Adallah is mixing some smelly stuff in a small, dirt bowl that she quickly made. She spits in it and jabs her finger to add blood. The twins and I watch her intensely. We need answers as to what is going on with us, and after the mountain, Adallah has reached the end of her patience. She says conjuring memories is a complex ritual that she will have to pay a price for. At this point, if it's not her life, we will pay whatever for answers.

Izzi and Kade refuse to eat. They have been sitting in silence for a while. Just sitting. And holding hands. I want to throw a ball of light at him, but that would probably make Izzi mad, so I will let him be. I should let him be. He fought so bravely today. He is pretty good with a weapon. Who am I kidding? The guy has skill with a knopesh. I have never used one before.

I think of how he had my back on that mound today, him and Assim. I guess I should lay off, but it's kind of hard when I have eyes for the princess, as well.

"Almost ready. Princess, please join us for this. I may need you and Neenho to make it work," Adallah says.

I watch Assim as he watches Izzi walk over. She is still gripping

Kade's hand tightly. Assim sighs as the two plop down on a log near the fire. We meet eyes for a moment, and then I look elsewhere.

Somebody is super jealous, I think.

Bastet jumps on Adallah's shoulder, and Izzi frowns at the cat. Finally! Someone else who doesn't look at the cat as if she's cute. She's weird! Where does she keep coming from?

Izzi continues to stare Bastet in her bright, golden eyes. Then she shifts to Chike's twins, who sit between their mother. They lay on her, and she hugs them both tightly. They could have died today, I think to myself.

"Whose memories are these?" Izzi asks Adallah.

"Mine, Neenho's, Adiah's. I pulled what I can from those I am closest to. Something from Drahzil and Zarhmel too, and what I can get from Nephthila."

Izzi tenses at her mother's name, but Adallah moves on before those feelings set into the air.

"Heki tu'br ayt cuso. Ashat he'y anapuaj," Adallah whispers, and then she glows a bright white. Her light is beautiful. I feel connected to it. She throws the entire bowl into the fire, and the flames completely disappear. Silver wisps appear, becoming a huge circle. I can see something moving inside. I inch closer, my face almost in it. I see moving images in the silver circle, and then I see people.

"Father was the first human pharaoh—Pharaoh Urbani. Drahzil was three, Adiah and I were one cycle of Shemu, and Zarhmel was a newborn. With no gods actively walking the earth, the Egyptians did not know how they were going to erect monuments, grow food, and be prosperous without their makers."

We watch the pharaoh—a short, plump man with an unlikable face—consult with priests and engage in prayer. The scene then switches to a meadow full of people heading toward the palace.

"It seemed the gods answered Pharaoh's prayer. A new race of people came to seek refuge in our land from theirs. They were very strong and very skilled in all manner of labor and the arts. Deities would appear, and with their light *He'ka* from the gods, Egypt was back on track to becoming a grand world," Adallah tells us all.

We watch everyone work in harmony, the gods blessings on all. This is a lie. It feels wrong. I think. I chance a glance at Izzi, and she slightly nods. She agrees.

"But then, Father became prejudice and greedy. The new beings, we called them, Father would not pay them. He made them live on the outside of Asir's gates where the Nile ran dry and the flood waters hit the hardest. The Egyptians received all the good jobs and better homes. Then there was a divide. That part is true, I think.

"Father claimed Amun-Ra came to him and said the new beings were a gift to him, to work for the pure blood of the land. There was a fight. A woman, who was their leader, got some of her people out of our lands, but the rest were trapped."

We watch as he enslaves them. Some of the Egyptians were all for this, and others parted ways with the palace and formed their own villages.

"Then Father fell ill. Deathly ill. No one knows what really happened to cause this. Then the worst thing to ever happened came about. Sekhmet was set loose on all of Egypt. She went from village to village. Not one part of the earth was left without blood on its grass and sands. Father prepared his people, but none were a match for the savage goddess. She killed Father and our new mother, Silia."

We watch as the lioness pounds through the earth, ripping her teeth into anything that she crosses—women, men, children, animals, everything that breathed.

"Drahzil was crowned at the morning sun at thirteen years of age. Zarhmel became the prince at ten. I and Adiah were named the princesses. We were eleven. Drahzil, believe it or not, ruled with a warm heart. He did not believe in this slavery term and wanted to move the new beings into the better villages and pay them. Zarhmel, on the other hand, did not agree.

"I did not care about the politics of our world. I was the princess. I had no worries. Adiah, like Drahzil, was troubled. She spent all her time in the temple of Arc'ale, Isis's temple."

We watch as the images change from her family to a grand party.

"I was twelve years old when there was a feast thrown for Drahzil, to honor his first pyramid completion and his marriage. I cannot tell you the full story, because it confuses me. I need Adiah to make sense of it. But the queen was having an affair with Zarhmel."

I don't glance at Izzi. Refusing to look her way, I stare hard into the flames.

Izzi lets out an involuntary gasp at the sight of the girl who we watch in red, dancing with Drahzil then sneaking off with Zarhmel. All harmless stuff as they sit and hold hands in the garden.

"From this night, everything changed somehow. My brothers and sister were acting strange, like a secret was towering over them all. In the midst of all the celebrations, Adiah came to me. She told me something terrible would happen soon, to her, to our family, and Isis chose us to help. She talked in riddles, and I wanted nothing to do with it. She told me that Isis wanted to tether us. I did not know what that meant. I went with her one night to the temple, and Isis, the goddess in human form, was there."

The scene is disfigured. We can't see what is happening in the temple.

"Isis told us many things to come. Our mission as her earth hands, eyes, and ears was to secure the amulets and keep them safe. I refused."

Three jeweled pieces appear in the orb. The beetle a bright green, the Wadjet eye in red, and the life ankh in purple. When fused together, they glow gold.

"Isis said they were made of the blood and flesh of Amun-Ra himself. The gods could not find them, so she needed us to. I wanted no part in this. I just wanted to be a princess.

"On our way out, Drahzil confronted us; said he heard everything. He wanted the amulets. He and Adiah had words. She accused him of being like a reptile; said he hid around corners like a lizard in disguise. He threatened to have her punished before Asir."

I hang onto every word Adallah says.

"I stayed away from my sister after that. Some Ahket's went by, and Drahzil seemed normal, and then ... Drahzil disappeared. His chambers were soaked in blood, and half of his army was gone.

Zarhmel was crowned and took the queen as his. No one understood how, but in only a few short days, the queen was pregnant. And even wilder, she gave birth in her garden as the sun rose. Adiah and I were there. We ran for help, and when we came back, the baby was not there. And this is where I am lost."

We all lean in and see an isle, water, red eyes, a sarcophagus, and we hear a woman screaming. We see Adiah pick up a baby. We see a desert and the glass pyramid.

I let out a gasp. The glass pyramid … it's real!

"Speculations spread far. Whose child was it? And Adiah disappeared. Only I seemed to realize she was gone. When she returned, she was a different person, with light. I had no choice but to fall in line. But what was scarier was that Adiah was in possession of the amulets and two babies. I never asked how.

"She asked me to help her protect the children. The queen had told people that the baby could not be seen yet. Truthfully, she had no idea where her child was."

The palace comes into view. It's under attack. Fire is everywhere as we watch Drahzil and his men. But they do not linger at the palace. They head east.

"I got out and ran to the hideaway home that Adiah and I established in the new Pakhet tribe. I got there and waited … and waited. Then I saw it—two bright stars in the sky, one above me and one near the palace."

In the orb, we see Adallah drop to her knees.

"I knew then Adiah was not coming." Adallah watches herself cry in the orb as tears fall now. The Adallah in the orb does not see the man approaching her.

"Thoth. He had a child in his arms. I knew what it all meant and what I had to do."

We watch as the man helps Adallah to her feet. Then, together, they enter the house, a purple hue encasing the home, and then the entire orb dissolves. The bowl melts away, and the orange flames are back.

6

IZZI-RA

No one is breathing that I can hear. That story was hard to hear, and it must have been hard to tell. It was definitely hard to see, and I saw everything in Adallah's mind. I saw the crisp clear vision in her mind, not what was in the flames.

My mother consorted ... the new beings ...

"Where did the second child come from?"

There, if there was any air, I just sucked the rest of it out of the circle. No one even flexes a muscle.

I catch Adallah's eye as she shrugs. "No one knows but the queen and Adiah."

"And these amulets?" I pull the one I have out and let it fall on top of my dress.

"Adiah never told me everything. The ankh piece is filled with his blood. The beetle is said to be his flesh. And the eye, his human eye. The possessor of the amulets will have power beyond Ra."

"And Neenho and I? Where do we come into the picture? Why do we have light?"

"That, I cannot answer, Izzi. That, I never knew the answer to. I thought this memory would show me something I missed. Thoth may know all, but he only knows what a collective knows, and then the future is revealed to him in many ways and many forms," Adallah tells me with sadness in her eyes ... for me.

I nod. I am used to being the art piece in the room that everyone regards, but right now ...

I get up and walk away.

"Let her be," Assim tells, I assume, Kade.

I find a hidden area under a tree and flop down. My head is spinning. My mother. Drahzil, Zarhmel. If I am her child, Lizard Man could be my father. Zarhmel could be my father, too. But they all said they never had an affair. So, who is my father?

Neenho's face and my father's face swim around in my head then fuse together. And his smile is like the rising sun. When Neenho smiles, he makes everyone around him want to smile. He brings calm, just like my mother. Neenho could be the queen's son.

I have always felt alone. I have always felt like I did not belong. I have always felt like things never added up.

I let myself be a thirteen-year-old girl. A thirteen-year-old girl on her birthday, whose mother is dead. I have no mother. I have no father. Neenho has no mother, and he has no father, even if it is them.

I lay there and let myself cry. I cry until I fall asleep.

The drying leaves on my face become soft grass. A hand is caressing my face and smoothes my hair out. I hear the faint flow of the Nile and smell the scent of flowers around me.

"Happy birthday, *saat*," my mother says.

I sit up, finding myself in her garden. I turn to her, and there she is. Her hair has grown a considerable amount, as it usually does. Her curly, stiff hair is fluffed out around the small, gold crown she wears. She is in a white dress, like mine. She looks beautiful. She always looks beautiful.

"I went to the Underworld and back today. I barely ate, and I cried myself to sleep. Naturally, I dream of you, Mother." I have no energy in me to cry anymore. I know this is a dream.

"You are here with me right now, *saat*. I know you have had a rough day. And I am sorry for that. But I am glad you made it. I waited and waited, and I said she will come. Because every year, since she was two on her birthday, we sit in the garden, and we have honey-soaked bread. Extra honey-soaked, that is."

She pulls a circular honey-soaked, date bread into view. I always have a giant honey bread on my birthday that everyone enjoys. But it is always so over the top. I like honey. Mother said, on my second birthday, she snuck us out here, and we sat and ate our own. And every year since I can remember, we meet here when everyone else is in bed, and we eat honey-soaked bread, and we talk. My subconscious knows this and brought me here, where I want to be.

Mother shakes her head. "No matter what I tell you, you will believe your brain is creating this for you. You are the most powerful goddess, Izzi-Ra, and for that reason, you are in danger. You can shed the power if you put it back in the amulets. But if you possess the amulets and your light, the gods cannot stop you. They will try to destroy my child."

"Am I? Am I your child?"

"In every way possible, *saat*. In more than one way," she says, tears swelling in her eyes.

"I will never know the truth now, because you are dead, and I am so sorry for that, Mother. I am so sorry I let that happen." I move into her arms and let her cradle me. This feels so real. Her smell, her beating heart, the warmth of her skin, the way she breathes on me, it is all too real. I hate this dream so much because I never want to wake up.

"I am not dead, *saat*. I am very much alive in the palace. I cannot die that easily. I am home, waiting for you to come back."

I sit there stiffly. This is a dream. It has to be. I am someplace else. I cannot be here and there and not know that I came here. That is impossible, right? She feels real, though. She feels so real.

I perk my ears and hear the Nile. I hear the guards at the gate. I can even hear the horses in the stables.

"After everything you witnessed today, you question the power of astral travel, *saat*? I tell you, child, you are something else." My mother's laughter rings out, and it makes me smile. This has to be a joke.

"Astral?" I ask.

She smiles and nods. She is about to explain something when ...

"My Queen, are you out there?" My father's voice carries across the Nile and through the gardens.

We both freeze. Is this real? This is real?

"*Saat*, this is not a dream; this *is* real. Very real. You must get to the Isle of Murku. Get what she has, but *saat*, you must leave her trapped. She is very dangerous. Do *not* release her. Drahzil is a threat, but the gods are not your allies, either, my child. I will tell you ... I will let you come onto me and see everything. You and NeenhoKano must trust one another *always*. Do you understand? You will know when it is time to come for me."

"You know Neenho?"

Mother nods sadly.

I want to say something, to ask her a thousand questions, but I cannot form any words as I feel dried leaves on my face and the warmth of a fire. I am waking up. *No!*

"Mother, I need you. I am so scared. I do not want to do anything anymore. I want to go to Shiza and be a wife. Mother, what is happening to me?"

She holds me tightly. I do not want her to let go, but she does. She takes the bread, breaks a piece off, and eats it. Then she nods for me to do the same.

I grab a small piece, with a shaky hand, and reluctantly have some, but I am glad I did. It tastes so good. The bread is so moist. This treat is the best ever.

"Happy birthday, *saat*," my mother says again.

I put the other piece in my mouth and smile at my mother. Then I hear drumming.

Mother studies me, and I study her, because the sound is coming from her. The drumming is in her chest. I lean in until my ear is touching her chest, and there it is. I fall into her, and she falls backward.

I roll over to help her, but she is not there. I am back in the valley. Someone has moved on a rough patch of leaves near the fire.

"Princess, are you okay?" Assim is there, sitting up against a log, no doubt watching me sleep.

I crawl over next to him and lay my head on his shoulder.

He stiffens. I do not think I have ever touched him in any kind of way before.

"I am not okay," I answer him. I lick my lips, and my eyes widen. The taste of honey just exploded in my mouth. I must be dreaming. This is not real.

I close my eyes and snuggle as close as I can to him, putting the dream out of my mind. My final thoughts as I fall back to sleep is, *He smells like Neenho, and his chest feels like the clou.*

7

NEENHOKANO

The fire crackles near me as I lay on the ground and stare up at the stars. Just for a moment, I pretend that I'm home, on the roof top. I close my eyes and take a deep breath, trying to remember the smell of my village. The farm outside of our villas usually sends the sweet smell of figs and pomegranates my way.

I shiver a little, not sure if my thoughts gave me the chills or because of the changing weather.

Ahket is over. We are heading into Pèret season, the season of cooler air, dead leaves, and the games that probably won't be played now, because of me. That kind of tickles me. I think of stupid Annut hearing that the games have been canceled because Neenho is a powerful something and someone who resembles a reptile wants to kill him.

I open my eyes and continue to stare at the array of stars, still pretending that Adallah and her damn cat is below me in our home, fast asleep on the rug in front of the fire. Maybe I can sneak off and go have a run with Ishiva? I smile at the thought. Not only can I outrun her, but I can also probably trap her with my light now. I grin bigger, but then my smile fades, thinking of Ishiva, with the body of the girl that man thing killed. Because of me. I wonder if the village is okay.

I can't wait to show them all that I am someone. I'm practically saving them. Annut and his smug bandit of buffoons will have to kiss my feet. I giggle to myself. I think I'll even slap him around a little with my light. Yeah, just a little slap here and there.

I laugh aloud at this then cover my mouth so as to not wake those around me. I glance around to make sure I didn't disturb anyone and see the flames are dying. I wave my hand, and they resume to a nice, big glow. I feel the heat from the flames and scoot back some.

As I lay back down, my thoughts shift again as I notice I also feel warmth growing inside me. The power.

It's growing. I can't explain how I know, but it stirs within.

"Almost like a snake trying to break its way free."

I jump at her voice, and a small scream escapes my lips.

She sits up and peeks around at the sleeping guard. Then she stands and walks toward the trees in a shadowy area. I follow.

"Call your *clou*," Izzi demands.

I glance up into the sky and hear the melody come from my lips. A small wisp of air forms before us.

Izzi gets on then lies down. "Take me up, Neenho."

I get on, and then we soar up a little, just shy of the trees.

Izzi lies flat on her back and puts her hands behind her head. "This is how you look at stars, young male."

I glare at her. "Is anything I think private?"

"Well, young male, you do not shield yourself. You are wide open. To me, anyway. And your thoughts are really loud. Woke me right up."

"You were never asleep," I shoot back. "So, what are your thoughts, anyway?" I ask. "Bet they are more serious than mine."

She laughs. "I wish, Neenho. I wish I could have gone through the last two days and still think about normal stuff. I tried to pretend I was in my bed at home, in the palace, but ..."

I decide to lay next to her and study the stars again. "I've decided we are in a very, very long dream," I tell her.

The laughter that comes from her now is more carefree than the stiff one from before. "Neenho, this is a horrible dream! That mountain, I have never been so fearful in my life. I prayed to wake up so many times." She laughs again.

"Not being able to feel you was the scariest part. Not knowing what happened to you kept the three of us out there, fighting." I don't even feel embarrassed saying it. Well, maybe a little. But it's the truth.

I shake my head, feeling a little lightheaded, almost in a dream-like state.

Izzi is hugging me in my mind. That's new. She allows me to feel her full emotions and hear all her thoughts right now, and she is so grateful for what I just said.

I smile. *Points to me, none to them*, I say to myself then regret it, knowing she heard me.

She giggles again. I love that laugh. It's so beautiful and full of her light. I lighten up and laugh, too. *Oh well, I like you*, I allow myself to think. Who doesn't like the princess?

"Pharaoh does not. He does not love me. I am so confused, Neenho. There is so much we do not know. Did you see the look on the goddesses' faces? They looked as if they feared us." She burns the image bright in my mind.

"Um ... Izzi?"

"Neenho, not now, not that," she says, shutting the inflow of emotions off from me.

"I've grown up thinking my father was killed building a temple, and now ... She is your mother, Izzi, no matter what. Just like Adallah is my aunt, no matter what. They raised us."

Izzi sighs. "Today was a nightmare, Neenho, and it just gets deeper. And we went somewhere today. Remember the crown room? The woman on fire in the water!" She sits up suddenly.

"Izzi, there was no woman on fire in water?" I try to remember, but I didn't see that. I saw red eyes I think.

"I know that art. My mother has a picture of her there on that island. Neenho, that temple with the crowns. That is Hauhet Khames. That temple sits above the palace. We must go there. There are answers there!" There is excitement burning in her eyes.

I crinkle my nose. *Another adventure that could cause us death*, I think.

Yes, she thinks back to me.

I look away from her beautifully determined face.

"Hey Mister I'm-Gonna-Go-Slap-Around-Mean-Boys-In-My-Village, do you not want to find out what is happening to us? The answers are at that temple. Maybe we can even contact Osiris, the ruler of the Underworld and find my mother. Maybe I can bring her back."

"Maybe I can find my parents, too," I say, not really caring. I don't want to go there.

"Neenho, have you thought maybe we are related? Maybe she had us both?"

"I have, but it doesn't feel like we came from the same mother." I can tell she agrees. It feels true. I know that I know Izzi. I feel that connection, but I do not feel like she is my sister. "Well, Osiris married his sister," I joke.

"We are not gods, Neenho."

"No, we are much more."

She smirks then lies back down and surprises me by snuggling against me.

"You are so small, NeenhoKano."

"For now, Izzi-Ra."

"Happy birthday, Neenho," she whispers.

"The happiest to you, as well, Princess," I whisper back.

We lay there together, thoughts running wild and intertwining. We drift off into sleep.

I see Izzi in a garden with the queen, eating sweet bread . Then I see Izzi around the fire with Assim, but I feel her here with me.

My head fills with chaos as the end of our birthdays and the season comes to an end.

8

DRAHZIL

Drahzil is at the top of the palace on the west guard's tower. He has the perfect view of Asir from where he stands. To the north, the battlegrounds and the best view of Hauhet Khames. The east has the gardens and the Nile flowing around the kingdom and right through it before it gets back on track and heads north. The south has the entrance gates, and the royal villas and the market farther away. He can see farther west, where the new beings live, and the latest worksite. There are time obelisks in every area, and one big one up here.

This guards tower is his favorite spot. As a boy, he would spend so much time here with the guards during his father's reign. At eight, he started training as a man of the watch tower. Unlike his brother, Drahzil made it a point to train everywhere, from tower to kitchen. Drahzil would even visit the new beings' villas. He knew them. He knew what they needed to do the work that they were gifted to do. They liked him. But now ... well, things change.

In the far distant south, he sees what appears to be a fire, where his army decided to take up camp. They are off the grounds and surrounding the palace. If the children come back, he will be ready.

And if his brother tries to turn on him, well, he will be ready for that as well.

He scrutinizes the grounds, the remaining new beings who are finishing the end of their day. He clucks his tongue. His brother really is following in their father's footsteps. Drahzil did not rule this way. He paid his workers. Egyptians and Nubians—what they call themselves—alike worked side by side, with the aid of deities to build. That was how Horus had done it, and just as Osiris had started.

He shakes his head, wielding his new *He'ka* to clear him of the haze that just clouded him. What is he thinking? Why is he thinking this way? He felt his old humanity for a second.

A soft wind passes, and he stiffens as her scent hits him.

"She ruled by your side. She was always at your side. She loved night watches on this tower with you," she says.

He does not turn to her. "She will rule again, and you will take her place," he says through clenching teeth.

"When will you accept that she is I, and she cannot be changed?" She is close, at his ear.

He feels agitated, flexing his muscles, trying to calm his nerves. He cracks his neck then rolls his shoulders, trying to not let her voice cloud his mind.

"Is this a permissible conversation? I warned my gullible brother that I would not hurt you ... for now. Be gone, Nephthila. Now."

She steps next to him and looks out over the grounds. The torches are being lit as Ra has ended the day with a blanket of stars.

Drahzil closes his eyes, not wanting to see her. The smell alone makes him want to burst in flames as that honey scent wafts his way, making him shudder within.

"I need your help, Drahzil." She sighs. He refuses to open his eyes as she continues, "I need you to tell me who was the robed man you were talking to? The night of the party, the night everything changed."

"What are you going on about?" He faces her then steps back as if he has just been hit in the gut.

She stands before him, dressed in her white, fitted gown, gold bangles around her neck, arms, and ankles. Her crown is tall on her head. She gazes at him with pleading, brown eyes.

"Drahzil, the man you were talking with at your birth year festival. Who was that?"

He wants to yell, but he takes a moment to play this game. *A man?* He does not remember a man at the festival.

Without notice, Nephthila puts her hands on his head. He cannot control anything as there is a whooshing sound, and then they are in a haze. He notices they are in his mind, in the past. Nephi is searching and comes to what she is looking for.

He tries to use his light, but she is stronger.

They are in the grand hall. People are milling about, having a good time. He sees his brother, so small, so young and lonely, standing off in a corner. If he did not know any better, Zarhmel looks like the boy! The way his locks fall around his small face, those wide eyes, and that scrawny body.

Zarhmel watches a beautiful, young Nephi dance with a good-looking man. Zarhmel is jealous.

Then he sees himself and stops trying to fight Nephi's power. He takes in his appearance. His smooth, brown skin, his smile that seems to show every gleaming, white tooth. The green emerald on his finger.

He was Pharaoh. This was his seventeenth Shemu celebration. He is beloved by all. His sisters stand at his side, smiling, identical fifteen-year-old twins. Adiah whispers in his ear, and they laugh. He laughs freely with them. Drahzil remembers exactly what she said. It was about Zarhmel.

All in an instant, Nephthila is sweeping over to Drahzil, and they dance together. He twirls her around in her beautiful red dress. She whispers in his ear, and they giggle. Then they walk out the room together.

Present Nephthila urges Drahzil to follow their memory selves.

They follow, Drahzil not seeing it then, but now he sees his brother dancing with Nephthila, as well!

Present Nephthila feels Drahzil trying to fight her out of his head, but she holds on and pushes further, blood seeping from both their noses.

Drahzil and his Nephi are in a room, kissing, when they hear loud thuds and muffled sounds coming from the room next door. Young Drahzil and his Nephi barge into the next room to see about the commotion. The handsome man who Nephthila was dancing with earlier is being held down by a man in a black-hooded robe and ... Nephthila?

They all lock eyes, and Drahzil yells.

He pushes Nephthila out his mind, but instead of being back on the tower, they are in an empty grand hall.

"Take us back now!" he yells at Nephthila.

"It is no longer me in control, Drahzil," she whispers.

A woman walks into the center of the room, her hair floating around her, red dress seeming to ooze on the floor around her. Nephthila watches the Nephthila that has Drahzil's full attention.

Nephi tries to move but is stuck. Then the room shatters, and they are not standing in the same space, neither here nor there. Just the three of them.

The Nephi in red holds her hand out to Drahzil. "Save me," she whispers.

"Drahzil, do not listen to her. Please. She is not the one. She is not the one you love."

Drahzil looks pained. He remembers that night. He remembers how he walked in on Nephthila. That he discovered ... He saw ... But he cannot put any of it into a full thought.

"Save me. She knows where I lie. I am alive, my love. I am waiting for you." Her voice is like a bucket of cold water being splashed on him.

"Drahzil, that is not her. She is not the one you love."

"Sister," the other Nephi says. She laughs loudly then slaps Nephthila.

A small drum sounds and grows louder and louder. The sound seems to come from both Nephthilas' chests.

The one in red looks at her sister with recognition on her face. "You have one, too?" she says accusingly.

"And you will not get it, Kawaad." Then Nephthila raises her hands, and a blast of white light hits the other one, a loud whooshing sound overcoming their ears.

Nephthila and Drahzil are back on the tower.

He lowers her hands away from him slowly. "Was that real?" he asks.

"I think I saw the man's face you spoke to. She has everything to do with him. She will use you again, Drahzil. Trust me. Let the children have the amulets, please."

"You take me for a fool! She's alive!"

"She is not the one, Drahzil. Please, listen to me!"

Nephthila wants to tell him that was not real, but her other half broke through her power and came forth.

Izzi, having one piece, must have awoken her. No one can imagine Kawaad. She is gaining strength, and they both saw.

"Drahzil, you will make another mistake," she tries to warn him, but she can tell he will not listen. "You will stay a monster if you try to help her ... if you try to help *that one*."

Drahzil stares back, anger fueling his every thought.

She does not flinch at the death stare he gives her, but she knows his mind is made up.

He runs at her, and she stands, waiting for whatever he will do, but then he changes course and hurls himself from the tower. He rises on his flamed horse and flies off into the night.

He fumes from his encounter with Nephthila. She got into his mind. He had not remembered that party in a long time.

He exhales loudly, trying to shake it off. His mind feels foggy with thoughts and feelings that he does not want to feel.

He flies over his camp, a world of fire below, but instead of landing, he veers in the air and goes west.

Who was the robed man and the man being held down? He cannot remember that ever happening. That memory was wiped from him for a reason, and she brought it back.

He exhales loudly, wanting to yell into the night.

All of a sudden, he sits frozen. Heliaj slows down, sensing her riders fear.

She was there. She broke through and came to him. She is alive. But he saw her *ka* in the Underworld. He saw her down there. How can that be?

Tired of questioning himself, he leans in close to his horse and urges her to pick up speed.

He flies into the dark, deserted city of Jaquel, ignoring the thing below, and flies right over the waters and through the entrance to the Underworld. He flies over the Red Nile and through the passage that leads to the black palace, landing at the gates and leaving Heliaj there as she lights up the entire area. He enters the palace and heads down the dark corridors.

Entering the dimly lit chamber, he pauses, seeing Montu perched on the neck of the broken statue in a small glow. He floats, cross-legged, and has his eyes closed. He does not break his concentration, although the god knows that Drahzil just entered.

Drahzil turns from Montu to Anubis then takes a step back.

The god is not covered in his black robe. His skin is grey and peeling. In the center of his chest is a black burn, flesh badly burned around it. He winces in pain as he moves.

"You are becoming less and less of a man as you continue to visit here," Anubis says without opening his eyes.

"I am the rightful pharaoh. I am not a man," Drahzil says coolly.

Both gods let out small laughs.

"You humans," Anubis starts, but then he stops as he winces in pain again.

"I thought gods were immortal. How can you be wounded? And by kids, at that? Heal yourself."

Anubis and Montu both snap out of their concentration, both annoyed with this human.

"I can only be wounded by a god! I can only heal by the power of a goddess. Only they have healing powers," Anubis sneers at Drahzil, but Drahzil only cares about one part.

Did he say only a god can wound a god?

"The boy had purple light, and the girl pure gold. No speckles. Seems we have underestimated the entire situation," Montu says.

"What do you want, Drahzil? We did not call for you coward. We saw you fly away at the sight of the goddesses back at the mountain," Montu continues, waving him away, wanting to kick him into the vortex.

Drahzil came to demand answers as to the memory that Nephthila dug up that he has no recollection of.

"Be gone, mortal fool," Anubis snarls.

"No." Drahzil braces for pain, but he can take it.

Enough with the games, he thinks to himself . He wants answers, and he wants them *now*.

The heavy drape behind Anubis flutters, and Drahzil catches the sight of dim, blue light. He charges up the steps and snatches the drape down. Neither Montu nor Anubis try to stop him as he enters the other room and stands before the case, Osiris staring back at him.

Between the fight at the mountain, Nephthila, and the returned memory with the new information, this new development has his head reeling.

He examines the god, his markings, his admirable structure, his perfection.

"He is a fallen god. The day the children were born, it seems he wanted to syphon what they had in them, as well."

Drahzil listens to Montu but is still staring his god in the eyes. He cannot believe this. Not Osiris.

Amun-Ra created man, but humans did not live realistically. When Osiris became Pharaoh in his human form, he and Isis set the tone for humanity. They taught humans and ruled with the teachings of what all mankind would need in their time and in the future. Osiris was who Drahzil sought to emulate before all of this.

"The human emotion that spews out when their god is not what they thought. Paintings in temples a little off ..." Montu taunts him.

"What are those children? What are the amulets? Why do you need me?" Drahzil asks.

Osiris's eyes dart around.

No one answers.

Gods.

He goes back into the chamber, finding it hard to break from Osiris without asking the questions he desires to ask. He observes both gods, waiting for a riddle. Anubis looks on the verge of a real death, and Drahzil wonders if the vortex could swallow him up.

The gods glare at him. Then Montu stretches his wings then flies down to face Drahzil.

"Gods and goddesses, whether they admit it or not, take pleasure in ... well, pleasure with humans. Your creator's greatest weakness. Amun-Re fell in love with a human woman during his time as Pharaoh. She died. She was buried with the child that she bore with Amun-Re. Shortly after, Amun died and ascended."

Drahzil does not cut the winged god off. Finally, he is getting a story and not a riddle.

"Amun-Re did something he had never done before—raised the dead. He only told one other god what he was doing. That god accompanied him as he went to the small tomb that he had erected for her. Inside was his love and a smaller sarcophagus. Amun only wanted her, so he brought her back. However, the *He'ka* he used seeped into the smaller sarcophagus, and a small child rose, as well."

Montu continues, "His love turned into a goddess. The goddess, however, had no memory of her past life or who the child was. The child could not ascend to live in the kingdom. So, she remained on earth.

"Amun's brother took the child; said he would find her a human family to raise her. Amun couldn't care less. He had his love back, and the child possessed no light at all. She was not a threat.

"As they left the tomb, the child began to cry. She was screaming and tried with all her little might to go back into the tomb, but they would not allow it. There was something in there that she wanted, but they did not bother to check."

Anubis sighs deeply. "We know this information, but no one else knows this. You ask yourself: why?

"When a person dies, who makes the journey with them? Their journeys were reversed and everything that lay at peace in that chamber was brought back."

Drahzil glances at Anubis, who would know who the goddess was and who she used to be. He contacts all *Ka*s. He is the first stop. Maat would know, as well.

"Where did Amun's brother take the girl?" Drahzil asks.

Anubis's breathing is becoming shallow. He looks in real pain, but Montu ignores him.

"When humans pray to their god or goddess, we always hear the call. Some are weak, but some come in very strong vibrations. Amun-Re was getting the strongest prayer vibrations that he had ever received. We all felt the call.

"It was his child. She went to the temple every day and night and prayed to him to help her find her family. Amun-Re never went to see the child. Instead, he directed a thought her way. He told her, in her mind, to visit a mountainside. There, she would find answers."

"She found the amulets there?" Drahzil has heard of her. The Princess of Amun-Ra. Where the tales began.

"She is real, and she is dangerous. You have seen her Drahzil. You have contacted her. You have even had relations with part of her."

Drahzil shakes his head. He would know if he had met this …

His thoughts trail off. The memory Nephthila showed him. He discovered there were two Nephis, that much is clear, but … that cannot be. The story of the princess of Amun-Ra has been told since Osiris ruled, for over three hundred Pèret.

"Do you know the earth queen's birth? Who her parents are? Where did she come from? Did you ever ask your love her age?" Montu asks.

Drahzil stops thinking and stops wondering. He asked Zarhmel the same question about his queen, and yet, he thought he had her figured out himself.

"For once, you display intelligence. There is hope for you after all," Anubis says weakly.

"The girl discovered that the amulets can open the gods' realm, and many other worlds to her. But she has to be a god for that to happen. She was born of one, her mother is now one, but she needs more. She needs to birth her own child. Only with all three amulets can a child be born. The child would possess the gods' power and, with the amulets, whoever can sacrifice the life of that child would then gain all from that life. Osiris failed," Montu finishes.

"Once the children find all three, and the power of the amulet is possessed, they can see into our realms. Once they are theirs, the holder can destroy all gods and goddesses. There will be nothing for you to rule once this is all over," Anubis says.

Knowing that the gods can read his mind in their presences, Drahzil thinks of nothing of value. However, he lets himself think freely *why are many gods and goddesses on the children's side? Why do these two not have more on their side to help?*

With that, two gold beams of light fall from the ceiling. Nekhbet and Wadjet step outside the lights as they dissolve. Nekhbet goes right to Anubis and, with her golden light, she heals him.

He stands up and flexes his muscles. Then he transforms his head into that of the jackal and bows to her.

"What do I owe you for this?" His voice booms from his animal form.

"Nothing," Wadjet hisses nicely. "We do not trust Isis or Re. Those children and those amulets are going to destroy us. We need to do something about it."

Montu turns to Drahzil. "Well, it looks like our ranks are growing."

9

IZZI-RA

I feel myself slowly waking due to an ache in the arm that I lie on. I notice that Neenho's *clou* no longer feels warm and comfortable, but hard, cold, and damp. The sun must be rising because bright light shines.

I stretch on my back, yawning as I open my eyes. Instead of seeing blue sky and trees, there is brick above me. I sit up fast, snapping my neck from side to side. I am back in the door-less chamber. I am in the center of the crowns that shine specific hues. The four walls are all changing pictures, as they did when Neenho and I were here. Different pictures, all the time of the creation, man, the rise of the pyramids, and then they flow together. Water for miles, and a lonesome isle in the middle. I move from the center of the crowns and to the wall straight ahead. The isle seems to be growing closer, those red dots appearing under the water as they did before.

Again, it looks like the art on my mother's wall.

"*Saat*, help me," a voice calls.

I nearly scream. I was not expecting that.

"Mother?" I manage to choke out.

A small something appears in the art and grows closer. "*Saat*," the voice whispers to me again. She fills the rest of the wall. On all four walls. She is painted with no cloth, her black, wavy hair flying around her. Her big, round eyes are locked on mine. It is the painting from my mother's room. "*Saat*, save me please," she whispers.

"Who are you?" I surprise myself by saying.

She smiles at me, a smile that does not reach her eyes. She may have her face, but she is not her. Her grin widens. "Come to me, *saat*."

"You are not my mother." I lift my hands to throw a ball of light.

She lifts her hands at the same time, and I am hit with a gust of wind and fall backward, screaming. I open my eyes, still screaming, but hands cover my mouth.

Above me is Neenho, his wide, brown eyes staring at me, hushing me.

I sit up, breathing heavily, beads of sweat rolling down my face. I am back on the *clou*, the moon shines brightly above us. It is still nighttime.

"Neenho, what ...?" I start, but he holds his hand up to me and points. I notice he is crouched down on his knees, looking down.

I follow his finger and gaze out. Our camp has been invaded. Men have our guard hostage. They have taken their weapons and have them lined up.

"They are like mountains," Neenho whispers.

Indeed, they are. There are only four men, but they are huge. They wear black waist pants, no shoes, and have that pale pink skin of patches all over their arms and back of their darker skin. They have the same haircut, as well— shaved on the sides with locks only in the center of their heads.

"Neenho, let's use our power to help them. We can take them out."

"I bet we could, but something tells me to hold back. And you do not look very good at the moment. You were screaming in your sleep. I don't know, but the *clou*, I think, masked your scream. Assim didn't even glance this way. I tried to wake you, and then I heard the commotion down there. What were you dreaming?"

I watch the men as they question Chike, who seems to be the only one being talked to. I have no idea how to answer that. "Later. You say they did not hear my scream?"

"The whole of Egypt should have heard you. I wonder ... Hey, Mountain Men!" Neenho shouts. Then we both cower, but no one looks up. Interesting.

"Assim!" I shout, but he does not glimpse up, either. I cannot see anything around us, but I feel it shielding us.

"I want to know what is going on. I think I can read their minds," I tell him. Then I calm my breathing, still feeling the effects of my dream, and focus on everyone below me. I feel the lightheaded fuzz and know that I am in.

Kade and Assim are being guarded by one man. Kade is terrified and worried about me. He is thinking of ways to escape. Silly male. Assim is calm. He is not thinking anything as he glares at the man, right in his face. Must be that army training. Adallah is not panicked, either. She hopes Neenho and me are safe.

I switch to the twins and shake my head. The twins are being held by one of the huge men. He has a gigantic hand on each of their shoulders. They like it. They are enjoying this. Crazy, but they are. At least I know they are all okay and not in any immediate danger.

Chike is glaring at the fourth man, who seems to be the leader. He stares down at her, disgust all over his face.

"Dare ya sho ya face?" he says to her.

"What's happening down there?" Neenho questions.

I elbow him to be quiet.

Chike glares up at the man with no fear in her face or voice, "Sho'te, I have my reasons. I want to see her. If there is punishment, so be it."

The man slaps Chike across the face. I see Kade and Assim stiffen.

Ta'li thinks this is okay, that she can take it. Umi thinks along the lines of being prepared for this. They scare me.

Chike spits out blood. "Take us to her," she says without a quiver in her voice.

The giant man, Sho'te, raises his hand once more, but the man with the twins strides over in two steps.

"'Tis not fer ya ta decide, Sho'te. Let her decide wut iz ta be done wit dem," the boulder man says.

I frown, thinking of how they say words. Interesting.

Sho'te continues to stare death blades into Chike's eyes. "I 'ope she kills ya."

Chike is not moved. "I welcome the peace, Sho'te, something you need." They stare one another down for a second more.

"Head out!" Sho'te yells, stumping out our fire with his bare, big foot as the others are marched down the hill.

"Follow them," I tell Neenho.

"Well, duh. What else am I gonna do? Go back to sleep? Although, I would like to because, Izzi, you slept with me." He grins, raising his eyebrows.

"Wipe that goofy grin from your face, Neenho, now, and follow them."

He urges his *clou* down and forward. We stay several feet back, but if anything goes wrong, we have the advantage. I think.

"See the markings on their head?" Neenho whispers.

I nod. I have been studying them, as well. Three circles that loop around one big circle with three circles that loop together. I have never seen that symbol anywhere in the palace or the temples on the grounds.

"Aunt Adallah has a book. It documents the first one hundred Pèrets of the humans. I saw that symbol in her book. They were of the first tribe, Izzi."

They stop walking, and Neenho swiftly goes above so that we can see what is happening ahead. They have reached a dead end. I see the first signs of the sun rising. There is nothing but a mountain before us all. No way to climb over that.

One of the men goes to the jagged wall and rubs. He stops at a space then pushes the slab of rock effortlessly out the way.

"Go," Sho'te snarls, and then my guard is pushed forward through the tunnel.

"Neenho," I whisper, feeling panicked.

"I don't know, Princess. I don't know if we can."

Everyone is inside the tunnel, and the man who opened it is about to close it.

"Here goes nothing." Neenho dives down and shoots right into the tunnel, almost hitting another boulder man, but missing by inches.

The other man pushes the slab of rock back into place.

Neenho and I are as high as we can be against the ceiling, which is not far at all, considering the height of these men. I hope they cannot hear our pounding hearts.

The man strides toward us, and we brace for him to hit the *clou* and expose us, but he brushes right past. Then he stops and looks up, right at us. He sniffs the air then plugs his nose.

I glare at Neenho, seeing the sorry expression on his face.

A torch is lit by one of the boulder men, and then he lights another one for his companion.

He obviously cannot see us, because he decides there is nothing there and continues. We both let out a sigh of relief.

Neenho urges his *clou* forward, and we float behind. I feel some anxiety being in a small cavern like this. It feels like I am back in Meretseger's mountain. I shudder at the thought, thinking I could not do that again. Ever.

We continue for some time. The path, at times, slopes downward then upward. There is no art on the walls; nothing that would suggest who these people are or where we are going, or even what direction we are heading. I mentally pop in and out of my guard's feelings. The twins are eager as always for an adventure, Adallah and Assim have the same game faces on, Kade is about to break at any moment, and Chike is feeling anxious now. We must be getting close.

"Princess, what was wrong earlier?"

"I think I was dreaming. I … It felt so real though. I was back in that chamber with the crowns and the art on the walls. That island appeared again and, this time, I recognized where I have seen it—a painting of my mother's. Only, I no longer feel like it is my mother. The woman in the art tried to speak to me. She … I do not know. She told me to save her. This ..." I trail off, unable to form words that make sense.

But, it's not just that. I had a dream of my mother last night. I was with her in the garden, and then I fell asleep with Assim, I thought. But then I woke up and got on the *clou* with Neenho.

I am losing my mind. I have already lost it. Half my *Ka* is in the ruins of the mountain.

"Maybe she was my mom," he says.

Like I never gave that a thought, I think to myself. Neenho has no parents, and yet he was born the same day I was. We do not have similar features, so he cannot be my brother. He does not feel like my brother either. We both know this.

Neenho may be an outsider, but he is pure of the heritage. I know that much.

The group is ordered to stop walking. Neenho and I hang back. Then one of the men lets out a loud call, almost like the bark of a dog. We glance around, but the men just wait.

Neenho floats back more, not sure what is about to occur, and I think that is smart. I dart my eyes from wall to wall, looking for where the opening will be. I notice we all stiffen as the sound of clicks fill the cave.

Neenho and I look around again and, without any notice, a slab of rock falls from right above us. I scream, and Neenho ushers his *clou* inches from the crash. We slam right into a wall, and the *clou* dissolves as their torches blow out.

"Wut wuz dat!" Sho'te snarls.

He advances over to the darkened corner where we lay exposed. Neenho crosses his arm over me, and I prepare for the large hands to grab us.

He looms right over us, bends down, and then sniffs. I dare not breathe, staring right into his black eyes. With his large nostrils, he sniffs again. I am in shock. He cannot see us?

Neenho is stone stiff, not moving a muscle, his heart beating at an alarming rate.

The man's face closes in on ours, inches from my nose. He cannot see us. How?

Neenho is gripping my leg tightly.

Another mechanism opens, and fresh air and light pour in from the hole. We are in the light, but Sho'te decides there is nothing there and stands. He advances on Chike and raises his hand.

"What are you punishing me for this time?" she asks.

A wooden ladder drops down the hole. "Up. Now," he tells her, pushing her toward the ladder.

She glances where we are and smiles, knowing no one can see her. Then she heads up.

The others are forced up the ladder. One of the other men pushes open a trap door in the rock ahead of them, and the men go through. Sho'te does the call again, and the ladder is pulled up as another slab of rock reseals into place. Sho'te glances around one more time, right over at us, and then he goes through the opening that the other men walked through. He closes it and leaves Neenho and me in darkness.

We let out heavy breaths, and Neenho lets go of my leg. I feel a ripple dissolve around us. I light my hand so we can see one another.

"You made us invisible, Neenho. How did you do that? How did you know to do that?" I rush out. I was scared, so scared.

He shakes his head, pushing his locks out of his face. "I didn't know that I did until he was close to us." Neenho lies back against the wall and relaxes with his eyes closed. He looks drained. That amount of power he used must have been something. He is getting stronger; I feel it. I tuck that thought away for later.

We are on the same side. We will never go against each other. Right?

I get up and walk over to where our guard went up. I stand back and lift my hands, my light bright in both palms.

"Wait," Neenho says. "We go through there." He points to the wall that the men went through.

"No way." I snort at him. "Why would you want to go where they went? Our guard is this way."

He stands and walks over to the wall where the giants went

through. He uses his purple light to slide the slab of rock aside. "Because it won't be guarded."

Okay, he is right, but I will not tell him that.

The sun is shining fiercely. We see a path leading into trees as we exit and Neenho covers the hole again. He whistles that melodic sound, and his *clou* appears. We jump on and head up.

"I knew I heard something," he says.

Right above the cave is a battle field. More mountain men are engaged in combative training.

"Scare tactic. They make sure whoever they capture see right away that they will not be able to fight their way out," Neenho says.

I focus my eyes around the general area. There seems to be nothing but mountains and hills beyond the training grounds, and behind us is a small forest, and then ...

We both stare, eyes wide.

There lays a village, which sits in what I can only describe as a sinking pit.

"What is that? I have never seen anything that resembles that in the palace art."

There are many tall structures, and color, lots of color. The structures are splattered with different colors. Blue homes, green homes, yellow pillars, blue columns, and orange obelisks. I have never seen structures colored like this. Odd.

Neenho shrugs as he urges his *clou* to the ground, skirting the area. He lies flat, gazing downward, stopping at the start of the path into the trees. "Here, tracks. They all went this way."

I frown. "So, you are a hunter now?"

Neenho snorts, shaking his head, his locks hitting his face. "No, just spent loads of time in the Pakhet valley is all." He urges his *clou* forward.

Just as we hit the entrance to the trees, the *clou* dissolves, and we fall. I scrape my leg on a broken branch, and Neenho falls flat on his face.

"*Bestou.*" I dust off my leg and watch as the blood flows from the small cut.

Neenho spits dirt out his mouth. *Bestou.*

"What is with that thing? Can you not control it anymore?" I scold him.

Neenho stares at the trees then glances all around. "*Heka*," he says. "Do you feel it, Princess? It's rippling off my skin." Neenho steps forward and backward near the start of the path.

Since when did he get so enlightened? I have not felt anything since the mountain. Maybe I am drained, tired.

He turns toward me, smiling, every inch of joy reaching his eyes. His smile calms me.

I walk over and step from dirt to grass, and then I feel it. I step back then step inside again. I feel the ripple around me. It makes the hair on my arms and neck stand on end.

"I wonder if our light will not work inside here," Neenho says.

"Looks like you will not be any help in here." I scan the ground and find a long stick. I wield it and swing to make sure it is a sturdy weapon. "I can fight without *He'ka*," I say, turning the fighting staff in my hands around my back and in a pose right at his head.

Instead of looking envious, he grins at me again. "I can run. Even faster than before. Any sign of trouble, Princess, I will run while you fight."

"Such a gentleman, NeenhoKano." I bow to him.

"Okay, well, let's go on the next adventure, shall we? No sleep and no food. I'm as excited as the twins. Ladies with weapons first." He bows.

"You noticed how weird they are, too, about danger?"

Neenho nods. "I think they should have been born with this curse, not us."

I agree with him silently.

We face the trees. *Here we go again.*

As I pass the barrier, I feel all my *He'ka* disappear.

10

NEENHOKANO

W e walk in silence, only hearing the sound of our own feet breaking small twigs. My ears are perked, listening for any kind of movement, treating this as I would if I were out running from Ishiva. Normally, I wouldn't wear shoes, but a goddess made me these. I have never had such nice shoes, and they are gold. I will make all the noise in the world, I guess, not taking these off. I glance up, trying to listen for anything.

"There's something off about this place," I say.

She nods in agreement. "No birds, no bugs, and the leaves drip as if it just rained."

"Why would our *He'ka* not work in these trees?" I wonder, because nothing seems scary.

"A god or goddess is my guess," she says. She is thinking about the mountain, and I agree.

I look up as we walk, not paying attention, and walk right into Izzi.

"Oh, my goddess!" Izzi screeches.

"I'm sorry. I was looking up," I try to apologize, but then I see it's not about my clumsiness.

The trees stop and lead into a circle. The trees have been cleared out of the middle and line the perimeter. Cow-headed statues with the body of a female are in the center. Rows and rows of cow statues. They stand at attention toward the two giant statues that tower above them. A goddess with a lion head. Sekhmet, it has to be. Next to her, tall and slender with his ankh cross staff, long goatee, and the three looped rings on his crown is Ptah.

I run through the statues, touching as many as I can. This is so cool.

Izzi is standing before the gods in disbelief.

"The symbol on their heads, the big men, they wear the mark of Ptah. Do you know what this means?" I yell to Izzi. The two statues are so tall that I have to crane my neck up to see them. "Do you know where we are, Izzi?" I'm excited. Finally, I know something.

For the first time since meeting her, she is speechless.

"Ptah, his queen, Sekhmet. Hathor's fertility grounds. We are in Kemet, Izzi. Those boulder men are Kemetians. The stories are true. Chike and her twins, the patches on their face. They are Kemetians. Remember I said Aunt Adallah has a book? Yes! It all makes sense. Thoth wrote her that book. She read it to me every night. Ptah is the first creation god from the goddess Nun. Then yadda, yadda, yadda, and then our creator was born. Ptah created the first race of humans. Kemet is where god and man walked together. Amun only took over as a technicality."

Izzi looks horrified.

"You had to have known they were here, Princess. The pharaoh does business with all villages, except us. Right?"

"I was told—taught—that Kemet was destroyed long ago, and their village lay in ruins," she tells me, still filled with disbelief in her voice.

I laugh. "Well, Young Queen, looks like you better get down to that village there and demand why they haven't been paying their dues to the palace."

She frowns. "This is no time to joke, young male. This means the stories I know are not true. Your village and this village exists. What other villages are out there, just ready for the chance to bond together and go after my Egypt?"

I don't respond to her, because she's right. Pakhet planned to overthrow Upper Egypt, and by the looks of things, so do the Kemetians.

"Let's find the others. They could be in danger."

I nod then turn to walk away from the cool monuments, but I can't. I try to move my legs. I hear Izzi straining behind me, too.

"I can't move, Princess!"

"Neither can I!"

"What do we do?"

"Neenho, let's sink into the ground and maybe we won't be stuck anymore."

"Great idea. How?"

"Neenho! We have no *He'ka* to sink into the ground, you idiot. We ... What is that?"

We hear rocks shifting, like it's breaking apart. The ground shakes.

"Princess, I think we're about to discover why our light doesn't work here."

" Wow NeenhoKano, you think so?"

A shadow looms over us.

"No way!" she screams.

I'm afraid to look up, but I have no choice as I hear the deep growling sound above. My scream is stuck in my mouth as the stone head of Sekhmet comes down on us, jaws wide, sharp teeth glistening from the sunlight. No time to try anything, we are sucked into darkness.

We are falling fast. Wind swooshing past my ears so fast that it sounds like whistles. Whatever is at the bottom is sure to kill me, I just know it.

I flip over to see ground below us, and I close my eyes, waiting for the impact. This is a stone lion, so is her belly stone? I wait for the impact, but it never comes. I peek, finding my nose inches from white marble flooring. My arms are outstretched, and I can feel the tip of Izzi's fingers.

"Can you move?" I ask her.

I hear her breathing heavily.

"Who are you? I can feel you there."

I try to see what she is talking about, but I can't move. My whole body is still frozen.

"It is you, isn't it?" she asks.

"It is I, NeenhoKano of Pakhet," I say.

"Shut up, Neenho, not you. Him."

I'm so confused. What is she going on about?

"Izzi, have you gone mad?"

In an instant, we snap upright. I let out a small, tiny scream. Maybe it was a little louder.

The marble ground had me thinking we were in a chamber, a nice, grand hall, but we are ... well, I don't know.

"Izzi?"

I don't know what is above the sky, but the priests always talk of what it may look like, and I think this is it.

The moon seems as though we could jump on it. The sun is off in the distance. There are giant circle balls in the air, here and there. One red, another one blue with a ring around it, and a giant orange one. I have never seen anything like it. White lights of some sort zip by fast. Pressed against the black of the sky here are colors that seem to flow in and out of existence. We stand on a platform.

My body loosens, and I have full control of myself again. We are just floating through the air, stars twinkling all around.

"Where are you?" Izzi asks.

"I'm here, Princess. Can you not see me?" I stand in front of her face.

She exhales loudly and pushes me to the side. "Show yourself, please," she asks the air.

I pinch myself, making sure I'm awake. Then I pinch Izzi, and she slaps my hand.

I glance around frantically. "Izzi, I think we're dead. Izzi?"

She's kneeling.

I look behind me and almost faint. Then I slowly turn and bow, not taking my eyes off the god before us. His long, black goatee reaches down to the end of his white robe. His moss-colored skin is flecked with golden light. His small face is calm, his eyebrows thick, his jawline soft. I notice he has a black dot above his upper lip. Something the artists need to remember. *I'll tell them*, I think. His staff is gripped in his long fingers.

"Izzi, he really has moss-colored skin. God skin, whatever it is. Am I whispering?"

"No, no you are not," she says as she stands up.

"Where are we?" she asks him.

"Neither here, nor there. You are nowhere, dear. You are where you are," Ptah answers her.

11

IZZI-RA

Ptah tilts his head, his eyes sparkling with curiosity at us. He holds up his staff and a gold orb with three green-colored rings appears. Inside, I can see my guard. They are being held in a cell. They do not look hurt, and they are all together, except Chike. I do not see her. This furthers my suspicions.

"Are they going to kill them?" I ask.

"My people are a peaceful people. We do not harm."

Neenho and I both raise our eyebrows at him. Sho'te was not at all peaceful with Chike.

"What do you want from us?" The amulet is exposed, and I grasp it.

"I am not interested in the amulets of Princess Amun-Re. They belong to you, after all."

He glides toward us and gestures to my hand. "May I, dear?" he asks. He smells like happiness. Happiness has no smell, but that is what fills my nostrils.

I hesitate, but his twinkling eyes and the warmth of his melodic voice tells me I have nothing to fear. I place my dirty hands ... I yank it back to study my nails! I cannot believe this. Then I reluctantly place my dirty hand in his hand, and his eyes orb over.

"By the gods," he whispers. He drops my hand then delicately grabs Neenho's, not even asking Neenho for permission. Not like he would object, anyway.

Ptah's eyes are still orbed over as he tilts his head back. "Do you see, boy?"

"No way," Neenho says.

Ptah's eyes are back to normal. Still holding Neenho's hand, he bends over so that he is eye to eye with him. "Do not hurt her. Please. Any of them," he says to Neenho.

I am confused. He did not show me anything or say anything to me.

"But ..."

Ptah squeezes his hand to silence Neenho. Then he drops his hand and grabs his staff that was standing straight up without his support.

"What did you see?" I ask Ptah, even though I know I am not going to get an answer.

"When the gods created their very own people, and then the chaos erupted and emotions were born, we agreed that there would always be one rightful leader in each region to rule and keep the Maat in order. Egypt's village is in danger. My people will help."

"Egypt is not a village; Egypt is the entire world." He may be a god, but my honor and pride go before anything.

He is not moved by my words. "Kemet is the foundation of your world, child. Egi is just a part of it. And neither of you know this. Thoth is not answering the prayers of scholars on earth, is he? Tsk, tsk."

"Why did you summon us and take our light?" I am irritated, but he knows this.

He whips around with amusement on his face now. "It was not I who summoned you. You asked me."

Neenho and I glance at one another, neither of us wishing to have been sucked up by a giant lion head, but then I know Neenho probably did.

"Your *heka* can never be taken from you. You allow it to be blown out like a candle in the wind. You can relight it anytime you want. True, there are barriers that will shut it off, but all you have to do is blow it alight again." Ptah blows on his staff, and it goes dark. He blows again, and it lights up.

Neenho begins to blow on his hand several times and nothing happens.

"See? He has done it." Ptah beams at Neenho, and Neenho smiles back. The two of them are on my last nerve.

"Nothing happened," I say.

He winks at Neenho then turns to me. "Your visit has been very interesting. And I answered questions you both have had burning in your minds. Until we meet again, Izzi-Ra. I do not like you very much though. You are just like the others of your kind." He bows to me.

I am in shock. I have never had anyone tell me they did not love, let alone not like me.

Neenho is gawking. I see him trying to suppress a smile, and I glare at him, daring him to smile.

"Pharaoh." He bows to Neenho.

This gesture throws me over the edge. I want to scream at him, but he bangs his staff on the ground then disappears.

I frown at the empty spot. *What?* The floor cracks from under us, and then we are falling again into the dark unknown. Just as we are about to slam into the grass below us, we slow down then drop. My face goes right into the grass, mouth open from screaming.

Spitting, I get up, not even bothering to dust myself off. We are in the heavily treed area again. No signs of the lion goddess statue or Ptah.

Neenho glances around, shocked as well. Slapping his locks out his face, he then grins with dirt smudged on his face.

"Another god. We just met Ptah. A creator god at that. And he said he doesn't like you." Neenho cannot help himself. I let him gloat.

"We keep meeting these gods and goddesses, and they tell us nothing but something. They talk in riddles! Princess Amun-Ra and a world called Kemet?" I think about what Ptah said, as well. We need real answers. If we summoned him, maybe we can summon Ra himself. First, we need our guard back.

I notice the moon is shining, and I instantly flare up in anger *again*.

"Neenho, it is dark. It was sunrise when we got here." I stomp my foot. "He robbed us of time! Where are we now?"

Neenho looks around, sniffing. Then he walks quietly through the trees. I follow reluctantly until we see lights and hear music. We creep closer and peer through the branches.

Some sort of celebration is at hand. More giant men sit around a large fire, making music. They play many types of hand percussions. The men seem to be more colossal than the ones who took our guard. Although they appear scary, they are cheerful and colorful. They wear leaves around their necks and arms and grass skirts. Odd. If I am not lying to myself, they have radiant smiles, I must admit.

We watch as they play away on their hand drums and shake bells in tune to the high rhythm beat that they are playing. I was tense, but now I notice I have relaxed.

Off in a corner, I see the mean man, Sho'te, leaning against a tree, looking solemn. I notice all the men wear only bottom covers, but his arms and chest are covered.

I turn to study Neenho, who is slightly frowning. I do not need to see into his mind to know that he is thinking the same thing I am.

I wrap my hand around his upper arm and squeeze. He yanks it away, and I hold back a giggle. Our thoughts are also on another observation. Where are the women?

The upbeat rhythm changes to a slower yet soulful beat, and we turn our attention back to the crowd. I see Sho'te walking away. Must not be the party type.

The beat continues. The men that were clustered together now break into two rows, facing one another, still playing their instruments.

"*Ooo ...*" Neenho breathes out.

Women in colorful, plant-like dresses dance their way into the circle. Neenho is at attention. I do not sulk as he did. Yes, they are stunning, and they move as if they *are* the beat of the drums.

"Their skin," I whisper as I will my eyes to focus in on them. They have the same white splotches on their faces, arms, and legs like Chike and her twins. The ladies are holding something in their hands, and then it alights in flames. They dance, tossing fire around. The men beat the drums, cheering them on. *The Egyptians could do that*, I think.

"Neenho, snap out of it. We must find Chike and the others."

I feel him before he yanks me up, but it's too late. Sho'te has us both by the neck.

He emerges from the shadows of the trees, us dangling from the grips of his boulder hands. He is not choking us, but this is uncomfortable, and he will regret treating the Princess of Egypt this way shortly.

The music stops, and a flurry of whispers fill the air.

Sho'te drops us in the center. We scramble to one another, standing back-to-back. We have no *He'ka* here. What will we do? As we continue to circle, trying to keep everyone in our line of vision, in the distance, I see a giant, colorful statue of Ptah. He is green, and I can see the twinkle in his eyes. I almost feel like he is truly there.

I raise my hand slightly and, like an idiot, blow as if I just blew out a candle. My feet tingle first, the warmth snaking up my legs then filling my body and arms. It reaches my neck, my mind, and I feel the charge in my body. I feel my power surging through my body and assume Neenho feels it, as well, returning. My mind is open to him, and he tells me that he's had his light back since being in the sky with Ptah. No time to argue with him about that, either.

I glance around at the many faces, no fear on my face.

"Who sent ya here!" Sho'te yells in my face. This guy is always so tense and mad.

I never break eye contact. I feel Neenho's shoulder on my back quiver some.

"Brotha, please. 'Ave peace, Brotha Sho'te. I will take it from here."

Sho'te growls in my face before reluctantly turning away and joining the crowd.

"Who are ya?" I hear a soft male voice.

"I am NeenhoKano of Pakhet," Neenho says proudly. He almost makes me feel like that's a real title of someone special.

A whisper through the crowd. Sho'te continues to glare like he wants to eat me, I think.

I drop my head, close my eyes, and take a deep breath. When I open my eyes, I see small feet. I slowly look up at the person who stands in front of me.

Splotchy legs that shine from the light of the fire, a moss-colored skirt above curvy hips, and a bust covered in plants. I reach the face of a woman about my mother's age, maybe older. She has green makeup on her eyes, lips, and wears a green-feathered crown over her bushy hair. Her eyes are a sliver mist, like Chike's, and her nose flares out with rings in them. I have never seen such things. Her ears have small spikes in them, and she has a small spike through her eyebrow. What is this? Over her right eye is a white patch that takes the shape of a butterfly. There is no way around it. It is in such detail.

"An' ... An' who may ya be?" she says in that deep voice that I thought was a man's. She gives me a once-over before resting her eyes on mine.

"Izzi-Ra Urbani. But you know that."

She clucks her tongue, and everyone does the same. Then she holds up her hand for silence.

"I know da face of Nephthila when I see it."

"Tell me something I do not know," I snark.

She grins. "I did not say ya looked like her."

My eyebrows furrow. What is that supposed to mean?

She walks toward her people, walking around the circle. "I wud say welcome ta Kemet, but ya are not welcome here. We generally do not 'ave guests wander upon our lanz, and for good reasons. I 'ave no idea how ya even got pass our security unnoticed, but I will be lookin' into dat." She stops in front of a group of men, shaking her head at them. They drop their heads, disappointed in themselves.

"We do not murder, so please calm yurself of dat fear, young male. I hear it in ya heart."

I feel Neenho exhale.

"We will knock ya out an' 'ave someone take ya to the boarders of our lan. You do not belong here, an' no Egyptian royalty is welcome here *eva*." She clucks her tongue, and two people break from the group.

"Wait." I move toward her. "You have our people held here in a cell. We need them back, and only then will we leave peacefully."

I sense a shudder around the circle as the woman faces me slowly.

"Iz dat so?" She does a series of clucks with her tongue and holds out her hand. A woman with a red hawk-shaved hairdo hands her a long fighting staff.

"I thought you were a peaceful people?" I mock, my power tingling in my fingers, ready to fly.

"I said I wud knock ya out. I do not wish ta 'arm ya."

Two other women flank her. They pull fighting staffs from their backs. The red-haired one gazes at me hungrily. I have a lot of aggression that I need to get out, so she will get it.

"Here we go," I tell Neenho.

"Yep," he whispers back.

They charge at us and, together, Neenho and I throw gold and purple balls of light right at them. The ladies all go flying out of the circle. However, we do not stop. We whip lashes at the boulder men and knock down anyone else who looks like a threat, which is ... well, everyone.

It all happens in a blur, the natives wondering what just happened, watching us in fear.

Good, I think. Just how I want it.

The leader is back on her feet, holding up her hand and doing her clucking sound again. The fresh wave of fighters—all women—halt. Then her eyes lock on my neck. The amulet must have come loose from under my dress.

"Who are ya?" she asks, this time with a little quiver in her voice.

Neenho's hands are glowing purple. I am in a gold ball that pulsates around me. That is new.

"I told you, I am the Princess of Egypt, and you have my damn coven! I am dirty, hungry, and in need of a real pamper session. Do not make me do that again. Give me my people, and we will go!" I yell at her, my light radiating all around me heatedly. I want a bath and my nails cleaned!

"Please," Neenho adds softly.

"Chikenna, now," she demands.

Two men scurry away. Within moments, they are back, dragging Chike behind them.

"Do not toss her, either," Neenho surprise me by saying.

They think about it then gently untie her.

Neenho runs and hugs her then stands in front of her, guarding her.

The leader clucks her tongue fast. This must be a language, because Chike begins to do it, as well. They go on for a few moments.

I notice Sho'te is angry, but everyone else is intrigued.

"How did you get into the village?" Chike asks us.

"It was so cool. So, Sekhmet ate us—that statue—and then we were someplace like in the sky, and we saw the moon and the stars, and Ptah was there. And he is green. He really is green. And he is super tall. And he said he likes me, but he doesn't like Izzi. And then he told us to blow on our hands—"

"Ptah dropped us right over there," I cut Neenho off, pointing in the general direction of where we found ourselves. "He said that you all would help us once you found out who we were."

Everyone gasps.

I need this dramatic crowd back at the palace.

"Chikenna, ya 'ave my deepest apologies," the leader says.

"Thank you, Laila."

They both do that cross of arms in the air to one another.

Laila throws an evil glance at Sho'te. "We will be honored ta serve ya an ya quest. Welcome home, sista." Laila opens her arms, and Chike runs into them.

On cue, the crowd claps and cheers. Some women rush over to Chike and hug her.

So, this is where she is from, her home? Ptah made Chike?

12

NEENHOKANO

"I'm never leaving!" I sit in a circle pool of foaming, hot water, being scrubbed by two beautiful girls with smell good soap. Their patch marks are on their hands and arms only. They have those nose rings like the leader and wild, blue hair. They finish with my back and shoulders then they climb out. They wear these silk, skintight, green bodysuits. They go to climb in with Assim, but he declines their service. Kade also refuses. The girls bow then leave the bath chamber.

"They can come back and scrub my toes anytime. That's the best thing that has ever happened to me," I say, laying my head back on the soft cushion thing that they gave me.

"You would love the washes at the palace, then," Kade says.

I'm way to relaxed to even care that he talked to me.

"What? Is there gold floating around the bath?" I ask.

Kade snorts. "Something like that."

Assim actually laughs. That's the first time I've ever heard that sound.

I peek over to see what a smiling Assim looks like.

"What's so funny, guys?"

"Nothing. Some of the guys really call it a golden bath. Just funny you said that," Assim says.

I glance from one to the other, and they look at one another and burst into laughter.

"Tell me." I laugh along with them, wanting to know. "Does Izzi give out baths?" I ask, and they really crack up now.

Assim's eyes widen as if I just cursed her.

"You should ask her," Kade says.

"You know I can look in your mind and see what you're talking about," I warn them.

"Neenho, no, we're just having a laugh," Assim says with his wrinkled hands in the air for a truce.

I use my light and go into Assim's head. I want a special bath at the palace one day. I jump back, full of regret.

"That is just wrong!" I yell.

The guys are in full laughter now. I think I see tears in Kade's eyes.

I'm disgusted. "I'm telling Izzi."

Tears fall from how hard they laugh.

I use my light and gravitate bubbles into a ball.

"Don't you dare," Assim warns.

"Do it, do it!" Kade cheers me on.

I let the ball of bubbles go, and Assim ducks. It hits Kade full in his face. Now Assim and I are laughing at Kade.

Seeing the look in Kade's eyes and the bucket that the girls used to fill the hot baths next to Kade, I say, "No."

But Kade fills it up and throws it at me as Assim grabs a bucket off the ledge and fills it. He throws it at me, too. However, I stop them midair and send it back at them. Bubbles are everywhere.

We hear a throat clear and look up to see Ta'li.

"Very mature," he says.

His bath is next to mine. He pulls the garments from his body and stands there for a moment. We all turn away, uncomfortable. I hear him sigh as he dips into the water and leans his head back.

The three of us are silently throwing looks at one another, trying our hardest not to laugh.

I lay my head back and close my eyes. That was kind of cool. I have never had friends before.

We finish our baths then get into the clothing that the girls left for us. Soft green leg pants with soft green shirts and some soft slip-on shoes with a green tie belt to hold up the pants. I will hate this color by the time we leave this village.

The community bath houses are away from the villas. We were told to follow a lighted path that will lead to a dinner being prepared in our honor.

We take the path to a picnic area where food is being served. I sniff the air and almost faint from the delicious smells, and then *whack!*

Adallah hits me over the head with a rolled-up scroll in her hand.

"Good to see you, too, Aunt Adallah."

She snatches me into a back-breaking hug and kisses my cheeks all over.

Kade and Assim leave us to it.

"What a mess these last few days have been, boy. Are you okay?"

"Are you? Oh, Aunt Adallah, don't do that right now."

Her bottom lip quivers, and she gazes at me with the saddest eyes.

"Neenho, I do not know ..." She shakes her head. "I knew one day things would change, but for the most part, I just wanted to always keep you safe. I wanted you to have a regular, boring life, like I never had."

I hold her soft hands tightly in both of mine. "Aunt Adallah, we were never normal from the start or ever had a boring moment."

She gives me a weak smile.

"But what I do know is that I see your love for me. I see your love for me right now, and everything we are going through, me and you will keep each other safe. Okay, woman?"

Tears run down her face. "How did you become such a wise, wonderful man?"

"The day you gave up your life for me and started raising me."

Someone whistles our way, and we break from our moment. Assim waves for us to join the group.

Adallah puts her emotions wherever she stores them, and then all business, no play Adallah is at the ready. Still holding hands, we walk the lit path.

"Adallah?"

"Yes, NeenhoKano?"

"Don't you ever pick me up again and throw me over your shoulder."

"I had to save your life, boy." She laughs.

We walk through the winding path of lights until we come to a clearing. There are small fires all over, and people sitting around each one. Assim waves us to join our group at our own little fire, where there are big cushions to sit on.

I sit down next to Izzi, and Adallah sits on my other side. She is not going to let me out her eyesight anytime soon. Assim is next to Izzi, which I find funny. Kade is on the other side of the fire with Chike. There are strings of light all around the trees and tall torches throughout, warming up the area. The natives keep chancing glances at us. We hear laughter mixed with clucking.

"What are they saying, Chike?" I ask.

Chike peeks around. "There has not been outsiders in Kemet in hundreds of Shemu. It is frowned upon to leave. I am lucky to be here right now. Some of them love us and cannot wait to talk to us, and others want us dead right now."

"You could have left that last part out," Adallah says.

The twins are sitting with another group, laughing and carrying on. I have never seen them interact with others. Back in Pakhet, they only talked to themselves and me.

Umi and Ta'li are in matching green robes, and both their hair in tight buns. They look identical. I used to wonder what Ta'li looked like naked ... until today, because I wasn't sure if he was really male.

Izzi chokes back a cough, and I smack my head. *Forgot you could hear me*, I think to her.

She wears a green dress, her hair is combed and braided into two plaits, and her nails are clean.

I smile at her, and she gives a weak one back then goes back to staring at the fire. I try to push into her mind, but I'm met by a brick wall.

I exhale. I guess she'll talk when she wants to.

I watch my guard, or whatever they are to me now. I'm thankful that we seem to have made it through another day.

A clap goes through the area. Everyone claps. Izzi and I clap too late. Then Laila comes into the circle.

"Dank ya all dat changed ya plans an' join us fa a special meal fa our guests. An' we all welcome home Chikenna and her babies. Family iz home. Eat and be merry." She does a series of clucking noises with her tongue, and the natives follow suit. Chike does the same, and I see the twins doing it, as well.

Laila claps her hands again, and then a few men standing off to the side pound some drums. Oh, are the ladies coming back to dance? Because I would surely love that.

Women with trays of food come into the area. Three girls circle our gathering, and another comes around to pass out plates and goblets. The others then begin to serve us food.

My stomach is rumbling. All this saving ourselves has left no time for food.

The girl piles my plate high with lentils, a roasted meat, and a bowl of steaming stew made with lots of greens and the same roasted meat. Then another girl fills my goblet with some sort of purple drink. I dig in, hoping that speech was the prayer.

After we eat our fill, we go on a walk through the village with Laila. She tells us a little of Kemet's history and how Ptah created his own humans, putting only women in charge. Hathor, his daughter, ruled here first. Sekhmet never wanted to rule as a human; she always remained in goddess form. She says women are natural rulers by nature—*yeah, yeah*—and the people do not engage in violence or any kind of war.

We walk through a small area that seems to not have been built yet, and then we emerge into their world.

The brick walkway is filled with colorful shops, and foot carts litter the area. We pass jewelry makers and seamstress shops that are closing for the night. A vendor throws me a bunch of grapes, and I almost faint at the taste.

"All of our foods are grown by our god himself, jus' like in da old days when man wuz firs' made." She smiles at the look on the twins' faces from a sample bite of a treat that they had just received from another vender that we passed.

I see the look in Izzi's eyes, but she will not say.

They have these tall poles that have hanging lights. In our world, once the sun leaves, shops close. Here, though, they have outside lights.

The path through the market ends, and then we walk up a smooth hill.

"Wow," most of us say.

Below are their homes, and they are built in heights that I have never seen before. Each painted different colors, windows above and below, and each home has a small statue of Sekhmet or Ptah at the entrance. All the homes are in a circle, because standing in the center of the entire area is another statue of Ptah, water spewing from his staff, creating a pool of water at his feet. The water seems to stay right in place.

"If ya did not notice, tha Nile doz not run 'roun our borders, but it doz flow under us on its way to the salt wata."

My group is in awe, except Izzi. She observes but has no expression on her face.

I have never been to the palace, but I will be comparing when I finally go.

She throws me a look, and I wink. I wanted her to hear that.

Laila gives us all our own living space, as promised, next to one another. They are one-level villas. She says they use these when families are building on to their homes, or when some families need time apart from one another.

I open the door to the home that I got. There is a cord hanging just inside on the wall, and I pull it. The home lights up with those strings of lights strung around. *Wow*, we need this at home where Adallah has to light all the lamps by hand.

The family area has cozy, blue cushy chairs, a small fireplace, and the walls are painted as if I was in the salt water with green floors. There is a small kitchen area that is neat and orderly. Everything is blue.

There is also a small hall with two doors. I open the door to the right and pull the cord, finding a built-in wooden bowl in the floor. I glimpse inside and can see the grass outside and a bucket right below it. *Whoa!* Back home, I would have to go to the community *khazi* that was behind our house. Every ten homes shared a *khazi*, and all the males are responsible for getting rid of the waste. Not only do I have my own, but I'm also pretty sure I don't have to dispose of it myself. There is also a stand with a small basin of water in it and a bar of that smell good soap next to it. I'm never leaving.

I go to the room across from this one and pull the cord. My heart drops. Centered in the room is a giant bed with blue, sheer hanging curtains. There is a rod to hang clothing, and a small, circular window, complete with a net to keep out the bugs. I pull back the curtains and crawl into the bed. The softness ... I have never ...

I roll around on it. I'm never leaving. Forget whatever else we have to do. I quit. Kemet is my home.

I look around. The walls are that water blue, as well, and above, on the ceiling, are stars.

Making sure I'm alone, I start to jump. I have never had a bed, let alone experienced this joy.

I hear a door open and close.

"NeenhoKano, you better not be jumping on that bed, boy," Adallah says from the family room.

I get a few more jumps in then go out to the family room, sweating. That was fun.

"Aunt Adallah. Hey, you. No, I wasn't jumping ... that much. Just maybe two times." I grin at her.

She inspects the villa. "I would rather have this ocean layout. I have a desert, and Chike has a jungle. This place feels like a dream," she says.

"Their god and goddesses are active in their lives. I wonder why ours have left us," Adallah says.

We sit in silence, looking around. "Why did you come over, Aunt Adallah?"

She turns to me, and I see she looks out of place. "I laid down then realized I have never slept away from you since I got you. I have never been away from you. Today, when they took us and I had no idea what happened to you ... At the mountain, thinking of you out—"

I wrap my arms around her, and she lets her head drop to my shoulder.

"Aunt Adallah, there's something I want to tell you. We saw Ptah, and he showed me something. He showed me a lot of things. Can I show you?"

13

IZZI-RA

I lay in a hammock suspended in the air. I did not want to sleep indoors. My room was of the southern, snowcap mountaintops. Although the room was cozy and warm, I felt as cold as the walls depicted. Kade and Assim were placed in villas on either side of me. Assim's room looked like Ptah's floating mound in the sky, and Kade's room depicted the flood. If I knew any better, I would have said Neenho designed it just for Kade.

Kade and Assim are beyond anxious because of me. Not to mention everything they have been through, because of me.

The sky is clear, and the air is cool. The cold season is here.

Everyone has been enjoying their time here. The Kemetians are strange to me. *Dey issa looka crazy*, as they would probably pronounce it. Between the way they say things and the clucking they do, my mind cannot grasp it all.

The women here have wild-colored hair, and they do not wear gold but grass and flowers. The men are all massive, and everyone has patches of pale skin over their bodies. I think that is beautiful. That, I cannot lie. It is art on them. Hathor blessed them beautifully.

I have not seen any children, now that I think of this place more.

I let out a deep sigh, my brain racing. My mother should be ready for her journey to the Underworld. A wonderful ceremony was probably planned for her, in her garden.

A tear escapes my eye, and I let it go freely around my ear then drip down my neck. The thought of her delicate body being wrapped ... them taking her insides out and wrapping them for her ... and then Anubis will come. *Oh no!*

The Anubis I saw is not a good god. He better not go anywhere near my mother.

I pray Osiris intercepts. I need to see Isis again. Maybe I can go to the statue of Ptah and ask him.

I feel the amulet cold on my chest and redirect my thoughts. There are two more pieces that I need to find.

I pull it out and study it closely. The beetle. Two emerald stones for eyes, gold paint outline for the wings. I tuck it back out of sight. It is mine. I do not know why, but it feels like part of me.

I stare into the black abyss above. No stars in the sky. No moon light, either. There is a glow around here, though.

A small wind blows, and I smell dirt and honey. I smile because that is how my mother smelled. She always smelled of dirt because of her garden and honey because of the oils that she used on her skin. I guess it is okay to let my thoughts roam to her.

I am glad she will not suffer from her sickness again this flood season. *I miss you, Mama*, I think, hoping her *Ba* can hear me. I let another tear fall and quickly wipe it away. I have to find these amulets, and then what? What do we do with them once we have them?

Lizard Man wants them, and the gods seem to fear them.

I think of the dream I had about my mother last night. She told me I need to come back to the palace. I have not told Neenho about my dream, how real it felt. When I woke up, I did not even let myself believe I still had an aftertaste of honey and dates in my mouth. Because it was not real. None of it was real.

I think of Neenho. He must be sleeping like a baby right now. I saw him sneaking more of that grape wine they gave us. Neenho has never had any before. We have plenty in the palace. He kept asking for more fruit water. I found it quite funny.

Footsteps below take me out of my thoughts. I look to my other side and see Chike running out the villas. Great, something else for me to do since I cannot sleep.

I land catlike on the soft grass below then run quickly and quietly in the direction I saw her go. The villas are all quiet, lights out and doors closed for tonight.

I do gaze in amazement at the villas again. How they are in an array of colors and shapes. The art either depicts Sekhmet or Hathor with many glyphs etched around them. Protection symbols. The magnificent art skill adorns the walls and the walkways. The soft patter of the water falling from Ptah's staff is like a lullaby to put you to sleep.

Gosh, the craftsmanship in this village should be contracted by the pharaoh. Well, not Zarhmel, but me. When I am Pharaoh I will have the Kemetians—ask them—help me build on my empire.

I peek around at the sleeping homes, wondering where Chike went. I perk my ears and listen closely. I hear faint noise beyond the villas. I head toward it.

The warm colors of the villas, the flowerbeds, and trees dim out as I go toward the boxed home ahead that sits in a field alone, surrounded by nothing but a few sad trees.

As I near, I can hear her voice inside. I go around the back and peer into a circular window. What in the goddess's name is going on here? There is only one room in this forsaken place.

Dingy walls, no art, grey as the clouds that bring the rain. I shake myself from the misfortune of the décor here and listen in on why I came here.

Chike is standing at the wooden door with her back against it. Sho'te stands far away from her, near what appears to be his bed. This man ... I shake my head. He needs a woman to spruce this place up.

I almost gasp at the quilt he is using.

"Sho'te, please, talk to me," Chike pleads with him.

Why would she come here alone? He slapped her back in the cave. I am so glad I came. I will be ready if he tries to hurt her again.

"I will not go until you talk with me. They would not want this. *She* would not want for you to turn your back on me."

I tense when I hear him growl.

"Ya are no kin te me. Lemme be now, or I swea' fo' ma god an' tha souls of ma peeple," he ends in a low rumble, balling his hands into fists.

"I know I should have never left. I know. All that anger and hatred you are trying to direct at me is nothing but sadness in disguise. I see it, Sho'te. I feel it."

"Tha' slap was a warnin', Chike. Go now."

Chike laughs. "I gave you that one, and you know it."

I hold my palm out under me, and a small ball of gold light blazes.

"No need fa tha', chile."

I swirl around to meet the eyes of Laila, who puts her finger to her lips.

"Shh ... or ya will miss ta res of dis encounter," she whispers as she moves next to me and peers through the window. "Dey 'ave not seen each other in fifteen Shemu. Dis shall be good." Her eyes twinkle as she watches.

Sho'te still has his fist clenched, but Chike is not taking the hint. She takes a few steps toward him, takes a deep breath, and then bows.

"No!" he rumbles.

Chike puts her arms to her sides, and then a small ripple of colors surrounds her.

Laila is beaming. I am lost.

What is going on? What was that?

Sho'te just stares at Chike, who seems to be ... not moving, breathing, or blinking. It's as if she is a statue.

His shoulders slump in defeat. Then he bows, and his arms drop to his sides limply. Those colors, small yet noticeable, ripple around him, and then he goes still.

"Ooo ... She hasn' loss ha touch. She betta do betta 'cause he will not hold back on her," Laila comments on ... nothing. She is giggling and gasping.

I look at her, worried for her.

She finally meets my eyes. "Expand ya mind, Izzi-Ra. Look." She points back through the circular window. "Look, Izzi-Ra. See."

I look yet see nothing but them standing there, staring at each other like statues. I am about to leave this confusing scene when I see a battlefield, and then the room again. I see dirt and trees, and then the room again. I hear grunts and yells, but then the room again. I scrutinize them more thoroughly as they face one another, and then the room completely changes.

I cannot see Laila next to me, but I feel her there. I do not see my body, nor hands, but I know they are there.

Ahead of us, Chike and Sho'te are in full combat.

I gasp. What is this? How is this?

"Dem cannot see us," Laila says as Chike kicks Sho'te straight in the gut, and he falls back.

"Stop holding back," Chike yells at him.

Sho'te spits blood from his mouth as he gets up then charges at Chike. He knocks her down and gets her in a hold around her neck. She punches him wherever her long arms can reach.

"A peaceful people, my—"

"Shh ... Watch an' learn, chile," Laila hushes me.

The sky overhead was sunny but turns to a threatening storm. The wind howls, lightning strikes, and the two continue to pound on one another. Chike takes it. She takes every blow, and even though she has barely any muscle, she is equally striking this mountain man. They run at each other and claw and punch on impact. They fall into the now muddy ground, panting.

"I tried, Sho'te, I tried. You know how hard it was for me. I could not tell a goddess no. I could not say no."

"Ya lef' family behin'. Ya tribe! Iziz iz not ya goddess. Mama wept 'erself to death." He tries to snatch her, but she scoots out the way.

Both battered and tired, she does a series of tongue clucking, pleading to him in their language. His eyes widen and, for a second, I think he forgives her. Then he snatches her leg so fast, dragging her near him. He pulls her up and starts to choke her. She gargles out something, and he drops her back to the ground. He pounds the ground and roars.

I hear Laila sniffle.

The colors ripple around them again, and they come back to life, back in the room.

Sho'te stumbles back and flops on his bed. Chike slowly drops to the floor. Neither look hurt, or wet, or dirty.

"Those two ... Those are my ..." Sho'te breaks off.

"I am sorry," Chike whispers. "Their names are Umi and Ta'li."

"Are they his niece and nephew?" I whisper.

Laila snaps her head so fast in my direction. "Chilens, Chile. Dey are married."

My eyes are going to get stuck in this wide, surprised expression.

"Come, Izzi-Ra, let us give dem privacy now." Laila gentle grabs my hand and leads me away. We walk in silence.

Once back in the center of all the colorful villas, Laila stops at the water statue of Ptah and says, "Wha' ya jus' witnessed issa gift from our god, Ptah. The *Kyst*. The *Kyst* issa frame o' mind where we go with those we are havin' problems wit. Dere, we work out our problems. We will na be permitted back until we have resolved the issue at hand. Ptah did na want a people who allowed da negative energies of dis world to have a longin' effect. Family and friends mean everytang. Da violence ya witnessed is not normal *Kyst* travels. But dose two 'ave so much pent-up aggression. No one can kill in da *Kyst*. And no, men do not take der wives dere to beat dem or vice versa." She smiles at me.

I do not know what to say, but then I ask her, "Why did he mention Mama if they are not brother and sister?"

Laila shrugs. "Sho'te wuz born to a young, vibrant couple. Oh, fa many moons, baby Sho'te cried an' cried an' never stopped. Nothin' worked. Even Hathor came in human form to try an' he would not stop crying. Dey were goin' ta put tha baby boy out of his misery.

"Dey went to da Shaman ta bless the *Ka* and *Ba* an' to call Anubis

76

to guide da baby to tha Underworld to be taken to Osiris. I was wit dem. We laid da baby down, took the dagger, and pierced baby Sho'te righ' in de heart. The cryin' finally ceased."

I gasp at her, bewildered. I can see it all as she remembers it.

"But da most extraordinary ting 'appened. The *Ba, Ka,* an' shadow all emerged. Tha baby was still alive, looking at tha life force 'bove him. Tha elements swirled together den slammed back into baby Sho'te.

"Tha torches wen' out an' we were all knocked out. I was de firs' ta wake up. Tha sun had rose high, not a clou' in da sky. I stood up an look on da pyre. Sho'te wuz dere, fas asleep. Fa tha firs' time, he was sleepin'. I started cryin'. I wuz beyond emotion. When de otheas awoke an seen wha' I was seein' dey were filled wit so much joy jus' as meself. Restful, cryin', unhappy baby Sho'te fast asleep, wit a baby gal cuddled next to him. Dey say we come from a place before here. I know dat to be true, 'cause Sho'te could not be here witout wuteva it was he left behind.

"Ya see our spots, but Chike is different. She iz him reverse with black spots. Sho'te's skin. She 'as a black spot on her body, ova her 'eart, where her beloved blessed her wit life." Without another word, Laila turns on her heels and walks away.

I watch her disappear into a yellow and orange villa. I stand where I am for just a moment longer.

What am I supposed to do with that story? Is this a hint of some kind? A love that is so strong that it creates a soulmate?

I do not remember walking back, but I make it to my hammock.

My last thought is, *Did either of us create one another? Because I feel something for him light in the pit of my stomach.*

I continue to stare at the black sky, thinking of Neenho, until I fall into what I can only imagine is a dream.

Darkness, heavy darkness presses in all around me. Someone is there, but I cannot see them. Blue light flickers behind me, and I spin around quickly. A door has appeared and is open. The blue light is flowing from it. This must be a dream, but with the way things have been going lately ...

I do not even bother to feel for my power. Whatever is in there is not going to harm me. I know that much.

I walk through, finding a small, circular chamber, with just a glass case in the center. The case emits the blue glow around the room.

"Thank you for coming," a soft voice says.

He stands in the doorway that I just walked through. Inhumanly tall, with blueish-green colored skin, his locks hanging to his shoulders, goatee resting on his chest. He looks like every art depiction that I have ever seen of him, except he is missing his staff and *nefer* crown.

In a blink, he is standing right before me, towering over me. I am speechless as his big, brown eyes search my surprised ones.

"We know who each other is. No need for introductions. You wonder if this is a dream, yes?"

I nod then shake my head. I don't know.

"This is not a dream. I have summoned you here. I did not think it would work, but it did. I need your help, Izzi-Ra, and *only* you can help me."

"Osiris?" I mutter, feeling stupid.

We hear a bang come from the empty case.

He breaks eye contact with me to gaze into the case, his locks slapping his face as he whips them away. So much like Neenho.

"There is not much time. They must feel I have found a way to use pow'r. Izzi-Ra, I need you." He looks at me pleadingly. Those eyes, so pitiful, like Neenho.

"What do you, King of the Underworld, a high god, need from me?"

He is breathing heavily, searching my face. "Izzi-Ra, I am a fallen god. This case is my prison. I am trapped here. I have been for 12 Pèret. I was set up by the most villainous god, Nun, ever let come into creation. I need to get a message to Isis."

We hear the bang in the empty case again.

He glances at the case again, seeing something that I obviously cannot see, because he appears panicked and scared.

"How can a god fall?" I ask.

"Details. *Sh'lac si'gew g'met e'tha.* That is the message for my beloved forever queen. Have you seen her? She is my queen, my moon, my stars, my universe, my *si'jah mu'ht et.*"

I frown. Did he really need to add all that? I am not saying all that.

"As a native of Asir, I am pleased to serve you, but I am confused. What is happening to me? To Neenho? I need answers, please."

He grabs my hands and bends a knee to be eye level with me. "Izzi-Ra, do you know who you were born to?"

That question throws me off. He is looking into me. I hate how they all seem to do that.

"What?" I ask. "What do you see?"

"She is not dead. Nephthila lives. She did not die," he tells me, and my heart skips all the beats it needs.

Another dream that tells me that my mother lives.

"She did not come to you?" I manage to ask.

"No. Nephthila lives. But that is not the question. I need you to know who you were born to. You must not love her. That love will free her. You know ... You know the answer."

The bang is louder and startles us both. The room even shakes a little.

"What is happening, My God?"

"There is an Isle off the coast of Nu'el. Dangerous waters. You can die trying to get there. Only a god or goddess will be granted passage. You must get there; take what is yours." He points to a spot on my chest where nothing is. "The third piece is in here. Get the amulets, Izzi-Ra. Free Adiah. Free Anubis. Anubis is being controlled. He does not want this. Help us. Help us all."

We stare at one another; him searching me, and me searching him.

"Who caused all this?"

His mouth begins to form what looks like a snake, and the glass shatters. He grabs my face and presses my head to his. I feel my mind being sucked out; flashes fly before my eyes. Times, places, other gods. The island, the water, red eyes, my mother floating in the water, a tomb, and then a bright red amulet of the eye.

Osiris then yells.

I scream and hit something hard.

I have fallen out of the hammock and landed in the grass, mouth full of grass. *Ugh.* I guess it is better than sand.

The sun is shining brightly, and I hear children laughing and meaningless chatter off in the distance. I sit, huffing for a minute.

Osiris, he came to me.

I go to lift myself up, and my fingers catch on something. The amulet lays next to me, gleaming. I know where the second piece is.

14

NEENHOKANO

"You should not have done that, NeenhoKano. You think because you have these powers, and converse with gods, and can fly, you can do whatever you want! I should take my sandal off and welt your behind, boy. And then you ..."

Aunt Adallah goes on, and on, and on. I feel dreadful and, on top of that, I have to listen to this. I vomited a few times this morning, and she has had to wash me up. My head is spinning, and I feel dried-out and my eyes sting.

"Aunt Adallah, please. I know. I won't ever, ever drink anything besides water for the rest of my existence." I roll over onto my side. The cool floor feels great on my face.

I meet big, sun gold eyes. Bastet is in my face. *I have no energy for you*, I think to her, knowing she's enjoying this.

"Shoo, Bastet. Get away." I weakly swat at her, but she doesn't budge.

"Sit up now and drink this." Adallah sits a steaming cup down next to me.

"Oh no, please, I don't want it." The smell of it causes me to gag. However, I regrettably sit up because, if I don't, Adallah will snatch me up herself. My head spins, and my eyes take a moment to focus.

She's busying herself, poking the fire that heats the hot table she cooked her concoction on. I hate this stuff. Every time I have ever been sick, she would whip up a batch of this brown liquid that has a minty, nasty flavor.

"Drink it down, or I will force it down." She scoops up Bastet then sits in a chair that looks out the small, circular window.

I take a deep breath then drink a big gulp. The hot liquid burns as it goes down. I shake it off, though, and finish the rest, not wanting to hear her nag.

Even though I hate it, her drink always does the trick. I feel a small spark in my fingers, my light strengthening.

I study her sadly. She really takes good care of me; gave up her life for me.

"Aunt Adallah?" She hasn't brought up what I showed her last night.

"I know, Neenho. We should not discuss that any further. We will cross those dunes when they come."

I nod in agreement.

We stare at one another when a small knock at the door shakes us from the trance. Izzi enters without waiting for a greeting.

She took her braids out, so her hair is fluffy around her face, and her eyes look droopy, as if she didn't get much sleep.

"*Ti'ju*, Princess Izzi-Ra. Did you sleep well? Would you like some bread and butter?" Adallah asks.

Izzi takes in my room then meets my eyes. I'm still sprawled out on the floor. I feel a bit of haze, and I can feel Izzi is in my mind.

I stare back at her and tug at my *He'ka*. I need to start blocking her. I can't just get into hers whenever I want, so I'm not going to let her keep poking in mine.

We stare at each other. I see her pulling at stuff, looking and searching. *Block her*, I think.

A small ball of purple light pops up in my hand, and then it goes out but alights inside of me. I feel it creep up my arm, over my shoulder, and into my head. It forms a barrier around my mind, and I hold it there, holding her eyes. She was about to see what Ptah showed me.

I feel her trying to break in, but she cannot. Izzi does not let it show that she is upset with me, and I do not let it show that I just beat her at our first internal argument.

"Do either of you hear me?" Adallah's voice cuts through.

"I do not want anything. Thank you. Meet me at the Ptah statue. The one in the trees," she says to us then slams the door shut on her way out.

🐦🐦🐦

"*Nu'el*? Are you sure?" Adallah asks Izzi, who just finished relaying her dream to the group.

The twins, Sho'te, and Chike stand off to the side in their own little group. They all display the same deep-thoughted look on their faces. Neither said anything while Izzi relayed her dream, her vision, to us.

To the side of them is Laila. A huge man stands behind her, along with one of the gorgeous women who tried to attack us last night. Kade and Assim stand off to the side together, watching Izzi closely. Izzi, on the other hand, is circling the statue, rubbing every inch she can reach, looking for something.

"Nu'el, yes, that is what he said. We must go there."

Laila and her people laugh.

"'Tis not possible, aye. Nu'el was 'round about da time of de gods. Nu'el can only be—"

"Accessed by gods or goddesses. Osiris told me that part."

Adallah and I raise our eyebrows at each other. Izzi is always dismissive, but we are in Laila's lands, not Egypt. She needs to show a little more respect.

"What is Nu'el?" I ask, noticing Izzi wants that answer, as well.

"Nu'el hides the waters of Nun. No human has ever set foot there, nor been able to find the path through it. Dead man's quest, which Izzi-Ra is fully aware of," Assim says.

Izzi ignores him, still searching for who knows what? She stands back to take in the entire statue.

83

"Osiris pulled you to him in the Underworld? He told you he is a fallen god, that Anubis is being controlled, and showed you where another amulet lies?" Adallah recaps to Izzi, who just nods.

"He said get to Nu'el. He said save him, but we have to save Adiah first."

"Adiah is at Nu'el? Is that where that pyramid is?" I ask Izzi.

"There is only one way to find out. We must go there as soon as possible," Adallah says. I can see the hope in her eyes that her sister may be there.

Laila and two warriors start to cluck their tongues at one another. Chike and Sho'te nod to one another. Sho'te clucks his tongue, as well. He and Laila go back and forth for a moment.

"'Tis not possible!" Laila shouts. "Dere is no mon-made map to dis Nu'el. Ya wan' me to len' ya me peeple ta go farther west? Plus, dere is no god or goddess among ya ta get dere and ya 'ave no map."

Izzi grins. "Neenho," she says, and I jump. I'm not about to get into this. "Neenho, call your *clou*."

Confused, I whistle, and my *clou* comes from wherever it comes from. I jump on and soar into the sky. The breeze feels so good, my locks flapping behind me. Why don't I do this just for fun?

I hear Izzi clear her throat loudly in my mind. Oh ...

I shoot down and stop beside her. She climbs on.

"Up near his mouth, please," she demands.

We fly close near Ptah's mouth, and then Izzi leans out, rubbing the face.

"Ah-ha! Neenho, the staff. Get as close as you can, please."

I drop down a notch. Izzi leans over again, touching and feeling. I look down at Adallah, who shrugs. I see Bastet has joined and is now on Adallah's shoulder. Where does she come from?

"Yes!" Izzi twists the tip of the staff. She knocks the rock off, and it falls below. Then she jams her arm into the staff and pulls out a scroll. We hear the gasps below.

I take us down, and we dismount. The *clou* dissolves right as I get off.

Everyone stops acting like they are in different groups and come together in a tight circle as Izzi lays the scroll down. She then opens her palm and shines her golden light on it.

Nothing happens.

"Together?" I tell her.

She doesn't even look at me. What's with her?

Together, we send an entwined thread of purple and gold light at the scroll. It lights up green. It's blank at first, but then gold and purple lines, circles, and symbols begin to appear.

"With or without help from your people, I am leaving for Nu'el," Izzi tells Laila, who glances with wide-eyed surprise from the statue to the map. Then Laila and her people go off and have a meeting somewhere.

Izzi-Ra is being distant for some reason. She is in the back of her villa, laying in a hammock. She says she's just sleepy, but I know better. And the fact that neither of us is letting the other in just tells me more that something is going on. She says she wants to rest up for our journey. She thinks it may be something like Meretseger Mountain, that I should be preparing for our journey to this Nu'el place.

Assim stands guard outside her villa, because that is what he was born to do, he says. Kade feels hopeless since Izzi won't talk to him. Chike and her children are getting to know their mountain father, and Adallah is napping in a trance with Bastet. So, Kade follows me around. We sit around a common area with some of the natives.

There is a big grassy area, with a small pond. Children run and splash around it, and the adults just seem to come here to lounge. They did not let the children around us last night in case we were dangerous.

The female girls have colored hair like the adult females. The males are miniature mountains. Little boy sand dunes. They all have circle patches on them in random spots. Laila says their shapes will form when they discover who they are. When they realize what kind of warriors they are.

Huge trees litter the grounds, bearing pomegranates. The natives just grab them off the trees and crack them open, picking out the sweet seeds. Me and Kade have been trying to open one forever, neither of us getting it. Then I sneak and use my light to get ours open.

The Kemetians are really cool people. The only thing is they seem to talk really fast, have heavy accents, and pronounce everything weirdly. They don't sound like the Egyptians, but other than that, I like them. And I've noticed the boulder men are nicer than the women ... I think. All the men say, *lemme ask me mate* or *me mate said no*. The men make no decisions around here. They are just the muscle. Literally.

Near us, some men are playing a strange instrument that has tight lines on a craved, smooth, wooden thing. I see how his fingers press one of the strings down, and then another one, and music comes from the hollowed-out part in the center of it. Really cool.

"Packet boy," a boulder man says to me.

"Neenho," I correct him.

"Me names Rafa." He smiles at me. " Dat wuz somethin' strange ya did wit de purple light. Where'd ya learn dat at?"

"Gimme some o' those muscles, and I'll tell ya," I tell him.

He stares me down, and then we all laugh. A woman in the circle, though, does not laugh. She does not smile, move, or talk; she just rudely stares at me. Still, I smile at her. She clucks her tongue in that way they do.

"Oh, go off sum place else den. No one wants ya mood stinkin' up de place," Rafa says to her.

She clucks her tongue but stays right where she is, watching me. She has red locks that are slung over one shoulder. Her dark skin has pale patches up her arms, and one on her left cheek. It looks like the shape of a snake.

"Let me ask you people something. Why do you all have those patches on your body? No one in Egypt has that," Kade asks, stupidly.

"Ptah's daughter. She is Hathor, and she wanted her babies to look like her. Those touched by her, other half Sekhmet herself, will have animal prints in their patches. Only twins, a boy and girl, are born together," Umi says as she joins the circle. She flops down, looking extremely happy. She has been living in Pakhet her whole life. It must feel nice to be home. I wonder where I belong.

"There seems to be different ranks, like the women rule. That is interesting," Kade says, sounding even more stupid, in my opinion. That observation was quite clear when we got here when Laila wanted to knock us out.

"'Cause females are nest warriors. We are da most fearless. We fear no'ting. De men are strength," the mean woman says.

Umi gazes at her proudly. I wonder if Ta'li will become that big. He would look ridiculous with all that muscle.

"Yer purple *He'ka*, ya must be tha' chile of a great god," Rafa says.

I exchange glances with Umi, because I don't like Kade, so I don't want him thinking we can exchange knowing glances at one another.

I think about that for a moment. I have no answer for them, so I shrug.

I remember them saying we could not access the mountain without a god, and we cannot go to Nu'el without one. Maybe Izzi-Ra is a goddess.

I shake that thought away. We are not gods.

"Wha' god made ya, boy?" Rafa asks.

"We are on the path to discovering. But when I do find out, I'll tell you all 'bout it. I would love to stay here and be a Kemetian warrior."

They all laugh, Rafa patting me on the back. He then hands me a hand drum, and I start banging away. This feels so much like family.

15

ZARHMEL

Zarhmel sits on the deck of Nephthila's room. He stares into the water that flows past, lost in thought.

Izzi-Ra has gotten an amulet, his brother has taken down Pakhet, and his people, they know Drahzil lives. Problem after problem is arising.

There's no way around it. Izzi must be a goddess. She had the purest of golden light surrounding her. That look in her eyes ...

And Nephi, his queen, she knew. She has known. She gave birth to her. But, how? When Nephi said she was with child, he suspected the child could be his brother's. He was only thirteen Shemu when he officially took the crown and had never had any intimacy.

But Drahzil is not a god.

Nephthila was dead, in his arms. He knows this. He saw her gasp and take her last breath. His pain was unbearable for an entire night. He lay weeping by her bed. Then Obissi came to start the process and get her ready for the journey.

They both watched as she arose. Zarhmel was beyond belief. Obissi not so much, as he recalls. What is she?

His sister has been raising another child with god-like elements in the small Pakhet village all these Ahket's. He thought his sisters were dead. He thought his brother was dead. Is his mother and father going to reveal themselves alive, as well?

There is something going on, and he does not know what. He is Pharaoh! He wants answers, and he wants them *now*.

He hears laughter and a small splash. Lifting his head, he sees his queen on her paddle board, with her maidens, crossing the waters from her garden. This is a normal scene ... to the maidens. But not him. Not anymore.

He stands, all emotions pulled from his face.

"Pharaoh, what a surprise." Nephthila smiles up at him.

"Leave. Now."

Kolet and Sha bow then quickly hurry away.

"Pèret has begun. The flowers are closing, and I have noticed less creatures racing through the garden. I am going out tomorrow to advise the farmers on the best way to protect the crops from the freeze."

Zarhmel cocks his head to the side and really looks at her, letting disbelief show. With everything that has happened, she is talking about crops and flowers?

"Because there is nothing I can do about your troubled thoughts," she responds.

"What are you, Nephi? Tell me everything."

"All you need to know is that the child you raised, the child you allowed to sit on your knee and tell stories to, the child you crowned Princess, you have denounced her and tore her down from the kingdom as if she means nothing to you."

Zarhmel is taken aback. Nephthila has never raised her voice at anyone, let alone him, her king, her love.

"Things are not always what they appear to be, Zarhmel. You need to learn this, and you need to learn it fast. I am not the enemy here. He is." She points her finger up, and Zarhmel looks.

Drahzil is sitting on a column.

He jumps down. "Still have not learned to check your surroundings, little brother? Father's men were training, and this little guy was not paying attention. Walked right into one of their traps. We almost lost you that day."

Zarhmel knows what Drahzil is doing, but he will not get a rise from him. They are not children anymore, and Zarhmel holds the crown.

Nephthila has not once glanced at Drahzil, Zarhmel notices. He wonders if it is because that was her husband. Maybe she still has feelings for him. Or maybe his new features are too hard to bear. Even Zarhmel has trouble getting over the reptilian likeness.

"What do you want, Drahzil? My queen and I were having a private conversation."

Drahzil laughs. "Oh, little brother, nothing between you and the queen is private. Or true. Or what they seem. She is the enemy here, not me." Drahzil points a long-nailed finger at Nephthila, who still has not peeked his way. "Who is she, brother? Because I think I know a bit more than you do, at this point."

Zarhmel wants to shout, yell, and stomp his foot. He is Pharaoh! The disrespect, the disregard for his rank, and the way Drahzil speaks to him angers him. But he knows he cannot show this.

He stands tall and proud, hands sweating behind his back.

Nephthila only has eyes for her king, whereas Drahzil glances between them both. The air feels like its thinning, and Zarhmel feels like his throat is tightening.

What does he say to them?

Someone clears their throat loudly, startling the three from their awkward moment. All three sets of eyes dart to the entryway. Obissi stands there.

Drahzil and Obissi lock eyes for a brief moment. Drahzil looks away first, but not before Zarhmel catches the moment. Obissi was Drahzil's friend growing up. Drahzil was with Obissi the night the gods marked him as a priest.

"Please, excuse my interruption. Jabari is awake."

Zarhmel exhales, grateful for a reason to be able to leave. "I will deal with you two, separately, later. Lead me to him, Obissi."

Nephthila watches Zarhmel leave. Without glancing Drahzil's

way, she heads to leave but is spun around by a red whip coming from Drahzil's hand. He pulls her close to him, the whip getting tighter around her midsection. She does not struggle or seem stressed, but merely bored.

"Say what you need and be quick," she tells him.

"What was that memory? I remember that party clearly, and that is not what happened. How were you ...? I saw ... I know what I have seen!"

Another whip lashes out and snakes around her neck.

"You fool, tethered to a god. Do you know what happens once they release you? You did not think the light they gave you was forever, do you? It comes with a price. One you are not ready to pay."

"I will take my chances, Queen. You, on the other hand, what will your pharaoh do when I tell him about what you did? I know who you are, Nephthila."

With one finger, she lightly touches his face, and Drahzil shudders and his light dissolves.

"Do not underestimate me."

Drahzil studies his hands then lifts his eyes back to Nephthila.

She thinks for a moment. Then, instead of going through the door, she leaps from the marble steps and into the water, disappearing from sight.

Drahzil swears.

Heliaj flaps down, and he jumps on. When he is gone, Zarhmel steps back out onto the deck. He sent Obissi ahead. He is just as good at hiding in the shadows.

He stands, thinking about the small exchange that he just heard between the two. What memory did his queen share, and what does *tether* mean?

Zarhmel heads down the corridor that leads to the medical temple. Most temples are the color of clay or painted in gold, yet the medical temple is black. A statue of Osiris and the jackal stand at attention.

Jabari's wife and daughter stand outside the temple. They kneel when they see Zarhmel approach. He pays them no mind, walking right inside.

The walls are a smooth black. Few torches are alight. The place is to not make one feel like they are doomed but calm. A quite place to heal as you live, or as you prepare for the journey.

Zarhmel enters the chamber that holds several beds. The healer, Satsh, is bent over Jabari, checking him.

When Jabari sees Zarhmel, he tries to stand but weakly falls back.

"No need for all of that, Jabari," Zarhmel says as he pulls up a seat. "What happened to you, man?"

Jabari weakly gazes at his earth god as he thinks then shakes his head. "I cannot remember. I was here, watching the princess be married, and then I was here in this room."

Zarhmel does not know what to say. Nothing makes sense.

"I believe Jabari was knocked out during the chaos. See the cut on his head?" Satsh points out a thin line of dried blood that goes from one ear, across his forehead, to his other ear.

"It looks as if someone tried to cut his face off," Zarhmel states. He has never seen anything like this.

Satsh shrugs. He does not linger on the scar. Although he is not old—well, to him, he is not—he is younger than the hawaitis that they brought back from the Pakhet village. His soft, curly hair has not begun to grey yet, his brown eyes have not started to mist over as most elders' eyes have, and he is relatively fit. He studies the art of medicine to keep his mind and *ka* in tune with the gods, and that keeps his body healthy.

Satsh has been the palace healer since Isis was Pharaoh. He has seen many things and knows many secrets. But the palace folk only remember him when they need him.

Anubis is his god, and he is sworn to secrecy. Satsh has seen a mark like this, many times. But he will not betray anyone's trust and say a word. He can only hope Jabari will make it.

"A few more sun sets and some rest, he will be back to normal," Satsh tells Pharaoh.

Zarhmel nods. There is nothing more he can push on this matter. Jabari is momentous to his ranks. He lost a lot of men the other night, thanks to his brother. He is grateful Jabari was not killed.

"Get better. We need you." Zarhmel pats Jabari on his shoulder.

Jabari nods then lies back, closing his eyes without another word.

Zarhmel glances around the healing room. There are three more beds across the room, all empty and neatly made. He frowns.

"Let his family in, please," Zarhmel says as he leaves the room.

He walks off quickly toward his chamber, Obissi right beside him.

"Odd that he remembers nothing. And that scar ... how did he survive it? Do you think someone did something to him?"

"By someone, you mean Drahzil. And, if Drahzil had him, he would have killed him. Jabari is fine," Obissi answers.

"I did not see Kadir. Why was I not informed he was awake, as well?"

They pass the kitchen quarters, a sweet smell coming from the area. Zarhmel cannot remember when he last ate.

"Kadir's people were right at his side. He is on the grounds some-where. I was told he was sending word back to Shiza to warn them that Prince Kade has gone rouge and is to be killed at first sight."

Zarhmel smirks. *Perfect.* He was going to have the boy killed, anyway.

Shiza is now fully in Zarhmel's hands. He can send new beings there to start building.

A drum sounds, and they stop walking.

"Urgent news," Obissi comments.

The two turn around and head down another corridor, heading toward the gates.

Another attack maybe? Zarhmel thinks anxiously.

They reach the gates to the palace where about five men on black horses wait outside. The men wear armor with blazing blue waves on the chest. Their faces are covered by blue helms with five black tassels in the middle. They dismount and kneel.

Zarhmel approaches the gate cautiously. They should not be here. They traveled far.

"Satisians from Dejut Island, what brings you here?" Zarhmel demands.

The closest one takes off his helm, and then the rest of the men follow suit. They all watch Zarhmel with the same sky-blue eyes, their dark skin gleaming with sweat from the heat of the sun. Each man has a patch of white hair, braided into a tail.

"Queen Qui'l received revelation from her god that a war is on the rise. She sent us at once to let you know our allegiance to you as earth god has not changed. We stand with Egypt and our Asir brothers and sisters against any threat." The men pound a fist across their chest.

Dejut is on an island far south. The snowcap mountains of Vaarad, a mountain broken into three parts, sits as their backdrop. Vaarad is what floods the Nile every Ahket. The island sits high on a raised platform to allow the melting snow to go around them, flooding their land's soil, and the water around them, destroying Egypt.

Zarhmel is impressed. Queen Qui'l has let it be known that she would do anything to be his queen. She has always remained a fierce, loyal ally.

He did not get to choose the ruler of the island, as she was already in place. Well, her mother was. Qui'l's mother passed many Pèret's ago and left her the throne.

Zarhmel would never choose a woman to lead the people who follow him. *A mistake.* Zarhmel thinks women are meek lionesses. They should only breed and be pretty on the arm of a male.

"This act is much appreciated and will be rewarded," Zarhmel tells the Satis warriors.

"We also have word that the Princess of Egypt is outlawed. Our queen knows where the treacherous princess is," the messenger says.

Zarhmel and Obissi exchange looks.

"Where is she?" Zarhmel asks, ready to leave at once.

"She is in a village to the west," the messenger says.

A glob of something wet splats on Zarhmel's shoulder, and he looks up. Drahzil is hovering above on Heliaj. *He heard everything,* Zarhmel assumes.

The men also look up then back at Zarhmel. He notes how Drahzil's appearance, and his fire flamed horse, does not seem to move them in any way. Did their god tell them about the deformed men on fire camels, as well?

"We cannot leave the palace," Obissi says. "Do you trust this news?"

Zarhmel contemplates. "They have given me more news in this moment than you have in three days.

"You." Zarhmel points to the guy who seems to be the leader.

"Trisher," the man says, bowing.

"Trisher, will you and your men accompany me and my men to track down the rouge princess?"

All the men fist their chests as more come from beyond the shadows. "That is why we have come, ready to serve the earth god."

Drahzil lands, and Heliaj paws the ground. He goes as close to the gate as he can and peers through. The men look back at him, as if he is no one.

Zarhmel likes them even more. His brother does not scare them. Good.

"Me and my men are coming along, as well, brother."

"I would have it no other way. I always want you in my sight.

"Obissi, show these men to the guest quarters in the west wing. Izzi is not here to stake claim anymore. Let them rest and refresh. Send some of our fairest to aid them in their needs. We leave at half past the last shadow of the tallest obelisk." That said, Zarhmel walks away, alone.

Izzi-Ra's whereabouts is known. Queen Qui'l has impressed him. He knows this news will need to be repaid. She will be showing up to collect, too. He will deal with that when she arrives.

His queen knows something. If she does not want to tell him, maybe she will tell Izzi-Ra.

16

NEENHOKANO

I float above the group alone, laying on my back, looking at the clear, blue sky. There's nothing but miles and miles of sand dunes and sand ... and sand. I slap my hands to my face and moan. Three days of this! I don't think I can take it anymore.

I roll over onto my belly and peer down right at her. I scroll through the group, but my eyes must assess her again. She's resting her head against his back with her arms draped loosely around his middle as he steers his camel. I frown, wishing the thing would start acting wild, make her fall, and then she would get on my *clou* with me. The thought makes me chuckle, thinking of Kade flying into the sand and getting it all in his mouth.

Izzi's eyes are closed, and she's breathing deeply. My eyes are so good now that I can see the vibration of her heart thumping softly, right near her ...

I shake my head. I looked! Will she know? Can *she* hear me?

I glance again at her face, but she doesn't make an expression.

"Kade is a buffoon," I say loudly.

No one looks my way.

I rub my hand around my *clou*, feeling a hum coming from it. What god bas this and why do I? I tuck the thought away for now. I will find out these questions soon enough. "I'm bored," I sigh. I know the others cannot hear me but I was sure Izzi would be able to.

I focus in on the rest of our growing group. Leading are three mountain men who agreed to journey with us—Rafa, Odom, and Fa'teem. I watch their horses, feeling so bad for them having to carry a ton across this never-ending desert terrain. They stare straight ahead, not talking. They have slings full of weapons all over their bodies. Even leather ropes around their ankles, holding small knives. I wonder if they will teach me, but then I scrunch my nose. What? I have *He'ka*! Who needs a knife?

Behind the boulder men flanks Ta'li and Adallah. Ta'li has his head down on his camel's head, which must be uncomfortable, but so far, this journey has been. Adallah is looking at Bastet, who sits in front of her, staring at her.

I focus in. Adallah is talking. Talking to her cat, as usual. If I was any one of them down there, I would think that's weird, but I've heard her talking to that weird thing plenty of times.

Bastet looks right at me, and my vision clouds. I rub my eyes then look back at them.

Bastet is fast asleep in Adallah's lap now.

I rub my eyes once more, but the cat is still fast asleep. Weird.

Next battle, I'm zapping Bastet. I think she has lived long enough. Adallah can get a new pet and name it Maat for all I care.

I put the cat out of my mind for now, mentally building a list of concerns and questions.

Behind Adallah is Umi and Assim. They are riding close together, talking. I guess that shouldn't surprise me. He is an awesome guy and, well, Umi is beautiful.

She playfully reaches out and slaps his arm, and he throws her his brilliant smile. I wonder if Izzi knows what is blooming here and if it bothers her. I know that the princess's guard is bound to her. Her consort, he would soon become. Kade knows this, as well. I guess it's me who doesn't get it.

I glance back at her. Her eyes are still closed, but I can tell her breathing has changed. She's awake.

Behind those two is the mean lady from the village and her companion. They make me excited and frightened all in the same breath.

Her name is Marja'ni. Her red locks drape past her feet, and she wears only black lip color. She has two long, green staffs crisscrossed on her back. I bet she could throw her spear right up here and hit me. She looks like she should never be crossed.

Her companion is softer. Kofi is a little shorter than Marja'ni, and her patches are really cool. The patches on her arms are in the shapes of rocks, trees, and weapons. Two small birds are above her eyes, and her arms have wing shapes.

Ptah gifted her, Chike told me. She does not need physical weapons, nor does she have any visible weapons that I can see. She wears a green top cover and white pants that cut off near her knees. She has no hair, but the fuzz that is there is red like Marja'ni's.

Behind them is Sho'te and Chike. They ride close to each other and hold hands in silence. I notice how peaceful they both appear. Twin flames. I didn't know that was real.

I dart my eyes back to Izzi, whose eyes are open now. I wonder if we are twin flames. Did I make Izzi? Did she make me?

I take a deep breath and close my eyes, trying to remember something, anything, but I can't. I smell honey and dirt, and Adallah says that is what I smell like.

I sigh. I'm going to die out here ... Water? I sit up on my knees and sniff again, smelling a deep salt scent. I notice the group below has halted. They must smell it, too.

I see nothing but sand. High sand mountains.

I glance down and lock eyes with Izzi, who has no expression. Without having to read minds, because I can't do it regularly anyway, I zoom ahead. I fly over a few dunes, but still see nothing. However, the smell becomes stronger.

A wide mountain comes into view. I scale the edge as I fly to the top. Once I clear it, I halt my *clou*, eyes wide.

A large body of water is before me. The salt water spreads for as far as I can see. Nothing else in sight, nothing around it. Right in the center, though, not too far away, is an island. The island sits high on a mound of rock, calm waves washing up the sides but unable to lick the land.

My *clou* starts to back up as I think about needing to tell Princess Izzi and the others. This is it. The island we have been seeing in our minds.

I stand with the group as they face a garden of sand mountains. From above, when I flew over them, they did not seem to be this big or this many. There is no way to climb, because the sand just keeps falling. Only a narrow gap snakes its way through the sand mountains to reach the shore.

Sho'te and his men speak in their tongue clucking language. Whatever they are discussing must have to do with the sand and will they fall, because they keep touching the nearest one and watching as the sand rolls down at the slightest touch. The dunes are not stable.

"You can feel it?"

I jump, not noticing Izzi-Ra was next to me.

"That we are about to go someplace we are not wanted? Yes, I do feel it. Shall we turn back and just hide out at the Kemetians' camp for the rest of our lives until Drahzil dies?"

Izzi grabs the nape of my neck and yanks me closer. "We are going forward. There is no going back." Izzi is watching me but says this loudly and clearly to everyone.

"Prinzess, we do not feel tha' dis way is stable. We must find anozer way 'round," Odom tells Izzi.

Izzi swirls around to face them all. "There is no other way around? Look!" She waves her hands. "There is nothing but mountains of sand on either side of us and before us. Neenho saw where we need to go, and we will go."

"Princess, it is not safe," Kade says softly to her.

Me and Assim glance at him, my thoughts clearly visible.

"I know it is not. That is why I am flying with Neenho. We will be right above you all to help and spot danger."

Kofi steps toward the entrance to the maze and stretches her hand out. Then she steps back and withdraws a small dagger. But, from where? She has nowhere to put any weapons!

She stands back and throws it. Upon passing the first sand mountain, the dagger explodes into fragments of sand.

"Welcome to Nu'el. No man can enter," Ta'li says.

Kofi picks up a handful of sand and throws it past what we assume to be the starting line. The sand fizzles out.

"You want me to go in there?" Kade asks Izzi.

Again, Assim and I gaze his way, my thoughts clearly visible.

The twins start talking excitedly to each other.

"Do you two want to share?" I ask, annoyed, but then I regret it.

They come to either side of me.

"Nu'el is where Nun, Geb, Teftnut, Autum, Shu, and the other eight first lived together in god form down here," Ta'li whispers in my ear.

"I don't want to know the rest," I tell them as Umi throws her arm around my neck, pulling me closer.

"It is written, that before they left, they created a goddess. But she was not like them, she wuz sumting else." Umi winks.

Chike and the others look proudly at Umi. Izzi and I roll our eyes.

"No human can go into Nu'el. Only a god or goddess, or a being who shares a direct bloodline with one of the thirteen, can cross into it and discover what lies beneath," Ta'li says.

I didn't see a village, I think.

"So, they lived on an island in the salt water?" I ask.

"Island?" Adallah questions. "This is Nu'el."

"Well, the scribes did not document it properly because there is a huge island ..."

Izzi is in my mind, and she sees. The crown room, and the walls, and the woman. It is the island, for sure.

"Nu'el is a front. A lie. The thirteen did not live in here. They lived out there." My words are true. I just know it.

Izzi nods her head in agreement.

"Even if that is so," Kade says, "how do we cross into here to get to whatever you saw over there? If you have not noticed, we are short a god and a goddess.".

"Are ya all mad?" Marja'ni speaks. "Dat guh has gol' light. I've seen deities wit light, an' he 'as pure purple. Unless de scribes got our gods and goddesses stories wrong, dey share a blood line to one or many."

Izzi and I peek at one another.

I shrug. I've been thinking of that, but it's crazy.

"Well, there is only one way to find out." Izzi runs right into the maze, and everyone screams. Seconds pass, and we hear nothing. I don't even feel her. She then reemerges.

"Hold all questions. I feel the next piece. There is an annoying drum in my chest again," she says as she engulfs her entire body in light and holds out her hand. "Link up. Neenho on the end."

No one questions her authoritative tone. Everyone takes hold of one another's hand.

Kofi smiles at me as she grabs my hand. I can't help but give her a shy grin back. On her neck is one of those pale patches in the shape of the dagger she threw. Could it be?

Her hand is soft in my sweaty one as I ignite my light, wondering if I can pull weapons from her skin.

"Now, Neenho, try to fan your light out to meet mine," Izzi instructs. "Do not think, young male; just do. Tell it what to do."

I want to argue about that *young male* part, but she raises an eyebrow. *Later*, I shoot the thought into her mind.

She sighs.

I take several deep breaths then focus, trying to imagine my purple light spreading, overshadowing, as the sun does when it rises.

I hear Izzi in my mind, telling me to meet her, to come to her. Her voice makes my heart skip several beats.

I push it over the ones closer to me, willing it to protect all except Kade. Okay, him, too … I guess.

I open my eyes to see Kofi beaming at me. We did it.

"Do not break the link until we are all inside," Izzi yells back.

"What happens once inside?" Kade whines.

"Hopefully, you don't smolder to pieces." I chuckle.

No one else laughs.

We start to move forward. I glance back at the camels as they act so camel-like, not a care in the world. I wish I was a camel right now.

The front of the line is inside, and all seems fine. I feel a ripple and know we are completely in.

The sun is blazing behind me, where the camels and horses stand, but in here, it's cloudy and looks like rain. We walk farther in, our light keeping the path lit.

I bump into Kofi as we come to a stop.

"Let go," Izzi says.

The men all erupt into an argument. I think Kade is really crying.

Is Izzi insane? They could all die!

"Trust me. Let go."

Kofi, with no fear in her eyes, drops my hand. My light quickly dissolves, and we all stand in silence, waiting for the guard to burst into flames, or just Kade.

Nothing happens.

I step out of line to see we have reached a path with two ways to go.

"Break into groups. Neenho and I will fly ahead, as I said earlier, and guide you all." She sure is taking lead here. She did at the mountain, as well. One thing is for sure; Izzi was born to lead.

My *clou* fashions before us, and we hop on. I fly above them all, and we watch as they break into groups. Chike, Sho'te, Umi, Ta'li, and Kade take one path. The rest take the other.

"You do realize why we were permitted to enter, right?" Izzi asks as she watches them below.

"Because you are a goddess," I joke.

"Gods love riddles. Men have never made it through because thirteen came and thirteen went. They created a fourteenth god, but you heard the twins—she did not leave. You cannot come here alone without thirteen others."

"How did you figure that out? What if there was fifteen of us?"

"Simple," she says, "they all die. Go forward."

We watch as they weave in and out of dark spaces and corners we cannot see.

"So far so good," I whisper, messing up everything as a gust of wind blasts us, and we roll over, in the air.

"Neenho, go up!"

No time to look, I do what she says.

A dark cloud rolls over, covering everything below us from sight. Straight ahead, in the distance, we can see the island. Blue skies, sun shining, and clear water ahead.

"Don't even ask how that can be, Neenho."

"When I flew over before, all was clear. Why is it cloudy in here, but not out there? It can't be that simple."

My eyes are as wide, as shock-faced as I can get. Above us is clear blue sky but below us is a storm. We hear rain, wind, and shouts below. A part of me wants to just shoot for the island, see what's there, and get it over with.

Izzi has her head down.

I sigh heavily, making a loud mental note that here I go, saving her consort and husband again, as I dive into the storm.

17

IZZI-RA

We are level with the tip top of a sand dune, and I hear a burst. I am ejected from the *clou* and roll violently down the side of the sand mountain, sand in my mouth, hair, and anywhere else it can get, sticking due to the heavy rain that is pounding down. With a great thud, I hit a mud puddle.

I roll over to get air but choke on the heavy rain falling into my mouth, making the sand inside thick. Spitting, I manage to stand and try to clear what I can from my eyes.

"Neenho! Adallah! Assim! Kade! Anyone!"

Thunder rattles, blocking out any other voices or shouts.

Neenho! I shout in my mind. Frantically, I glance around. There are three pathways to take and one dead end. I back up to the solid sand wall and stare ahead, frightened. *Neenho!* I scream again in my mind. He's got to hear that.

I am soaked, my feet inching deeper into the muddy sand. What to do? What to do?

"Ahh, Neenho!" I scream.

Nothing comes back.

I cannot see clearly with the rain. Thunder cracks again, making me tremble and drop to my knees. I scuttle to the wall, pushing my back against it and burying my head between my legs and rock. I shiver. The rain is getting to me. *What to do? What to do?*

"Mother," I sob out.

Why am I panicking? Why do I feel lost? Why am I scared? The fear inside of me is not mine. It magnifies.

"Oh, *saat*, I am here," an almost sweet voice says.

I snap my head up. The rain is gone, the sun shines, and there is only one path ahead.

I stand, noticing that I am dry and in my royal wedding gown, complete with *hedjet*. The green beetle lay blazing in the center of my chest. The chain is vibrating around my neck.

I turn around to see that the wall is gone, too.

"Save me, *saat*."

I turn back, and she is there, standing in the pathway. She wears a long, red dress. There is no wind, but her dress and hair flutter around her, like fire. She has her face, her eyes, even the same smile, but she is not her.

"Who are you?" I ask her curiously.

She tilts her head to better observe me. "You know who I am, *saat*."

"Only my mother calls me that."

Her red lips turn up in a grin. She glides closer to me, but I put my hand up.

"Who are you?"

"You are so beautiful, Izzi-Ra. So beautiful. If only I could have had a chance, none of this would be. Come save me, *saat*, and find out just how much I love my child. I am going to destroy them for what they did to me and my child. I heard the cry. I heard it, and I never got a chance. Come save me and see."

"What?"

She glides a little closer. I raise my hand higher, frightened. I will my light to come, but nothing happens.

"You wouldn't hurt me, would you, *saat*?"

"Stop calling me that! You are not her."

She's getting closer. I keep backing up. My golden light flickers a little in my hand.

"*Saat*, you know. Give me the amulet." She snarls, getting closer.

"No, no, I do not know you." I am gasping, my heart pounding loudly in my chest and taking up the quiet space between us. The hum from the amulet giving me anxiety. I feel drops of rain again.

"Izzi!"

My heart skips several beats.

"Neenho, I am here! I am here, Neenho!" I scream, my throat hurting.

Rain begins to fall as the beautiful creature with my mother's face closes the distance between us. I hit a wall, noticing it is back. I try to make my light come forward, but it keeps dissolving in a puff of gold smoke. She laughs. Her laugh puts so much fear in me.

"I will take you into me, Izzi-Ra. I will make you mine again. The Book of Thoth, I will find it and rewind time." Her face is distorting, and a foul stench reeks from her. Her dress looks as if it has been on fire as holes appear.

"Princess!" Neenho shouts again.

"I am here, Neenho!" I hear pounding behind me, but I dare not take my eyes off her. She is so close and does not appear regal at all, but nightmarish. She holds out her arms as green beetles emerge from her neck, ears, and arms.

I scream. With all the force of my lungs, I scream.

She darts at me, and I duck, ready to feel a kick or something, or the beetles crawl from her to me.

I am screaming and shaking. Rain is hitting hard, and now she is shaking me.

"Izzi, look at me, look at me."

I snap out of it and open my eyes to see Neenho. I push up to see. The thunder rolls around the dark clouds above us, heavy rain still pouring down. The three paths are back. I stare straight ahead, half-expecting her to come around a corner again.

I throw my arms around Neenho, trying to remember how to breathe. He pats me on my back like I am a kitten.

"Princess, what's wrong? You just took a wrong turn. There is nothing to be scared of."

I am trembling. Holding tight to him, I frantically glance around.

"I know what I saw, Neenho. I know what just happened. She is here. She needs us to be here, but we cannot. We must go back."

"Who, Princess?"

A small wind circles around us. "*Neenho*," the wind whispers.

Ahead of us now is no longer three paths, just one.

"*Help me, Neenho*," the wind whispers.

I feel a small tug right in my stomach, and Neenho must feel the same, because he jerks forward. I hold his hand tightly.

"Neenho, do you feel that?" It is as if fear itself has a presence.

I hear footsteps crashing through the sand behind us, but that's impossible because there is a wall ... Where did the wall go? The sand wall that I coward against moments ago is now gone.

Assim comes out of nowhere, followed by Umi and Kade. Assim rushes to my side, but Kade grabs me into a hug. He is shaking. The fear on him is thicker than the rain. Kade's lips quiver, and his eyes look wild.

"We could not see. Everything was dark, and then something was there. We could not see, but we felt it," he stutters out.

Umi does not seem scared, but she does not say anything, either.

Assim's lip is bleeding. He wipes it away.

We hear more feet crashing down a path, but there is no one there.

Assim stands in front of Kade and I protectively.

"What happened to you two, NeenhoKano?" Adallah grabs him and hugs him, trying to shield him from the rain that is slowing down. Neenho has not moved or taken his eyes from the path. Where did Adallah come from?

"Where is my mother and brother?" Umi asks Adallah.

I step away from the others and to Neenho. I do not see his face, but I feel him strongly suddenly. His feelings are magnified. Not just one emotion, but everything.

"Neenho, what is it?"

The rain has completely stopped now, yet thunder still rumbles in the clouds above us.

Neenho is staring at nothing, and then he takes off.

Adallah almost falls from him as he pushes her away.

We follow him. The path is straight and narrow now. I get the strange feeling that people never make it out of this maze. Yet, for some reason, we are being allowed.

Salt becomes heavy in the air, and the crashing of waves against shore meets our ears. We take a final turn around a sand wall and come to a clearing. No clouds, nor rain. The huge sand mountains around us seem to dissolve. Behind us is nothing. We cannot even see our camels that we left behind. Nothing behind us, nothing around us, a lonesome island out at sea.

Ahead of us, at the shoreline, is the rest of the guard.

Umi pushes past me and runs to Ta'li. They do not hug but instead bump fists. Chike fusses over them both before deciding they are okay. The warriors have gathered and are clucking away. Except Kofi. She does not speak.

I focus on what Neenho is focusing on.

The lonesome island.

Thick, green trees cover the entire perimeter. Even with my new eyesight, I cannot even peek through the brush. The waves slap against the jagged rock that keeps the island from it. A humming sounds within me. I notice Neenho tense up, as well. He feels it, too.

"Wut iz dis?" Rafa asks in awe.

Assim is at my side. Unlike the rest who shiver from being wet, he does not.

"Izzi, where are we now?" Kade grabs a hold of my hand, his fear like a blanket that sweeps over me. I shake his hand off. I cannot deal with that now.

"Here nor there," Ta'li replies. "This is where our mother Nun arose?"

Kofi walks to the shoreline. Others make to follow, but she waves them back. She is in deep thought, careful to not touch the water.

"I have the deepest desire to swim," Kade tells me. His head is lolling a little, and his eyes glaze over before he begins to jog toward the water.

"Hold 'em back now!" Marja'ni screams.

Rafa grabs Kade around the middle and holds on to his squirming body.

"I want to swim!" Kade screams, fighting.

Neenho seems worried, heartbroken. Ta'li seems a little dazed, but he keeps shaking his head. Odom and Fa'Teem have sleepy expressions. Sho'te holds tightly to Chike's hand, but he is trembling. Another curse.

"Assim, are you okay?"

He does not look at me, does not move; just stands there as if he has been made into a statue.

Kofi finds a rock. She kisses it then, with great effort, throws it into the air over the water. The rock is about to make contact with the water when, to our astonishment, it freezes mid-air then dissolves. She lets out a whistle then pulls out her bow and arrow. From where, I have no idea, because she carries nothing.

In seconds, she sends three arrows flying over the beautiful water. Before making contact with the water, one explodes and two giant waves take out the other two.

"*Whoa!*" Ta'li and Umi say in unison. Assim shakes his head, with the same dazed expression in his eyes, like Kade, who is still struggling to get into the water. By the looks of Rafa, he is going to let him go soon ... and join him.

Assim heads for the water, but Odom is quicker, snatching him back.

"Wut tis 'appenin'? I wanna swim, as well. I feel like I need ta get in dat wata now," Odom says, trying to hold Assim down.

"Why are you able to fight it and not them?" I ask.

The boulder men shrug. Ta'li is on all fours, digging his hands and feet deep into the sand, lusting for the water.

Neenho is only focused on the island. The longing in his eyes is sad. He looks like he is on the verge of tears.

I feel a tug toward the water, but it feels dangerous.

"The men want to jump in the water. Whatever is here wants them to drown. Any females feel anything?" I ask the group.

Chike is struggling a little, holding Sho'te back. "I want to lay down and sleep. I am exhausted."

"Same," Umi yawns.

Kofi and Marja'ni yawn, as well. I did not even notice that Adallah has already lain down and closed her eyes.

"We have to figure this out fast. The longer we stand here, the more powerful this curse gets. Men get in the water and die, and women will stay on this shore forever and sleep to death, if that is possible. There is something that feels like it is tugging at me. The island is calling to me."

"How do we get there without dying?" Neenho asks with sadness in his voice.

"You fly us. Mere mortals cannot cross, but a god can."

Umi sits down, her eyes drooping.

"I'm not a god," Neenho says, sounding annoyed.

"Yes, you are. You both are," Ta'li says. "And Izzi's light is exactly like Isis's, and you two need to accept that. You just got us to Nu'el."

Neenho appears thoughtful. Then he whistles a small, quiet tune that is so beautiful, and his *clou* materializes right before him. I love how every time he whistles, he looks unsure. Then, when it comes, he looks shocked.

"Bastet. Where is Bast …?" Adallah is dozing in and out.

In his mind, I hear Neenho say the cat can die.

"Sho'te, we will go with him first." Chike pulls Sho'te forward. "We will check the immediate area while Neenho flies everyone else over."

Sho'te sits on the *clou*, taking up the whole surface. Chike then sits on one of his thighs and pats the other for Neenho.

I snort. I cannot help it.

Neenho glares at me, which is the first ever.

"No way am I sitting on a giant man's lap."

"Well, can you create another one?" I ask.

Neenho tries to whistle again, but it does not sound good. Once summoned, that is it, I guess.

I wave to Neenho as he guides his *clou* up, glaring at us all below. He straddles Sho'te's leg and one of his massive arms is wrapped around Neenho.

Kade and Assim are both growling and kicking, trying to get to the water. They are not even budging the boulder men, but it looks annoying.

I summon two balls of hot golden light and throw them into my guard's and husband's faces. At once, they are knocked out.

"I wuz goin' ta knock dem in de head wit de hilt of ma knife soon," Marja'ni says with a yawn.

I open up so that I can feel him, that aching and longing to reach the island suffocates me. He does not have that dangerous humming pull I have. I then feel him try to clear his mind as he moves forward over the water.

We all hold our breaths, expecting a giant hand to come out of the water and snatch them from the sky, but all seems calm. Neenho is soaring high. The water becomes still, quiet. And then the crystal blue shade of the water becomes a murky color. A small wave starts from us and follows Neenho's *clou* from below.

"Why is he going lower?" Umi asks, panic in her voice. "Princess, why is he going lower?"

For a moment, I am so focused on the water. I thought I saw eyes. Red eyes. I did not notice Neenho was, indeed, going lower. I expand my mind, pushing out to Neenho. I connect with him instantly.

Eyes on the island, there is a deep tug, that longing. He must get there. He has to, because it hurts. I do not understand why he feels this way.

Maybe the same curse on Kade and Assim has affected him, as well, in a different way.

Chike and Sho'te are yelling at him to go higher, but he does not even respond.

Neenho, I whisper to him, but he does not respond. I search his mind and realize he does not even know I am here! I summon my light and push it forward to him. I feel my body buckle and the sand digging in my knees. I feel hands on my shoulders, but I do not break my focus. I feel my light surge from me and hit him. The tug on him is lifted just as his *clou* is about to skirt the water.

Neenho soars back up into the sky. They reach the island, and I am snapped back into myself.

"What's happening Izzi? What do they see?" Adallah is trying to be frantic through her sleepy haze.

I focus again and expand my mind, but I am snapped right back.

"I can't," I gasp, the sand really cutting into my knees. I cannot feel or sense anything from him.

"We should have never let them go alone. Anything could have happened to them," Adallah tries to be upset but is too tired.

I feel like I am getting a headache. The humming within me is making me shake, or maybe that's fear.

"Princess ..." Adallah starts.

"I'm fine," I dismiss. "This strange hum is getting worse, like the ground is shaking."

"That's because it is," Umi says, surprised herself.

I snap my eyes open and glance to where everyone else is staring. The waters are calm on top and dirty, but there seems to be something disrupting it from below. We consciously gather into a bunch. I keep my eye on the island, watching for any sign of Neenho, the *clou*, purple light, fully opening my mind for him to intrude.

"Wut tis dat?" Fa'teem asks.

In the center of the water, two holes open, and then two canoes rise up, gliding toward us until they reach the shore. No one moves.

Eventually, Marja'ni and Kofi approach the canoes cautiously. They poke them with sticks, throw sand on them, and nothing happens.

I approach one, rubbing the shell to see if it is really real. They are pearl white shells. Giant shells. Deep and spacious. I rub my fingers across the rippling lines. How? Who made these? The gods? They are the most beautiful, crafted canoes I have ever seen. I want one! Nothing in the palace compares.

The ladies touch, examine, and even sit in the other one.

"They will hold us all. Maybe Neenho sent them." I shrug, having no idea.

We break into two groups to fit in the canoes. The two warriors, Adallah, and the twins are with me. The men are jammed in the other.

"Where are the paddles?" Ta'li points out.

We propel forward with no warning.

"Izzi?"

"It is not me." I shake my head, looking over the canoe to try to glimpse down. I meet a pair of red eyes and freeze.

"Um ..." I wave my hand for someone to see this, but the eyes go down and out of sight. A series of clicks sound, and then a dome wraps around our canoe, locking us in.

Kofi and Marja'ni began to pound on the dome to get it open. I can see the boulder men in the other canoe appear to be shouting. More clicks sound, and then we begin to submerge.

"Okay, everyone, stay calm," I say.

The other canoe is in full on panic mode. The warriors over there are ready for battle, I can tell. The glow coming from the twins, I expect. They are living their best lives right now. Adallah is worried, but not about us or herself.

We have completely gone underwater. I expected to not see anything because the water is so murky on top but, below here, everything is clear. Yet there is nothing under here. No fish, no algae, no nothing. There is not even a rock underwater. How is that island afloat then?

More clicks sound, and then we lurch forward, the other canoe moving with us. This cannot be good. This cannot be good.

"No hints, no legends, no stories?" I mock.

"Oh, you know what is down here, Princess," Umi says.

I frown. What is that supposed to mean?

"Once we left the outskirts of Mendet, that desert we were in for three moons has never been charted," Ta'li says in excitement.

The warriors look annoyed. I feel curious, because I do feel like we have entered a place no one was ever supposed to go. But we had the key to enter.

"Look!" Marja'ni points, drawing me from my thoughts.

Ahead is a wall of ... water. Thick, shimmering water. A waterfall in water? My nose is pressed to the dome. The water parts as if curtains are being drawn, and we pass through.

"*Shil te a mu aye*," I whisper.

"What does that mean?" Adallah asks, but I do not answer her, because I have no idea what it means or why I said it. I do not even have time to think about it, because the world before us takes my breath away.

An entire village. Underwater, black glass homes dart here and there. Statues have fallen over, covered in underwater plants.

A giant shadow is before us. *This must be the base of the island*, I think. But, as we get closer, I find that I am wrong. A ginormous statue comes into the clearing.

"She's gorgeous!" Umi and Ta'li shriek together.

"*Shil te a mu aye*," I hear myself repeat.

I have no idea where we are or who the goddess is. I have been here before, though. I cannot explain it, yet I know this place. I am home, *Shil te a mu aye*.

I stare at the statue before us, knowing she must be the one who was created and left behind. Only a goddess of our first times could have a statue of this magnitude.

Everything else may seem meek, but the statue gleams, as if it was finished yesterday. The blue water dances off the blue marble that represents her skin, her bright green eyes staring straight ahead. Her headdress is adorned with jewels of the sea. Her chest is bare, shells covering her breast, and her navel perfectly shaped. What is more interesting is the fishlike tail she has instead of feet, the fin curved in as she sits on her throne.

I bow my head to her.

Hatmehyt, the name is whispered to me. I have never heard of her, yet I have. She is not in the palace. We do not worship her. Then I think my mother did, and I know that to be a true thought.

"Look," someone whispers. What else could there be?

I do not even have to look their way, because I see it. Red eyes. Red eyes everywhere. We do not see the owners because the water or the light in the water seems to be dimming. I see a flick of something swoosh past, overhead, beside us. Red eyes everywhere.

"Umi?"

"Yes, Princess?"

"Are there people who can live underwater?"

"Ta'li and I have suspected, but ..."

Loud clicks again, and then a fizzing sound. Water is coming through the dome.

"I am dreaming. I am dreaming. I am dreaming." I panic.

Kofi and Marja'ni try to cover the small cracks with their hands.

The men in the other canoe are back to full panic mode. Kade and Assim will not even know they died, I think as water drenches my hair. A loud click is heard, and then the dome completely comes off. We float out of the canoes, which is jerked back the way we came. Adallah swims to me and holds on. She looks extremely scared.

Kade and Assim float nearby. Everyone is flailing around, going crazy.

No one else notices, but the statue of the goddess has turned to face us. We passed her. We should only be seeing the back of her chair, but I stare right into those sea-colored eyes, and she glances back.

The beetle around my neck starts to glow green. I feel the hum, and I just know. I should not be here. But I must be here.

The water around us shakes, and the sea floor opens to a whirlpool that sucks us all in.

18

NEENHOKANO

I lay on the ground, sweating. I've tried and tried to call Izzi, but I can't. I can't feel my princess. We have been walking and searching, but there seems to be no edge. How is there no edge? I climbed the trees and climbed as high as possible, but there was no top branch. I see the sky, I see the end of the tree, but I can never reach it. My light works, but my *clou* will not. As soon as we entered the trees, it dissolved, and we fell a pretty good distance. I, of course, was prepared mid-fall to land. Chike would probably have died, but her mountain man caught her.

The trees are thick, ground covered in thick moss. No tracks, nests, or the sound of life. What lives here, and where does it live? We are hot and thirsty. The other two are at a tree, trying to get water, while I lay here and pout.

"Do you feel that?" Chike asks.

The ground is rumbling. Lying still, I feel it. I jump up at once and grab a hold of one of Sho'te's massive arms.

I bury m face in his arm, breathing deeply, eyes squeezed shut. My heart is pounding in my ears. *Get it together, Neenho man.* I'm glad the others are not here to see this.

Sho'te does not even move his arm, and I feel Chike pat my back.

The shaking has stopped. I want to open my eyes and be in my poor village on my roof in my worn, old clothes. When I open my eyes, I want to see Ishiva.

"Neenho dear, we came to this island for a reason. It was calling you and Izzi here, like the mountain. The other amulets must be here. Adallah is safe on the shore, so do not worry. They will find a way here, or we will find a way to get out of here."

I gaze up at her and nod. Chike has always had this calming sense about her. Whenever Adallah is stressed out, Chike would show up, and she would snap into a better mood instantly.

I feel calm now. My heart is no longer trying to break out of my chest. I must do this for Izzi, my princess. The Princess of Egypt. I must do whatever needs to be done for myself, as well.

I breathe deeply and let my light consume me. Guide me. I concentrate.

Adallah is safe ... They are all ... Huh? My heart hurts so much.

I hate Adallah. She did this! She trapped me for life. I will kill Adallah! I will destroy the pharaoh and will rule everything.

I am breathing hard again, but not with fear.

I shiver with anger!

"Neenho?" Chike questions, backing away from me.

I shake my head. "Sorry, I'm trying ... I tried to ... to focus, but then ..."

"Neenho, did you hear what you just said?"

"I didn't say anything." I shake my head.

Chike, she's ... she's friends with the enemy. I must destroy her, too.

I hear those words, but I did not say them. Are these thoughts? I ...

Sho'te grabs his staff off his back, extending it in length, and stands in front of Chike protectively. He points it right at me. I don't know what's happening, but instead of being shocked at how defensive they appear, I smirk. Then I slap my hands to my face.

I shake my head. I don't know what ... Clouds? A sweet smell?

I feel her whispers all around me.

"Whatever is here has a hold on me. I ... I can't shake her. I need her. I must free her. Dead or alive, I will free her, and you all will take her place."

I heard those words, but I did not say them.

I sway a little, moaning in pain. I need to be near her. She loves me. Who loves me? I don't know.

I have to ... I see the frightened expression of my guard. "Please, don't throw that at me. Follow me, but stay back, because I don't know what's ahead or how I will be affected." I see their hesitation. "Trust me. Whatever is here and whoever is here, I can't block them, or it, much longer. Please."

Sho'te nods. "Try anyting, young male, an' it will be ya las'."

I face the thicket of the trees. It's there. In there. I let her—it must be a her. I smell her—consume me. I am lost. I let her have me.

I dart to the middle. Distantly, I hear feet behind me.

19

IZZI-RA

Dirt in my mouth again. Dirt in my hair. My sandals ruined. This awfully made attempt at a dress is dirty.

I pat my hair and almost burst into tears. I am damp and dirty. Seven days. Seven days ago, I was the Princess of Egypt. The best of meats and fruits gifted from the Nile right from the gods, silks of the best Egyptian quality, the palace, the parties, my mother ... She is my flower now that she is ...

Snap out of it, Izzi, I rant to myself while everyone else is checking on one another and figuring out our situation.

Hands are on my shoulders, and a face is in my face.

I want my mother. What would the queen do right now?

"My Queen, are you okay?"

I stare into Kade's eyes. "You are awake?"

"Awake? What are you talking about? My Queen, where are we?" Dirt is packed on his face, as well.

With a soft, firm hand, Assim cups my chin and turns my face from Kade's. He is just as filthy, his face emotionless as always, but his dark eyes tell me what lies beneath.

"Are you okay?"

I place my hand on his arm, allowing this brief moment, and then I remove myself from his touch. I shake Kade off, as well, and stand up, taking in our surroundings.

Thick trees surround us.

The warriors speak amongst themselves, the twins are as excited as can be, and Adallah is oddly staring her cat in the face, as if they are conversing. When did her cat get here? Has her cat always been with us?

"Noting!" Marja'ni shouts as she comes crashing through some trees. "I run 'roun' south an' den north, an' I cannot see de shore we wuz on or tha wata. I climbed an' climbed de treez and neva reach a top."

A whistle sounds above us, and then Kofi lands on her feet from above. She nods once to Marja'ni.

I am listening to the chatter around me but still staring at Adallah and that cat. When I get in Neenho's mind, he really hates the cat. There is something suspicious about it.

The cat stares directly at me and meows, but in my mind ... I think. Then it jumps on Adallah's shoulder.

"Can you feel Neenho, Izzi-Ra? Can you get inside his mind? Chike ...? Sho'te?" Adallah's eyes are leveled with mine, but it's her cat's eyes that I am locked with. The blacks of her eyes are flecked with gold, and her fur around her eyes are gold. Her black ears are perfectly perked, and her back fur looks like silk.

I know you, I say to the cat in my mind.

The cat nods.

"Izzi-Ra, look at me please."

I pull my eyes from the cat, but I swear I saw a nod.

"Neenho? Where is Neenho?"

"Have you all noticed how quiet it is up here?" Ta'li starts. "No bees, no animals, not a chirp. Where is the life on this place? Those red eyes in the water, I've never caught fish with those kinds of eyes."

"They were slanted in human form," Umi finishes.

"Izzi, concentrate. Find Neenho. Find Neenho, Princess. Please."

Adallah's big eyes pierce into mine. The love in her eyes for him ... I feel jealous.

I nod to her then close my eyes. I take deep breaths and try to focus on him.

Blank. A wall as high as the temple buildings that cannot be penetrated, like the thick, dried clay they are made of. I cannot feel or sense Neenho.

I snap my eyes open and stare blindly ahead.

The air around me feels compressed and stuffy. I can breathe but just enough to sustain me. My neck is stiff, as if I have not moved it in forever.

Free me, please. A whisper.

A tree branch snaps, and a small yelp follows.

I snap out of the trance. The wall is back up but, for a split-second, I heard Neenho.

"This way." I take off into the trees. There is nowhere to go but in here.

I hear the crashes and heavy breathing of those behind me. I hope there is no army waiting for us, because with all the noises they are making, we are easy targets. I see a little blur in and out my vision to my left and know its Assim. He's quiet, swift, and agile. Kade is not far behind, though. He is not making noise, either. He is ready to protect me.

I smirk. *My men.*

I hear something and skid to a halt. I hold a finger up to stop the others. Kade and Assim are on either side of me, neither panting, ears open for any sounds.

"You hear that?" I whisper.

"Water," Assim answers.

The others have caught up. They enter the clearing, looking around. We hear water, but we see nothing.

I walk the area, confused, as the others' faces match mine. The leaves and foliage are wet. The ground looks like the bottom of the ocean.

"By the gods!" Adallah shouts.

Rain. Rain starts to fall. Not on us but around us.

I look up but see no clouds or any source to where the water is coming from.

Just trees, not even sky, and ...

I snap my head back up fast. I am about to scream, but he puts his finger to his lip.

Neenho is high up in a tree. Their eyes cannot see him, but I can. I cannot even communicate with him.

I hear a whistling sound.

"Down!" Assim yells, yanking me to the ground.

I hear whizzing sounds all around us. Assim's strong arm locks me to the ground as he covers my head with his other arm. I use my force to knock his arm away then roll over. Things are flying all around us.

After what seems like a full minute, it stops. I crane my neck a little to see if Neenho is in the same spot. His eyes are wide in what looks like amazement.

"Is it safe?" I yell to him.

"I don't know," Assim answers me.

"I am not asking you. Neenho, is it safe?" I yell again.

He does a flip out the tree and lands catlike.

I roll back over onto my stomach and climb to my knees when I freeze. The others are frozen, as well. Water surrounds us. We are underwater.

I slowly walk to the wall of water that surrounds us. I stick my hand through.

Nothing happens. The water does not fall, just stands like a wall, as clear as the blue skies we cannot see any longer. Below, I can make out more of the village that lays underwater.

A whole world down here.

Adallah has snatched up Neenho and is fussing over him again.

"We ran into the thick of the trees. Rain started to fall, and then arrows were flying at us. I climbed a tree but lost Chike and Sho'te."

I want to rush at him and hug him and kiss him all over his

cheeks like Adallah is doing. I am glad he cannot hear that. Glad he is okay.

"Izzi, I see you, but I cannot feel you. How did you all get here?" Neenho asks me, his eyes telling me he wants to hug me as well.

"Long story," the twins say in unison.

"Where could they have ended up?" Kade asks.

Conversations are happening behind me, but I am more interested in this land. I see another area off in the distance. I want to try something, but the others will give me a safety chat. So, without any warning, I plunge through the water, hearing shouts and screams around me, but soon they are deafened by the water. I hold my breath. I see them all on the other side of the water wall, looking panicked. I float in the water, my hair flying all around me. I see nothing but old ruins and statues. Fallen over pillars with art. I am running out of breath and make the decision to swim to the next wall of water I see.

I reach it in seconds and plunge through. There I lie, wet and coughing for air on the wet ground. The trees around here are less dense.

Splash! Neenho bursts through the wall of water, he lies down, too, gasping for air for a minute. "That. Was. So. Cool!" He jumps up and looks around. Water surrounds this small area, as well.

"Look over there," Neenho points vertical through the water. It's a longer swim, but we can see a temple sits lonesome.

"Whatever brought us here is in there."

"It's not a whatever, Izzi. She. She brought us here. You feel her? She can control me, Izzi. She can speak for me."

A longing pain crosses his face for a moment, and then it is gone. He even looks confused for a moment. He does not look like himself, and then, in a blink, he is back to normal.

"Neenho, did she take Chike and Sho'te?"

He shakes his head. "I couldn't see who they were. We were running. Then it started to rain. I heard a shout and heard several arrows."

We stare at each other. I do not know if we are even thinking the same thing, but I can assume we are.

Kade, Assim, and the twins burst through. They fall to the wet dirt, gasping for air.

"This place is amazing!" Umi squeals. She and Ta'li ramble on between coughs about the atmosphere and whatever else. Their mother and father are missing. They should be worried.

"Underwater ruins. No scribe has ever ... We will be the first, Umi!"

"Izzi, please stop jumping through stuff. Let me go first," Assim says.

"How can I protect you if you act as if you do not need me?" Kade throws out there.

I ignore them both.

Neenho gives Kade the nastiest look that he can muster, and I snap my fingers in his face to snap him out of it.

"Are you okay?" I ask Assim.

He nods then looks around.

Ta'li and Umi observe the only monument that seems to be on land. A crumbled prayer area.

"Look at the art. That fishtail goddess is very powerful. See how she is facing to the left? With the *Ba* above her and water below her?" Ta'li is at his sister's side, looking over the broken prayer rock.

"I do not have a good feeling," Kade says.

"None of us do, Prince," Neenho spits out.

"You guys got to see this!" Umi shouts.

We all go behind the column to the other side. Another wall of water is there, and below, clear as the sky, is a what looks like a palace.

I feel heat around my neck. The beetle is glowing, and the drumming sounds loudly for me and Neenho alone.

I take the amulet off and hold it up.

"Neenho."

The chain sways as if the piece wants to get in the water.

"That is where we need to go." I follow my instinct and back away.

I slowly keep backing away and, as I do so, the green starts to fade away. I move farther away to where I cannot see the palace, and the chain lays limply and the light dies out. Holding the chain out, we all walk slowly back to the other side. Immediately, the chain sways and the amulet begins to vibrate and burn green again.

"Whatever is here is not meant to be disturbed," Assim says.

"Too bad we have to, though," Neenho snaps.

Assim is about to say something, but then he looks past me and squints.

We see it before he says anything.

Red eyes in the water, all around us.

"My Queen, you are not going down there." Kade shields me from the water and the eyes, with Assim on my other side. I see Neenho send a nasty glare at Kade.

As nicely as I can, I push Kade aside.

Red eyes gleaming so close to the water that I can probably touch them, I lift the amulet toward the water. The eyes crinkle into what is possibly a frown.

"I am going down there," I tell the eyes.

I hear the others gasp in shock, but I am not surprised as a torso and arms slowly materialize. A chest, neck, and then a head. The skin is the shade of seaweed, and his black hair flies around his young face. He shakes his head then raises his arms. A bow and arrow materialize, and he points it right at me.

"Izzi-Ra," Assim warns.

I step closer to his arrow, right on the other side of the water, aimed at me. "I am going down there," I tell him again. My entire body sets ablaze in golden light. Now he is the one with shock on his face.

I see the muscles in his arms shift just as he releases the arrow. Assim sticks his staff through the water at the footless man. The arrow comes through but flies over my head and explodes into water drops.

Assim pushes me down, making me fall on my back. I see the boy flying over me, another arrow positioned to hit me. It all must have happen so fast to the others, but I see every single detail—the water arrow that is turning solid. But that is not what catches my breath. Where he should have legs is a long, shiny ... tail? Specks of water glisten off the many colors of the ... tail?

He looses the water arrow, which flies at my head then turns solid, hitting next to my ear. He hits the other side of the water, and we see him circling back. This time, he is not alone. More red eyes have uncamouflaged their bodies.

I see the twins, Kade, and Assim try to follow their blurs, whereas I, and Neenho, I assume, can see exactly what we are up against— dark green people with fishtails. Their blazing colors appear like streaks of rainbows in the water, and their hair like clouds of smoke.

"I need to get to Adallah!" Neenho says.

I look over at the other side where the Kemetians and Adallah are. They have their backs to one another, weapons drawn. Fish people swim swiftly all around.

The leader, I assume, stops on the other side of the waterfall. He looks magnificent. His tail shimmers with different colors. He holds a long, golden staff with jewels embedded around the yellow stone on top.

I step a little closer, keeping his attention. His locks float around him. He reminds me of someone. He is largely muscled, face hard and scary. Beyond him, I can see his army flashing past us and around the others.

I hold my hand up, and a ball of gold light appears. He does not break eye contact with me. He does not give my hand a glance. But I see it. I see the flicker in his eyes.

He raises his staff, and his army stops moving before they disappear, though their red eyes are still everywhere. He then uses his staff to point below him.

"*He'est!* Mum!" Ta'li points toward the temple.

We see Chike and Sho'te. Two fish people are dragging them down as they struggle to breathe and get free.

"I'm going for my *he'est*," Ta'li tells us.

What the heck is a he'est? I think, looking down to where Chike and Sho'te disappear.

I look back at the fishman as he disappears before my eyes. The tail vanishes, the torso becomes water, and his head dissolves. All that is left are red eyes.

I hear a deep swallow behind me. Kade looks like he is about to faint. All of this is too much for him. However, he has not tried to run away, so I give him credit for that.

"I'm going with you," Umi whispers.

"That's too long of a swim. They will kill you both," Assim tries to reason with them. For a split-second, I notice he reached for Umi protectively before he stepped back next to me.

The red eyes have faded away, but I know they are still there.

I see the others looking our way from the other area.

"Look." Neenho is inspecting the corner of the water wall. "Look closely." Neenho emits his light in his hands. Then he takes a deep breath then plunges through.

I expect his light to go out and the underwater people to come and snatch him, but he is still standing there.

He smiles then pokes his head through. "It's a path. It looks like it leads all the way to that temple. And look, there is another one that leads to the palace."

I step through to see for myself. An underwater walkway?

It makes a square. We could have walked over instead of swimming.

We take the path quickly and make it back to the other side where Adallah scoops Neenho into a hug.

"Wut in dee gods are dos dings in de wata!" Fa'teem roars.

"We need to go for our mother now. We are wasting time," Ta'li says, frustration in his voice. I never heard anything from them before except excitement. I wonder if they can cry.

Then I hear it before it comes through.

The water arrows are flying through the water from every which way. We cannot tell where they are, because they are swimming so fast and even flying through the air above us from one side to another, shooting their arrows.

Enough!

I ignite and start throwing gold balls into the water. I see purple light flying every which way, as well. However, we are missing. Everyone else is swinging wildly and blindly, trying to knock them down. Adallah has white whips soaring around.

"I've got ta get to me mum. Now!" Ta'li exclaims.

Kade pulls me down as a swarm of arrows head our way. "My Queen, have you noticed that, once their arrows hit water, it becomes water again. It is only solid in here."

Another wave soars above us, arrows flying everywhere, and blurs of tails and long, black hair fly overhead, slamming into the water on all sides. At least fifteen slammed through the water barrier over us, loosed, and did not hit one another in the air before slamming back into the water. I see them as they swim around in circles, preparing for another attack.

Umi and Ta'li dart through the corner wall. I watch as they both walk fast on the narrow path, both armed with bow and arrows. Then the twins loose, finding their marks.

I scuttle to the corner and continue watching as they reach the temple and enter. I hope Chike and Sho'te are still alive.

"Neenho, Princess, we will all distract them," Assim says. I see a gash on his left arm.

The fish people are no longer attacking us. We look around, but they have completely disappeared. Not a red eye or flashy tail in sight.

"No," Kade says angrily, "I am going with my queen."

"She's not alone," Neenho puffs out.

Assim stands between them. "As her sworn protector, you think I like letting her go anywhere without me? Kade, you are with me. Neenho and Izzi, do what you need to do."

Neenho nods.

Kade looks shaken, as usual. He looks at me with that longing, loving look that he always has for me. Then he takes his pole and sticks it in the ground, pushing past Neenho.

"Kade, what are you ...?" Before I can finish the rest, he sweeps me into his arms and plants his lips on mine. They are as soft as they look, and sweet.

"I need you to stay safe, My Queen."

My face is burning. I do not know what to say. I ... Wow ...

He sets me down, and I stumble a little. Legs weak. Wait. What?

I dare not look at Neenho, though I see the blank expression Assim usually wears, trying not to unmask what he is truly thinking. The Kemetians are not moved, and Adallah looks away with a smirk on her face.

"All right, let's do this," Kade says. "Everyone pick a different corner. You can run through the path to the next area."

I cannot believe I have nothing to say. I do not know what to say!

"Ready. Ptah say to 'elp, den we 'elp," Marja'ni mutters.

"Warriors, Kade and I will cause a distraction. You all head to the temple and help the twins retrieve Chike and Sho'te. Follow the path in the corners. Weapons ready?"

Marja'ni and the mountain men nod. Kofi has her hands on her neck.

"Aunt Adallah," Neenho starts as she takes a deep breath and readies herself.

Everyone then rushes to the corners and go.

Kade and Assim tap poles then rush into the corner where Neenho and I need to go. Fish people appear. They poke their sticks through the water, clearing the path to the next land space. Neenho and I rush through.

Once we get to the next land area, water arrows begin flying everywhere. Neenho and I crawl through the area, water arrows turning solid as they hit the ground near us. Assim and Kade are already in the next pathway that leads to the underwater palace.

I peer over to the other path and watch as the boulder men take their weapons from their backs and poke them through the water.

Kofi pulls daggers from her ... neck? then throws them endlessly. How?

Marja'ni sends arrows every which way, along with Adallah's whip.

"Who are you going to choose?" Neenho asks as I watch the battles.

What a question to ask me.

"You," I answer then jump through the water and run on the path that my men have cleared for me. The guys stick their staffs in the water, trying to hit the fish people.

I jump over Kade, who fell, and pass by Assim, my eyes only on the lonesome, black glass palace.

A vibration so strong is coming from the amulet.

The path does not actually reach the palace. We must swim a short way. I plunge into the water and make the swim.

I am almost there when three sets of red eyes appear before us, and I halt, running out of air. The bodies appear, and there floats three strong fishtail men.

I look behind me to see what the plan is, but Neenho just keeps swimming ahead, his purple light in his hands. He throws it at the three things, and they dodge it.

I start to feel lightheaded. I need to get to that palace.

I summon my light and start throwing them every which way, which is difficult. My arms move slowly, but when the light leaves my hand, it goes where I want it.

I hit one in his side. Blood seeps from the wound, clouding the area. His red eyes round on me, and I see anger at its best. He speeds toward me like an arrow, but Kade swims fast in front of me and is knocked hard by the wounded fishman. Neenho throws his light at the other two, and they scatter. I see him reach the palace and enter.

Assim is there in a flash. I want to yell at them both! They were not to jump in the water.

Assim is losing air, as well, and trying to swing his heavy fighting staff at the two advancing on him, but he misses.

I throw two gold balls of light at the things but miss. They grab Assim by the legs and drag him upward.

"*No!*" I scream through the water, losing what air I had left.

The water around us vibrates as if I sent off an underwater explosion. The fishmen releases Assim, holding their ears.

What was that?

I watch as Assim floats away. *Oh no.*

Kade swims back up, reaching Assim.

I cannot stick around, so I turn and swim with all the energy I have left. Fear beyond fear is creeping into my heart and mind.

Is Assim okay? Is there even a way to breathe in this place?

The world around me closes in a dark, watery blur.

20

NEENHOKANO

As Izzi floats outside the water's entrance, I reach out and pull her inside. However, I don't think to catch her, so she hits the marble floor hard. Hopefully, she will think she did that on her own.

She lies there motionless for a moment then starts coughing. She rolls over and spits out water.

"I hate water. I will never bathe again. I will never drink it again. Ale for me for now on. I will demand and command and enforce this new law when I am Pharaoh." Izzi stands, coughing a bit. Then she looks out at the water-framed doorway.

"How does the water hold up like this?"

We crane our necks to peer up at the land space where we just left our guard. I try not to let images flood through my brain, because Adallah is up there with the fish people.

"Neenho, you swam right past me so fast. You did not even look back to see what was happening, if I was even okay. Kade and Assim, they came back and were attacked."

I see the little hurt in her eyes but, weirdly, I don't care.

I shake my head. Why would I think that?

I saw them dive in as soon as Izzi dived into the water. I want to defend my actions, but sadness creeps into me. I want to free her. I need to free her. I feel her. She calls to me.

I shake my head to clear the fuzz. As fast as it came, it's gone.

Izzi is still watching me.

"We will discuss this topic later, when you can think for yourself. I feel unimaginable fear," she admits. "It is not my fear, though. I can discern that it's being put there. Can you tell?"

I don't have an answer for her.

I turn from the water. "That thing is brighter than it was up there." I point to the beetle that is bright green around her neck.

"Right, Neenho," she says with that I-will-deal-with-you-later tone.

We walk through a tiny corridor that opens to a larger chamber. Even with its haunting, dead look, the flowers and trees that litter the area must have been glowing with colors in its prime. In the center is a large archway, vines taking it hostage. Above us is a glass dome. We can see the water. It's as if this was an observatory at one point. Why?

"An underwater garden?" I say aloud.

Izzi looks as if someone finally told her this journey is taking the shine out her hair as she walks around the room. There is a large tree off to one side of the room, all its leaves gone. She touches the tree like it will crumble if she is too rough.

I approach her and tap her shoulder. She jumps like I was never here to begin with. I have not known her long, but I have never seen this type of reaction from her. Her eyes look glassy, and her lips keep forming words that don't come.

"Princess?"

"This is my mother's garden. This is an exact ..."

I listen to her mumble to herself. She's in real disbelief over this ugly, dead garden.

"How? How? *How!* How can this be the exact same? My mother's. This is my mother's garden, and it looks as dead as she is." Izzi drops to her knees at the tree, resting her head on it.

Oh boy. The princess is heaped in a ball, and I think she's crying. She never cries. Maybe just weeping. Her shoulders shake, and her sobs are heartbreaking. I don't know what I can do for her. Kade and Assim would know.

I sit down and lift her face up. The tears spill, hitting my hands. We just look at one another, as we often do.

"I am terrified," she whispers.

Whatever, or whoever, is affecting me is affecting her, as well. Izzi would never admit that.

She is so beautiful. She's so mean, and yet here she is, looking like a wilted flower that's a part of this wasted garden.

"Maybe your mom is from here. Maybe this was her home. The only way we can crack this is to keep going, Izzi-Ra. Together, we will avenge the queen."

Her gold light flickers in her eyes. She agrees? Did I comfort her? I feel funny inside as she continues to look at me.

I keep my caring face on, if that's even what I'm doing. My heartbeat picks up, and I feel heat rising in my face and other parts of me. What is happening?

Izzi continues to look into my eyes. "Neenho," she says, leaning closer to me.

"Princess?"

Her face is closer. I feel her breath on my bottom lip. My heart is pounding my chest, sending blood to my brain that I don't need. The princess is going to kiss me. My first kiss, and with the princess!

I release her face go and scoot back. For a brief moment, the lust in her eyes for me reared the hatred that I have been feeling for everyone.

"Neenho," she says, breathing heavily.

"Let's find whatever is here."

She nods in agreement. Neither of us meet eyes again, fearing we will be controlled.

We stand, and then Izzi pulls herself together.

I point toward a pair of doors, assuming that's the way. Well, it has to be.

Without looking back, she heads out.

I have a little triumph dance. Point for me, none for the guard and prince. Izzi almost kissed me. Well, something almost made her do it, but I won't tell them that.

We walk in silence through a narrow corridor. The walls are wet and smells like the sea. At the end are steps. They go down into a place that neither of us want to go, but this is the way.

The pull is stronger as we descend. It's dark, but the stone walls seem to glow from the dampness of them, as if the water emits a glow.

Once on the last step, I can see nothing, so I summon my light and throw it out around us. Torches light up immediately.

"No way ..."

Along both sides are statues of the greatest craftsmanship that I have ever seen. Black marble, about my height, of males and females with no legs, like the ones who attacked us. The walls are alight with stories of what looks like battles. People in water with spears fighting those on land. Osiris and a god who I'm not familiar with are depicted with their backs to one another, both arms raised to a goddess. At least, I think she is a goddess. But she has one of those fishtail, as well. No legs.

Osiris's green skin gleams. He is his human pharaoh depiction, wearing the Urais and clean, white garments. His staff stands alone at his side.

The other god wears just a bottom wrap, his chest dark and strong. His head seems to be a mixture of different animals, like a camel or giraffe mixed with another. His staff has fallen at his feet.

Izzi walks the length of the corridor, marveling at the art as she trails her hands along each marble statue that she passes.

"Neenho, how is it possible to live in a world and know nothing? These people ... You feel it. I know you do. Our world is only supposed to be five hundred Ahket. But this ... this suggests longer."

"Humanity in Egypt is only five hundred Ahket, Princess. This, and the others, are much older. I do feel that. Their time can't be put into a timeline. They just are."

We reach the end, which is only a wall, no apparent way through. Izzi pushes, taps, knocks, but nothing.

The tug is so strong right here. Whatever brought us here is behind here. Even Izzi's neck is blazing from the amulet.

I stand back, taking a deep breath, and then I ignite my purple light in both hands. With sure force, I hurl the light at the stone, and it goes straight through.

Izzi rubs the spot. "Just like the mountain."

"How do we get through to you?" Izzi whispers to the wall.

We wait in silence, but nothing happens.

"Same way we got in," I say, surprising myself. It was me, but not me.

"Is it her, Neenho? The woman who looks like my mother? Is she pulling us here?"

I shrug.

"It is a woman, huh? Even if it is her, what are we supposed to do? Walk out of here without getting the piece? Maybe she knows what everyone else won't tell us," I say.

"I feel her danger," Izzi tells me.

"I feel her love!" I blurt out then regret it. "I'm sorry, Izzi. I didn't mean to yell at you."

"You think she is your mother?"

I look away from my princess, a tear escaping my eyes, but it's not mine.

"These pieces that make the amulet have the answers we seek." I engulf my entire body in my light. Then I walk at the wall, half-expecting to bump right into it. I see Izzi out the corner of my eye, looking horrified. Then I see nothing, and then I am through.

I peek my eyes open. I'm in a small chamber. Nothing to the left or right of me, but before me are stone steps that lead up to a tomb, red light encasing it. I walk slowly up the steps until I reach the top. A gold sarcophagus lays encased in the red light. Gold crown, braids, and arms crossed over a bosom tells me a female lies here.

"Who are you?"

I feel a ripple and snap my head around as Izzi comes through as a gold ball of light

21

IZZI-RA

Once fully inside, my light extinguishes. I see Neenho standing on the raised platform, a sarcophagus before him. Fear, anger, regret, and hatred swirl around my legs. They attach to my skin and, little by little, up my legs, wrap around my thighs, consume my torso, pierce my heart, and swallow my brain. I cannot move. I panic.

How can I fight her? How can I block her?

"Neenho?"

The torches go out and are replaced by a red firelight. The wall we just walked through dissolves and is replaced by standing water. Shimmering, red water.

"She knows we are here, Neenho."

"I know."

I make my way up the steps and stand on the other side. The amulet is burning intensely and vibrating. I take it off, and it flies from my hand to hover above the sarcophagus.

"We have to," Neenho says.

"I am terrified," I respond.

"No, you're not. She is."

Why am I so scared? Fear is exploding in every inch of my body, brain, my Ka. I should not be here. I cannot be here.

"Who are you?" I whisper.

"I hope you never find out."

Neenho and I both swing around, lights in our hands as we ready ourselves to fight. A breeze blows around us, although there is no window, but we spot the source.

He is short, light, airy. He looks from both of us with wonder in his bright eyes, a look I am used to getting as a princess. He holds his hands together in front of him, his white robe blowing from the mysterious breeze.

"Shu?" Neenho asks.

The man nods.

"You know him?"

"No. She told me," Neenho answers before turning back to the man.

"You come here a lot to make sure she's still here."

The light in the god seems to dim. "You should not let her in, NeenhoKano. Block her."

"I can't." Neenho is shaking, the veins in his neck visibly popping.

I glance at the sarcophagus and, for a brief second, I am in the sarcophagus. I cannot breathe, neck stiff, anger and fear pouring through me. I stumble back a step.

"Imagine if you let her out. Look how she affects you, and she is not even into her power. Please, come with me. I can get you all off the island and to safety."

I want to go. Now. I want him to take me from here and back to Asir.

"What do we have to do with these amulets? Why do we have these powers? Who are we? What have the gods done to us?" All this spews from my mouth as I shake, my own anger and emotions getting the best of me. My gold light burns brighter in my hands.

He looks from our faces to our lights, curiosity all over his face. "Pure gold light from an apparent human child. And purple. No ..." Shu trails off.

Neenho steps back, closer to the sarcophagus. The room grows a brighter red. Panic crosses Shu's face.

"I would very much like to talk with you two. Very much. But not in here. Not around here. We can go anywhere. I will take you anywhere, to anytime. But not here."

Neenho whimpers.

"It will get worse. I will not let you open that sarcophagus."

My fear eases a little. I do not understand why.

"We have to open it!" Neenho blurts out.

"I will not let you," Shu repeats with what should have been authority, but Neenho and I have been through way too much to care about a god making demands.

"Who is in there, and why does she want us to release her? We saw fish people. There are fish people! Why does that lizard man want us, and why did my mother have to die?" I rush all that out because, whatever is about to happen, I do not want it to happen and Neenho is slipping. Whatever is pulling at us has more of an effect on him than the fear that is pressing against my chest and mind.

Shu feels all is about to be lost, as well.

"She was put here," Shu starts.

"Imprisoned," Neenho sneers.

"That is exactly why you must not open that sarcophagus. I know you are powerful—maybe even more than Amun himself—but look at how she can control you."

Neenho looks possessed, but I see in his eyes that he is fighting it.

He takes a few steps toward the red veil that engulfs the sarcophagus.

"She is dangerous. More dangerous than any entity in the universe. You let her out, she will never be contained ever again. Egypt will fall forever, and the gods ... we cannot save our people if you do so. Neenho, Izzi-Ra, if you free her, all is lost. All will be lost for us all. We will fight, but we will lose."

"*You* will lose," Neenho says angrily.

I step away from him. I have never seen him like this.

The sarcophagus begins to vibrate.

"We are here for something. And it lies inside with her. And we have to get it." Neenho's eyes are in slits as he stares at the god.

Goldish yellow threads snake out from different parts of Shu. The wind around us begins to blow harder.

"They're around here somewhere. I know it!"

Through the water where the wall once was, I see Kade and Assim. They are looking right at us, but it seems like they cannot see us.

Shu never even turns to look. I bet he can see out the back of his head. Or he knew they would not be able to see through the water.

"Only you two could find this room. Not even the Murri."

"Murri? Mur-people." I vaguely remember my mother telling me a tale of people who lived underwater with a gorgeous water goddess. I have known of this place all along.

Neenho looks menacing.

I form another ball of light in my other hand; one for Shu and one now for Neenho. The way he looks right now ...

Shu never takes his eyes off me. Neenho seems to not even be a threat to him.

"See what she is doing to him? Imagine what she can do to the mortals in your world? Assim or Kade. Or Adallah."

He should have not said her name, since purple threads snake out of Neenho.

"Neenho, please fight her," I beg him.

"Shu, I am sorry, but we must open it," Neenho snarls. "We did not come all this way to leave empty-handed."

Neenho throws his light at Shu, who ducks then lashes his threads at Neenho, missing.

I feel stuck. I do not know what to do or whose side I am on. We came for whatever is in that sarcophagus. We have to open it, and Neenho feels protective of the mummy that lies inside. Anyone from our guard could be dead. Kade and Assim could be all who survived. We cannot make this journey for nothing.

I watch as Neenho and Shu battle, lights slapping each other midair.

"I am really sorry god of air." I dash to the sarcophagus and, just as I am about to place my hand on top, a thread as hot as a stick in a fire wraps around my arm and yanks me back.

"I am so sorry, Little Princess, but I cannot let you open that!" Shu yells. At least he addressed me properly.

Another thread of light wraps around my foot and drags me away from the sarcophagus, down the stairs, through the red water veil, and out the room. I see Neenho throwing balls of light as fast as he can manifest at Shu, who is blocking every single throw.

"My Queen!" Kade yells from down the corridor. Him and Assim look relieved to see me.

I want to hug them both, but I blow up into a golden ball of light and dash back inside.

The guys are pounding on the water, I assume it must be a wall to their eyesight. Assim is pounding and Kade is stupidly trying to stick his stick through.

No time for them, and no time for this anymore, I make my decision. All the frustration, and hunger, comes through, and my entire body becomes engulfed in hot gold light. I scream. I scream, and small rocks fall from above. Shu's light goes out as he covers his ears. Neenho's light goes out as he, too, drops, covering his ears.

I run across the path and ram my entire body into Shu, sending him flying across the room.

Neenho hurtles a ball of purple light at him that strikes him straight in the chest. A gust of wind swirls around him, and then a beam of light shoots down. In an instant, he is gone.

Breathing heavily, Neenho and I watch Kade and Assim try to get through. Neenho's eyes have no light in them.

"Neenho?"

He does not look at me. He goes to the sarcophagus, places his hand on it, and then pushes.

The top does not budge.

He throws his light, but nothing.

I walk over to the other side, my *Ka* screaming at me not to do this. *Everything* within me tells me not to open this, but this is what we came here for. We must.

I place one hand on the top and one hand in the middle, on top of the moon. Neenho, with a vacant look, places his hand on top and the other on the sun. Then, together, we push down and push all the way until the top falls and cracks.

Eyes closed, breathing deeply, I finally look, and I turn into a statue.

22

NEENHOKANO

My legs collapse, and I feel like the sarcophagus has been lifted off my mind. I was not in control. I was fighting. I was fighting so hard, but this aching, sad, angry ... *something* was holding on to me.

I open my eyes, shaking off the haze. That was intense. I beat another god!

"Izzi, we ..."

Izzi is stone stiff. Across the room, we hear Assim and Kade banging on the water wall. I finally look into the sarcophagus to see what treasure we have won.

A long, red dress hugs her body. Her arms are crossed so peacefully over her chest. Her bushy, black hair is a pillow beneath her serene face. Floating above her is a piece of a jewel. It burns sun-red. An eye. The piece is of an eye. The Wadjet Eye, or Eye of Horus. Amun's eye. Whatever tale one wants to go with.

The green beetle floats down, and the eye clicks into one of the wings of the beetle. Together, the green and red burn bright then the two pieces fall to the stone floor at Izzi's feet.

I look up at Izzi, who has not looked away from the woman. From the rise and fall of her chest, she is breathing deeply.

"Princess?"

"She looks just like her," Izzi manages to get out.

"Is this the queen?" I ask.

"Shu said she has been locked away for a long time. She has been sending emotions to us. I saw her back on the shore when I got lost."

Come to think of it... "Izzi, I think she was calling me when we were in that room with all those royal crowns. I remember now."

Izzi nods. "My mother has a picture of her painted in her room. She looks exactly like this."

The woman is well-preserved, I think. She's not mummified, though. I wonder why. Well, if she looks like the queen, then they have to be sisters. Maybe this is ... She could be ... I mean, we don't know. She did control me easily.

"Neenho, let's close her back in," Izzi says.

That's a good idea, I think. We got the piece.

We shrug then both look down to see that the woman's eyes have snapped open. She looks from Izzi to me a few times. Then the woman rises as if she is floating.

Her hair is blowing from no wind that I can feel. Her red dress flutters all around her. She stretches and feels her body before she suddenly smiles, showing all her white teeth. She looks like fire. And I have a feeling that she burns like it, too. I hope Izzi breaks the ice here with conversation, because I'm not feeling up to it.

She finally stops admiring herself and looks at me, or Izzi. Us. I'm not sure. I have managed to side-step around the sarcophagus and stand right behind Izzi, holding her arm.

Is it okay to be scared? Izzi shows no fear. So glad we are back to normal.

"Who are you?" Izzi demands.

The lady in red takes a deep breath, her black eyes never leaving mine, or Izzi's. I can't really tell who she's looking at.

"Be not afraid of me. I will never hurt you ... intentionally."

Her voice makes every nerve in my body spark. I don't know if it's from being locked away in a box for so long, but her voice is dry and dark, and cracks, and she can't seem to control her facial expressions. It's how I felt the whole time we've been on this island.

She looks pained, and sad, and like she wants to cry. Then she switches to anger and disgust.

"You are so beautiful. I held you lovingly as a baby. Just once." She is trying to keep her emotion in place.

Izzi seems to be choking. I squeeze her arm to give her the only backup I can.

"Queen Nephthila, do you know Nephthila? Are you sisters?" Izzi asks.

Her face goes from disgust before pain eases in, and then nothing.

"The queen is I, and she is what will become of me. We are of three Ka's that have never been whole. A broken pyramid."

I slap my hand to my head as Izzi takes a deep breath.

"What the ...? What is that supposed to mean?" I am so confused.

"Drahzil? Does he mean anything to you?" Izzi searches for a reaction from this woman, whose eyes narrow at the sound of his name.

"You know nothing of the one you call Mother!" the woman spits out.

Izzi sighs. "I know nothing of myself, either. I am sure you know more ... Kawaad."

Izzi has finally piqued her interest.

"Did she tell you of me?" the red woman asks.

"My mother is dead," Izzi says. "Stabbed by the pharaoh in his pursuit to kill me."

Kawaad—I guess that's her name—smiles. This woman is scary.

"Nephi? Dead? No, she lives. If I stand here, she lives. You know nothing of the one you call Mother."

Kade and Assim are back to pounding on the water wall, yet she doesn't even look their way.

"Consorts!" She licks her lips as she raises her hands, and small, red threads snake past us and through the veil. It lashes at Kade but goes right through him.

He felt it, though, because he looks right at us, not seeing us. Like the babbling buffoon he is, we watch him talking animatedly to Assim, pointing at the wall.

"My light? Where did they hide my light?"

Now all her attention is elsewhere, her eyes darting all around.

The amulets! I let them fall to the ground. I dare not look. Izzi will kill me.

Kawaad searches frantically then stops on the broken lid to her sarcophagus. She grins.

The amulets are behind a broken piece. Can she see them? I peek down then back to the two, trying my best not to let them know. Maybe I should stop thinking it before they read my mind.

I peek down again, unable to help it and do a double-take.

Green glyphs are snaking around the two staffs on the broken lid. A wilted flower, I think, bent to the left. Another one bent to the right, three circles, and three feathers pointing upward. I wish I listened in studies. I have no idea what that means.

Izzi surprises us both by laughing, taking my attention away.

"Riddles. Talking about nothing that means nothing!" Like a fire being lit, Izzi is a ball of gold light. "You are getting back in that box until I can figure out who you are and what to do with you," Izzi tells her.

I can't tell what it was—maybe fear or even shock—but the woman is in awe of Izzi's light.

"Pure gold. Not flecked," she whispers.

Now the mysterious lady looks right at me. "Neenho, my dear boy, are you going to fight me? You know who I am. You know deep down inside." Her voice caresses and holds me. I can't shake her.

"Neenho, stop being weak and block her now," Izzi says without turning to me.

I shake my head, the fuzz coming back. She is in my mind. I see her face ... nothing but her face beaming down at me.

She smells like the sea. I see her face now clearly. I can't stop myself.

"Neenho, would you let Ishiva catch you that easily?"

I didn't notice I was whimpering. She is inside, and that heavy weight is back on my mind. I wish I could blow it away. Bring light into this darkness.

"No!" I yell to myself, feeling a sharp pull as my body burns purple.

The red lady gasps.

Izzi must have been waiting for this, because she throws a gold whip at the woman in red, knocking her out the air. A red blast erupts from the woman.

I have a ball of light in my hand, but I don't want to hit Izzi. Instead, I throw two large balls at the water veil. It stops shimmering and goes still.

"Neenho!" Assim yells, looking all around the room now. They can see inside.

"Hey, guys!" I yell back.

The grunting from the fight on the floor grabs all our attention. Izzi is straddling the red woman and slaps her hard across the face. The woman has Izzi by the neck, squeezing tight. They look so beautiful tussling with one another. So ... so ...

"Neenho, help me!" Izzi screams as she slides across the floor.

Kade and Assim were both mesmerized by the fight, as well. However, now they try to break in.

"Move back!" I yell to them, throwing another ball of light. The water wall shatters and comes rolling over us all like a wave.

Izzi gets washed off the women in red and bumps her head on a step. Kade and Assim are clumsily trying to get to Izzi first.

As the water recedes, the amulets are washed out with them. We all watch as the red lady dives for them.

Izzi scrambles to get up, knocking Kade and Assim out her way. I try to run through the knee-deep water, realizing that it's impossible.

"No!" Izzi screams.

The red lady has the amulets, but instead of making a run for it, she rushes toward me. Green light is becoming brighter, and my attention is back on the broken lid and staffs. Where have I seen this light before?

"Neenho! The sarcophagus lid! It has her power. Do not let her get it!" Izzi shouts.

The red lady is already up the stairs and facing me.

"Not my power. A piece of me."

She stomps on it, and white light blinds us all as she is blasted off the steps.

23

IZZI-RA

W e all get washed out into the corridor. When the water recedes, I spit out what is in my mouth. I promise I will ban water!

Sitting at the foot of the steps that Neenho and I came down, from the corner of my eye, I see gold chains. The amulets! She must have been blasted by the light and released them. I scramble to get them and put them around my neck.

I hear Kade, Assim, and Neenho coughing out water, as well.

"Where is she, Izzi?" Neenho looks around frantically.

"My Queen." Kade is at my side, helping me up.

"I am fine. You two, I will deal with later. You could have died."

"Where would you be if we were not there to distract them from you?" Assim asks me.

"The Queen! She lives! How did the queen get trapped down here? Why were you and your mother fighting?" Kade's confusion is normal. Assim, on the other hand, is not interested in that question or the answer.

"Assim, you knew about her?" I ask.

"We will discuss it later," he says, looking around.

"It sure did get hot down here," Neenho says.

He is right. The cool, damp air has turned into a dry heat wave. What is going on and where ...?

A flash in my mind of my mother in her garden, praying by her oversized tree. She places her hands on either side, and white light seeps from her and into the tree.

"It's her! I know where she is. We have to hurry." I dash up the stairs, hearing their heavy footsteps behind me.

I dart into the corridor and back into the dead garden area. There she is, kneeling at the tree, hands placed upon it, and light, red light, seeping from the dead roots and into her.

"No!" I yell, throwing a ball of gold light at her back. It hits hard but does nothing. It's as if she absorbs it.

The others finally reach the garden and freeze behind me.

She sucks in the last bit of light from the tree and stands up. Her hair and red dress flutter around her. She turns to us, fire in her eyes. Then she raises her hands, and this time I know the light is going to make contact.

"Run!" I yell at them.

Instead of hiding, Kade charges at her, and so does Assim. Neenho and I both hurl light at her. With no effort at all, she knocks Assim down, and a tendril of red light wraps around Kade's neck. She throws him across the room. More tendrils extinguish our lights with ease.

"I have missed that. Oh, I have! Do not make me hurt you, my child. We have just been reunited."

How dare she stand there, looking like my mother, pretending to be Neenho's mother.

I pull more power from within then unleash a whirlwind of gold light on her. Her light goes out, and she is knocked down. She actually has some fear in her eyes now.

"The third piece is just a heartbeat away, Izzi-Ra. I will get it before you." She said my name with so much hatred as she takes off running.

I follow at full speed, through the dead garden, through the last corridor, and back to where we came in. With no hesitation, she dives through the water. I follow, not even sure why I am still pursuing her. Maybe because she looks exactly like my mother.

There are no fishmen out here, and I cannot see the pathway, so I must swim.

We reach the top, both trying to catch our breaths. I look back in the water, expecting the palace down there to start crumbling. What I see is a giant shadow swimming fast toward us.

Kawaad looks, as well, and grins "Ah ... Hatmehyt has awoken, and she will not be happy." She takes off running again, her red dress billowing behind her. Then she dashes back through the water, and so do I do.

She swims quickly over to the other land space. I am right on her. We both splash through the water wall, gasping. I hate this.

She does not even stop to take a breath. Ugh, I hate that, too. But I have no choice. I cannot lose her.

I follow Kawaad, getting glimpses of the shadow in the water. There is a waterfall ahead. I skid to a stop, and so does she. The shadow in the water is before us, huge tail whipping around.

The shadow screams. Kawaad and I back up.

The shadow begins to transform as we see hair flying about and its fishtail swaying. The water parts, and she comes through. A glorified woman steps into the space, water glistening off her blue skin. Golden patches of skin go up her arms and legs. Her bushy blue hair has golden threads. Her amulet is a shimmering yellow stone I have never seen.

I want one!

Snap out of it, Izzi.

She has a long staff, made of water. Neenho will freak over that staff. The twins will want to be her.

"I cannot let you leave, Kawaad, without a fight. My people gave up their lives and families to make sure evil as pure as you will never tempt mankind again." Her voice is like a wave as she taps her staff, and more shadows appear around the waters.

Kawaad looks around. "I am supposed to go back into my tomb

and lay there for all eternity, Hatmehyt? Because of the mistakes of my father?"

"Yes." The goddess looks past Kawaad to me. Her lips move, but nothing came out. Regardless, I heard her. *"On the count of three,"* is what she whispered to me.

I count low then throw a huge whip of gold light at Kawaad's back just as the goddess sends bluish-gold light at her front. Purple light comes from above. Neenho is on his *clou*.

Kawaad screams, her red light meeting ours from all angles.

For being alone, she is holding her own against us. I am breaking into a sweat and feel like I am draining.

"Fight, Izzi-Ra. I need you to fight," the water goddess says.

She knows my name.

A new wave of energy comes to me, and I summon more power from somewhere and slam my light into Kawaad harder.

I look up at Neenho. His light seems to be hitting stronger, too. His light even looks a shade darker.

Kawaad is looking up at him, as well. Neenho, once again, looks pained and confused.

"Neenho!" I yell.

Neenho's light goes out then back on. He throws it at the water goddess.

"Neenho, no!" I yell at him.

Kawaad busts free. She leaps over the goddess and into the water, disappearing through the trees.

I jump up and follow her. We already ran around this entire perimeter, and there is no way to the salt water, so she cannot get away.

She is running straight for a large tree. She throws her light at the tree, and it blasts apart. I can see the sand dunes and the salt water. She dives into the water. I stop on the edge, Neenho right next to me, and then the goddess. We watch as a red blur swims through the water.

The goddess and I turn to Neenho.

"I ... um ... That sure is a nice ... staff you have." He puts his head down.

I slap Neenho hard on the shoulder.

"I'm sorry. She affects me more," he whines.

"We cannot let her go free," the goddess says.

I watch as Kawaad is almost to shore.

"We still have time," Neenho says.

I am fuming. This is his fault!

He walks away.

"Neenho, what are you doing? This is all your fault. If you would have just—"

He turns around and starts running right at me. "Oh, shut up, Izzi-Ra!" he yells, slamming hard into me, and we go flying over the edge. I scream.

Neenho whistles, and before we hit a jagged rock sticking out of the water, we land on the *clou* with Neenho in full control.

Breathing hard, still so upset, I just watch him as he flies fast toward her. She is almost to the shore.

Below us, in the water, I see colorful blurs and a ginormous shadow. The goddess and her people are with us.

We are almost to the shore ourselves when my heart sinks. A looming cloud of fire is heading over the sand dunes.

"Not this guy again," Neenho says. "And he has allies!"

Below, looking like a million ants on a fallen piece of meat, is the pharaoh's army. Beyond them, I can see men in blazing blue uniforms. The Satisians! I should have known Lady Qui'l would side with my father. And to think she is one of my favorite rulers.

We hover, keeping our distance. The fire cloud hovers, as well. Lizard Man has his eyes on Neenho and me. The army below stops near the shoreline. How did they get through the sand mountains?

Kawaad is still in the water, looking up at the fire above.

I do not see the goddess and her people anymore. The water is clear. I see nothing at all, but that does not surprise me.

A line parts, and a few riders comes forth. The pharaoh, flanked by Jabari and Kadir.

"Take me down, Neenho. Now."

I expected an argument, but his *clou* moves forward. We pass over Kawaad, who is trying her best not to be noticed.

"Izzi-Ra, quite the mess you have caused. Come, talk to your father. I will help you clean it all up." He smiles at me, my father. A hug from him usually does the trick, but then his eyes ... the warmth never reaches them.

"I am going to kill you." The words pour out my lips before I can even think them. It feels good to never have to pretend with him anymore.

His smile leaves his face. Now his eyes and sneer match. It is the look I know he has always given me behind my back, aimed right at me. We never have to play that game again.

Right above him, the lizard man stares right at us. The amulets are exposed.

"Surrender, Izzi-Ra, and—"

I burst out laughing.

I laugh. And laugh. I must look like I have finally snapped.

"And what? You will spare my life, Father! Shall we spark a deal? I help you; you help me. Oh, wait. That thing up there wants to drain my *Ba* and *Ka* and rip my shadow apart, in hopes that he gets my light."

My light bursts forth from me. I radiate it. I am angry as my father's face gets closer and closer to me. Or am I getting closer to him? I am gliding toward him, arms raised in the air, my light sparking around me. Am I flying without Neenho?

He draws his weapon, along with many of his men, but I do not stop or take my eyes off him. I hover right in front of my father's horse, Nehi, and pet him. I love this horse.

I hear weapons clink as the army behind my father have readied their weapons.

He holds up his hand, looking at me in awe.

"I will rid you of this rider," I tell Nehi before glaring at my father.

"I have always felt it inside of me, but I never knew what it was. I remember being asleep some nights and waking up, seeing gold light all around me, but Mother was there each time. She would say it was the candlelight burning. It must kill you to know that she knew all this time. It must kill you to know there was a god in the palace, but it was not you."

The veins in his neck pop.

I smirk at him. "Although your face says nothing to me, Father, I hear the blood in your heart pumping fast. I can hear your thoughts swirling about. You cannot focus. I smell your fear. You killed the only Ka who ever loved you and I both," I tell him.

This time, he smirks at me. "What are you talking about, Izzi?" His smile grows brighter.

"Bring her forth," he demands.

I float back a little, ready for the attack.

The Satisians part, and two horses come forth. A figure on one is covered. I breathe deeply. Who could they have captured to try to bargain with? Did they find Adiah before us?

My father snaps his fingers, and one of the soldiers snatches the cloth off.

I fall from the sky and into the sand, all my powers receding deeply within me.

"Mother?" This must be a trick. She looks as she did the last time I saw her. In my dream.

Her almond-shaped eyes swim with tears as she nods her head at me. Her hair has grown in.

I look back at Kawaad who is still watching from the waters.

"My queen is very much alive. Surrender now, Izzi. You and the boy."

I look back at Neenho, who is behind me, closer to the shore. He looks like he is concentrating hard.

I know what I saw. I saw her take her last breath.

Neenho is rambling on about me being able to fly without a *clou*. I need him to focus. My mother is alive. I saw her die!

"You and I both," my father says. He does not need *heka* to know what I am thinking. I cannot hold face. I cannot hold myself together. I am ready to blast away every single man here and fight to the death to get my mother.

I feel Neenho grip my shoulder with clammy hands and pull me up. I hear his faint voice in my mind, telling me to pull myself together, but I cannot. I thought she was dead, yet she is alive. She must be just like me. I am just like her?

"Surrender now, and your punishments may be light. You have no army. You cannot fight us alone."

Neenho and I stand there, minds racing. I see Neenho looking up at the cloud of fire. He whispers something about hating Drahzil so much, and then a spark comes through his fingers and zaps me.

"Let the queen go, and we may have mercy on you," Neenho says, loud and clear.

All eyes turn toward him, including mine.

"I do not want this to end badly, and I do not want you all to have to turn on each other, because that is what will happen here if you do not surrender the queen to us now."

They all laugh. My father's shoulders shake up and down. Roars and hissing of laughter above, and a small, weird noise from the Satisians, which I assume is their laughter because their faces show nothing.

"The boy my sister raised, you surely have her intelligence. I will take it easy on you."

His face turns hard. "Enough of this. Grab them!" my father yells.

"I wouldn't do that if I were you guys!" Neenho shouts over them. "See, those blue guys are going to turn their allegiance to us, Lizard Man is going to turn on you, Pharoah, and your men are going to scamper away like cowards."

I have no idea what Neenho is talking about. Too much water must be making him crazy.

Drahzil lands his horse, making us both jump back. We grab hands, and I feel our light buzzing between us, as it so often does when we touch.

His horse's wings are so beautifully inflamed with fire. It nods its head, spitting flames into the sand, leaving a small trail of fire.

"And, why would I turn on my brother?" His voice makes me sick.

"A trade." Neenho shrugs calmly.

I move to grasp the amulets around my neck, but they are not there anymore.

Drahzil spits.

Neenho holds up the two pieces of amulets, and a gasp goes through the entire area. They burn radiantly and seem to want to fly away, swaying.

"I know you want these. But you want this, too."

A large thread of purple light seeps from Neenho, heading into the water. I watch with curiosity, like the rest, as he yanks something and his light comes back. Tightly bound is Kawaad.

Drahzil slides from his horse. He has completely lost his cool. Whatever he was expecting, it was not this. Both of us have gotten a surprise today.

I peer over at my father, who is sliding from his horse, too, looking from Mother to Kawaad. Whispers spread throughout the army. *There are two queens!*

Mother shakes her head.

Neenho does not have his light around Kawaad's mouth, but she seems to be gagged, as well.

"Oh, and as I promised, those guys will not fight us because their allegiance is always to the water goddess."

Waves back at the island come forward. They grow gradually, getting larger. Once higher than the cloud of fire from Drahzil's army, she emerges, water glistening from her skin. She looks down on the situation.

Two more ripples of water come from near the shore, and a canoe shoots out. The dome opens, and Adallah hops out with Assim, Kade, Rafa, and Kofi. They spread out across the shore behind us.

Where are the rest? Were they killed?

I look back and nod to Assim, letting him know I am fine. Kade is staring at his father.

The water goddess raises her hands, and the dunes fall, making it flat land.

I see Adallah relieved to see Neenho, but then she shifts her focus to Zarhmel. They lock eyes, uncertainty in both, almost as if they want to hug one another.

Water springs forth all around us, and in the water, I see the goddess' people with tails, their weapons at the ready.

The Satisians are off their horses, on their knees. The leader scampers forward and drops to his knees. He starts speaking in a loud, annoying cry. It sounds like a bird being plucked of its feathers.

"We are here, and we have been here always. Depart from this land now. Return to Dejut Isle and let your queen know I will be there soon. Go. Now," the goddess speaks.

The men mount their horses and ride off, back through the maze of now water.

"Follow them," she says to no one that we can see.

Father's men are, indeed, scared. *People in water?* Father will have some explaining to do when he gets home.

I see Drahzil's army trying to stay away from the water. Not a good thing when you fly on something of fire.

I also notice that there is blue light wrapped around Kawaad now. She was caught in the water by the fish people. The goddess was able to trap her, and Neenho must have been in tune with all of this?

Drahzil is breathing heavy. Smoke seems to be coming from him. The woman he loved was not my mother; it was Kawaad. Kawaad and mother stare at one another.

I feel that chaos is about to erupt. However, I have tunnel vision.

I go for my father, dodging the water arrows. I see him trying to force his horse to move.

As I get closer, I hear a faint ticking mixed with a drum. An amulet? It ticks louder and louder in my ear. I smell honey and dirt. I shake it off. Must be the two I already have.

I look up to see Neenho above me, darting around on his *clou*. He is throwing balls of lights everywhere at the flying camels. I do not look at the shore to see what the others are doing.

Father's army is retreating through the now maze of water.

"You want her, Izzi? Fight for her. Fight for her without that light," He taunts.

I accept, picking up a gold stick that was dropped by a palace guard.

"Fight fair," I say, twirling the stick. He jumps from Nehi and extends his pole.

"I did not say anything about fair." He lunges forward, and we duel.

His spike slices my upper arm, but I wound his thigh. I used to play in his chambers as a small child. I know his open areas, and that dawns on him, as well. He rushes at me full force and knocks me down hard, knocking the breath out of me.

He said not fair.

I burst into a gold ball of light and rush right back at him. He hits the sand hard. Blood squirts from his mouth. I grab a knopesh and advance on him.

"I never loved you," he spits out.

"Same," I say as I bring the weapon down to his throat.

She touches my shoulder gently, and all my light is sucked away.

"He lies, *saat*. I know he has love for you and you him. Spare him, please."

I look into her eyes and melt. Anything for her.

I am about to drop the weapon when it is snatched from me and driven right through my side. I scream in pain, my mother screaming in my ear, as well. Neenho explodes in my mind.

I see my father's face swim in and out of focus. He grabs her, throws her on his horse, and speeds off. I hear my name being called from a distance. I feel warm suddenly. Warm and wet. I fall into the sand, my head hitting hard.

Drahzil whips Neenho out of the air and snatches Kawaad. Both Neenho's and the goddess's light vanish from around her. I see them take flight.

Where is Assim? Is everyone okay?

I let the wet, warm waves of my blood take me away from this devastating scene.

24

THE GODS

Two sekmis playfully nibble on one another. One hits the other too hard in the side, and the wounded one falls from above, landing in the outstretched hands of a god. The jaguar-faced god checks to make sure the sekmi is fine then gives it a little help to get back into the air.

Gods and goddesses lounge around a cozy, dimly lit garden. The sun and the moon are off in the distance as they coexist in this space. Stars shine blazingly above the gods who lounge around the area near a golden fire in the center.

Their attention is diverted to a nearby hill where a beam of white light appears. Shu steps out of his light. He sways then falls.

Goddesses and gods rush to his side. Horus picks him up and lays him on a lengthy chair. His white robes are singed, and there is a circular burn mark on his chest.

Sekret claps her hands loudly, and a burst of flames come from them, moving up and around the entire kingdom.

Within seconds, Amun-Re is there. He looks over the small god, whose light is bleak.

"Quick, Sekret, Meretseger, Maat, Hathor, heal him."

The others step away as the goddesses gather around Shu. They each lift a hand, and their lights come forth—Sekret's gold flecked with orange, Meretseger gold flecked with green, and Maat and Hathor's pure golden lights—and swallow up his body. Then the lights go out, and Shu lies motionless. A small swirl of wind comes from him, and his robes are restored. He opens his eyes slowly.

"Who do I get to kiss first?"

"How, Amun? How?" Maat turns on the god.

"How did they do this to you, Shu? They wounded Anpu, but this ... Amun, he almost died. A god dead? Human children with that kind of power?" The scorpions around Sekret's hair are hissing her anger to the crowd.

"That is because they are not human nor deity." Isis enters the area, looking at Meretseger. They do not say anything, but both are now fully aware of everything. Meretseger still needs time to process. Her family. Those humans are her family.

"Horus, son, I need you to save and avenge your father again." Isis then turns and leaves, Horus following.

Re addresses the remaining, "It has been many moons and suns since man has seen their gods and goddesses. Go forth. Show up in your temples and shrines to your most loyal. To the families you created. No matter the side you choose, all of Egi is in danger.

25

NEENHOKANO

The heat from the fire in the room makes my palms sweaty, and I have to keep regripping her hand. She would be so mad if she was awake and knew this.

I smile at the thought of her yelling at me. I want her to wake up and yell at me. I want to hear that shrill in her voice that she gets when I don't listen to her ...

"I need you to wake up, Izzi-Ra. I need you, Princess."

She lies stiffly, her body cold, despite the warmth in the room from the fire. She looks dead and was pronounced dead by Chike and Adallah. But I can feel her. Our *He'ka* is still connected. She lives, but where is a mystery. *I would know if the Ka left her body. I would know*, I convince myself. I feel her.

"Your mother is alive, Izzi. We need to go save her. She needs you."

Today's events press hard on my conscience. Fish people, white-haired army, two queens. What is happening? This is madding!

I lay her hand gently at her side then lean back, trying to relax. I need to sleep. I should be sleep, but I can't.

I look out the doorway, and my heart skip several beats, because a few dolphins are outside the door. They bob there for a few seconds more then swim away. This place is insane! I'm underwater, but I'm not in water. The water never comes through the threshold. This place is so cool. And I can't even enjoy it because the events of the last few days keep haunting me. The mountain, the island, and this red lady, Kawaad, who got away. She almost got the amulets, too, thanks to me.

Everyone is safe, even Kade. We could have lost him. We could have lost one man at battle, but whatever.

Everyone being safe is all that matters, and it's not by the grace of the gods. They put us in this mess. When I figure out how to get to their kingdom, I'm going to blow the place up, like they have done our lives.

I huff in a sweeping wave of emotion and feel my light flare up around me hotly. Then, in an instant, it begins to simmer. I feel light-headed. I know this feeling.

I look up, and he is there.

"Calm yourself, dear boy. You know how you get when you are angry."

"Thoth."

"The scale of Maat has leveled, and there so has the reigns on the steerer. Does a horseless rider have no path?"

"Thoth, please not with the riddles tonight. I never understand what you're talking about."

His eyes twinkle in the firelight. It's weird seeing him younger and cleaner.

His words swirl around my brain, and I mentally see them be absorbed by my purple light.

"Aw ..." he says as he sits on the edge of the bed.

"How can you say you and I are on equal playing fields? I don't see how we're examples of one another. Look what's happened! Adallah was almost killed today, we took the Kemet people into a siege, the fish people almost killed us, and I let Kawaad get away." I snatch Izzi's hand back in mine. "Look at my princess. She's lifeless, and Izzi is life itself in Egypt. How do I bring her back?"

"Once a wave crashes into another, another will follow, and

another. Amun himself cannot stop it. The stars are the maps to the end and beginning to every path. I know because I wrote them."

I frown at him, not in the mood.

"Okay, there is one true earth goddess, and you hold the hand. There is only one true earth god. Only one, NeenhoKano. The gods of Egypt do not share playing fields. Things are stirring, and Egypt will fall completely because of it. The Egypt I knew is gone, and the one you will build will be washed away and stolen. You living will make all that come about. That is what I have for you, and that is what I will give you." He looks at Izzi then back to me. "I hope you two will choose to join us and not get lost out there."

"You already know the answer to that, as well, because you wrote it," I say to him.

It's his turn to look surprised.

I know what he's saying, but I don't believe that. Izzi and I will not do what the gods and goddesses think we are supposed to do anymore. We have our own battle stirring here. And we will win.

Thoth smiles at me. He heard my thoughts, as I knew he would.

"That's my boy—excuse me, man. You are a man. Perfect. I must get back now. Neenho, when you need me, summon me, and I will be there for you. As for Izzi, you know where she is, and you can go get her."

"Wait," I call to him. "Is she ... my mother?" I look deep into his eyes, watching every slight facial expression I can catch.

"The womb is just the first home, and the heart you hear will bring you closer to that place."

"Really?"

"Really."

A warm beam of white light shoots down, and Thoth steps inside. He bows to me, and then he is gone in an instant. Another conversation with a god. But not just any. Dotthy. And he would never lie to me.

I go to the entryway to peer out without getting wet. As I am about to turn away, a shadow looms over me. The blue water has dimmed. The goddess appears right in front of the doorway. Her blue hair sways about like the plants below, her blue and gold skin bright in the water, her tail changing colors with every flick. She holds her long, gold staff in one hand. The staff would almost be something cool if the top was not just a rock. With her other hand, she waves for me to come.

I shake my head.

She laughs. I can't hear it, but the way she tosses her head back, and the smile on her face, tells me. She motions with a nod of her head for me to come.

I sigh. Either I plunge into the water on my own, or she will pull me by force.

She nods, understanding my thoughts.

I give Izzi one last glance. Nothing has changed. I have the amulets tucked safely around my neck.

I look back at the water goddess and prepare to hold my breath and go out. However, she holds up one hand to stop me. Then she purses her lips, as if kissing the water. No, puckering. What is she ...? Whistle?

She nods.

I push my body into the water, letting the saltwater grip me. I float there for seconds, scared something is about to grab me and pull me far away. The goddess looks even bigger this closely. Her tail whips around, bigger than Ishiva.

She nods at me encouragingly as bubbles come out my mouth. I'm losing my breath.

I let the air in my mouth out and, stupidly, try to whistle underwater. Instead of water rushing into my mouth, little bubbles escape. My *clou* forms, not in front of me, but around me. It closes in. I sit wet, bobbing in the water.

"What the ...?" It's a thin layer all around me. I can breathe. This gets cooler and cooler. Izzi will be so jealous.

"Only one god has one of these. How did you get one? He went through a lot to get this from Nun," she says.

"Hey, I can hear you now!" I tell her. "Tell me, what god has this *clou*?"

"You do not know?" Her big, round, gold—her eyes are gold in the water. So cool!—eyes peer right into mine as she tilts her head in thought. "You do not listen when your superiors teach?" She narrows her eyes at me, but she has a smile on her face.

"Uh ... No, I guess I don't. Who's the god? Who has a *clou*?"

"Come, Young King. I want to show you my world."

The plain rock on her staff begins to crack. The rock then falls away, and there is a yellow crystal stone there. Light begins to come from it.

"Not a jewel, Young King. A hematite, like my name. I was born of the rock in the waters of Nun."

She doesn't need to read my mind because my face says it all. I slap my hands to my face because I never bothered to ask her name.

She chuckles and continues on, "I am Hatmehyt."

She nods her head for me to follow then swims away. I urge my *clou* forward.

There is nothing below, but I see a couple of little lands above here and there. I am right on her tail, literally.

She looks back with a smile.

Finally, someone who wants to have fun! I feel for my light and let it out. A warm burst of purple comes through. I go over her and shoot off. My *clou* slices through the water as I look back to see how far she is and halt. She's not behind me. I look up, below, side to side, but she's gone. Where could she have gone? There is nothing but clear blue water. No life. Panic comes because I cannot even see where I left Izzi. I want to zip back, but then I think back to what she said, how I never pay attention when my superiors teach me.

I let my light flow, not where it shines around me but inside. I feel it around my mind, and my eyes sharpen.

I cannot see her with my eyes, but my light can. Her vibration is right below me, her thumping heart that sounds like a wave crashing the shore.

There is a flick of her tail. I see her! What do I do next? Yell *gotcha*? What would she do? What would Izzi do? Izzi would just go for it.

I keep pretending I have no idea where she is as I urge my *clou* a little bit ahead. I still feel her under me. I then open my palm and send a purple thread of light around her tail. She materializes, smiling.

"Gotcha!" I giggle, proud.

She shakes her head and points at me. She has blue threads coming from different parts of her, all surrounding my *clou*.

"Do not think, King. You failed this teaching. We will try again." She releases me but sends me flying back the way we came.

"No fair!" I yell.

I ignite my light and zip back toward her. We zip around, above, and next to one another. I see small fish here and there, and below me, sea nature start to come into view. The rocks shimmer like her tail, in many colors. There is a small mountain ahead. We both scale the rock as we go up. I notice the seaweed on the rock seems to reach out to her. She twirls around as she swims up, as if she's saying *ti'ju* to the rock and plants.

We reach the top, and I am ready to zoom off and continue our race, but I stop. I hope my *clou* does not burst with how close my face is pressing against it.

As far and wide as I can see, a monumental underwater land lays before me. If I thought Kemet was impressive, then I don't know what that means. It looks as if Egypt was built ten times over and placed underwater. Palaces! Large, small, and between sized palaces. They all gleam a black, shiny glass. In the far distance, I see a statue larger than Ptah's of the water goddess.

"Welcome to Murku. Home of the Murri. We are not fish people. We are Murfolk."

I cannot move.

One of her blue whips wraps around my *clou*, and she pulls me forward.

The fish—I mean, people—are all around. They no longer look scary with red eyes but golden. Their skin is a dark seaweed color. Their hair is thick and black, and it moves like the plants that sway from the moving water. Their tails are long and change colors with every movement. The women ... Wow, the women ... I can't even divert my eyes from the shells they wear. They are the biggest I have ever seen. The shells, I'm really looking at the shells. As we pass, they bend their torsos at their goddess.

"How?"

She stops at a group of older women. They bow to her, and then surprisingly to me.

"This is the water of Nun. The other thirteen came here. They lived for a time above. But Shu, he was interested in what more could be below."

"Shu? He created you?" I think about what Izzi did to him earlier. I hope he is all right. "How?" I stupidly ask.

She laughs. "The hematite rocks. The jewels that litter the saltwater. When the god of air came below, he sent wind through. That is the flow of waves. He picked up a rock, and his light infused in it. He created us. My sister and me. It was difficult. Some of the gods could not understand us. We could walk on land, but we yearned for the water. My sister, she yearned for more."

I am as confused as always. Izzi said fourteen came, and then there was fifteen?

Hatmehyt is staring at me with a smile on her face, no doubt listening to my thoughts.

"Five is unlucky, boy. Sixteen. True, I am a goddess, and so is my sister. The tales humans tell are mixed with then and now. There is a sixteenth created, or born, here. And she will lie in Hauhet Khames."

Fish pass her, and she swims around them in delight as murchildren chase them. I am so confused? How many gods were here?

"I never thought I would see them again. We felt her evil, and we knew we had to give it all up to save Egi. We were willing, but you came and ruined our sacrifice," she says.

I can't even respond. This land has me mesmerized. Am I dead? This is incredible.

We pass a group of males. The men all have twisty locks that float around their face. They stand, or float, at attention then bend their torsos forward. She nods to them.

I notice one glares at me. Even with his red eyes gone, and crack grey skin all healed and smooth now, I'll always remember he shot a water arrow at me.

"Lazlo, gentlemen, good to see you. Let us hold a feast for our people and our guests. Let us rejoice in having our homes and family back in order," she tells them.

The others smile, except this Lazlo guy.

We continue on.

"He was honoring what he swore to do—keep the evil here. You dishonored his sacrifice."

I look back to see that he continues to glare at me.

A small child, with a bright purple tail, swims to him, and he opens his muscled arms wide. The little girl swims into the embrace, and I see lots of bubbles come from her mouth.

"You all gave up your families to keep Kawaad here? Why?"

She looks among her world proudly. "She came here for refuge. A god brought her, with a baby. He made her a palace. I agreed to let her stay if she did not bother my people."

She had a baby with her? Izzi or me? Me or Izzi? I don't want to know.

The water goddess looks at me sadly. She knows. She knows I am not ready to know.

We go into a small cave. At first, it's dark, but then the walls begin to sparkle with bright, yellow stones embedded in the rock. It's the stone that is on her staff. Forget gold, I want one of these things.

We exit, and then the next part looks strangely familiar.

Hey? This is where we started.

Below is the palace where we let Kawaad loose. Across is the temple where Izzi lies. Above, I see the many lands where we were in battle with the Murfolk or Murri I guess.

"How did we ...?" I'm so confused.

"You pay attention to nothing, Young King. You and the young goddess need to quiet your minds. Thoughts betray us and leave you seeing only what you want to see. In your case, your powers are also overshadowing logic. You control it. It, not you."

Two dolphins swim around her. They make soft noises. She giggles and makes the same noise as them. They swim around her, and she twirls in a circle, their bodies touching. They then swim away, and she watches after them happily.

"Although you have ruined everything, Young King, I want to thank you and the young goddess for setting us free. Any time left together is better than none. Go. Save your princess."

"How ...? How do I save her?"

"You know where she is. She told you where she wanted to go. When you feel scared, you go where you are not afraid." She points her staff at my chest. Then she flicks her tail at me and swims away.

I urge my *clou* back to the lonesome place where Izzi lies. Before I reach the entryway, my *clou* bursts, and I am plunged into the water. I swim quickly through the doorway and fall to the floor.

Izzi is there. She lies in the center of the room on the overlarge bed. No change. The fire still crackles on.

I think of how Izzi told me about the many fires that burn throughout the palace, making it warm. What has our lives become? Izzi would so often wish she would wake up from this nightmare and be in her room. I wish I was on the rooftop ...

The palace!

"I'm coming for you, Princess. I'm going to save you, and I will never let you forget it, and you will be indebted to me, and I don't want to hear no back talk about it."

I laugh because none of that will ever happen. Then I rush to her side and grab her cold hand. I kiss her hand before tucking it back to her side.

The amulets lie dormant around my neck. When Izzi was wounded, they separated. Interesting.

I go to the door and peer out. No one around, just those two dolphins. I see the land above and want to get to. I hate swimming. This is starting to suck. Oh! My *clou*.

I whistle.

Nothing. So, I plunge into the water, floating there. I pucker my lips then blow out the air I have in my lungs.

Still nothing.

I swim back inside and hit the floor again. I hate this.

I don't ... No ... I can't ... Yes, I can. Because he said I can, I wander into a fit of thoughts. *Neenho, think about this. What if it takes you someplace else, far away from here, and you have no idea how to get back?*

"Oh well," I say to myself. *Here goes nothing.*

I close my eyes and take several deep breaths. I feel my light warm up around me and see purple. Bright purple. But that's not what I want. I put flecks of gold in the light and pull them together. Then I open my eyes, and there it is—that beam of light.

I turn back and smirk at Izzi because I'm not going to tell her how to do it.

I walk through it and think of Adallah. Then, with no sign or a countdown at all, I'm zipped away, screaming.

I feel like I've been stuffed into a tiny bag and flung across the entire length of the Nile. I want to look, but I'm too scared. What if I end up in the salt water around no one?

My throat is starting to hurt from screaming. I open my eyes, still screaming, scanning the room and seeing all the people around me staring in confusion. Some of the Murri have stuck their heads through the water walls to see what the noise is.

Ta'li and Umi are giggling. Adallah and Chike, and pretty much everyone else, give me that boy-is-you-crazy look. Assim, as usual, has no emotion either way. Kofi smiles at me. The mountain men do not.

"You have no idea what that was like," I say to the room.

"You stepped out of your light like the goddesses," Umi says in surprise.

"Well, crouched out," Ta'li corrects her.

"I wondered if my light could do it to. You don't look surprised, Aunt Adallah," I say.

Adallah and Chike sit at a clear, circular table. Inside, small orange fish swim about.

This place is insane. Everyone sits in comfy green chairs, except Sho'te, who stands near one of the water walls, looking around. The walls are a shimmering water. The Murri people—I need to remember to call them that—swim past.

This place is unbelievable. Everything is so royal-looking, and the colors are so peaceful.

I go to a water wall and peer out, seeing the village below, so brightly lit in this clear blue water. Their tails streak past, leaving rainbow colors.

"Since you are here, I will stand watch over Izzi-Ra," Assim says.

"No, Assim, stay. She is fine. Trust me. She can't be harmed." I'm taken aback by the authority in my own voice, and I think he is, as well.

I puff up more, looking for Kade. I want to boss him around.

Adallah grins at me. "Have you learned something, Neenho?"

"Thoth came to me. What's bound by men is not the tip of the pyramid, but the scales have been weighed, and they will fall, level, or outweigh the odds. *Ooo* ... I get it." I'm tickled a bit.

I clear my throat and pull the amulets out from around my neck. "We have to get the third piece of the amulet. We have to go to the palace. I have a feeling the queen knows something. She may know where the third piece is, and it may be with Adiah. The queen knows. Or Kawaad.

"Assim, I expected Adallah and Chike to not be shocked by the queen having a twin, but you know something more, as well."

Assim nods.

"We gon need mo warriors if we wan' ta take on da palace in Asir," Sho'te says.

"Me an' ma peeple will head back ta Kemet an' tell our queen wut 'as 'appened here."

"An', even if our god an' queen do not chooze ta fight, Kofi and I are wit the Prince of Egypt. We will find ya." Marja'ni fists her chest, and so do the others.

"Send us to the Isle of Kepri's. We will ask the sisters to join us in our fight," Umi says to Chike.

We really don't have time for this argument but, to my surprise, Chike stands before her children and fists her hand over her heart then puts her other arm before her. Umi fists her heart and puts her arm across her mother's. Ta'li then fists his heart, laying his other arm on top of theirs. Chike clucks her tongue. Umi responds in the same way, and then Ta'li. Adallah and Kofi are emotional watching them.

"You have the support of my people, as well," Hatmehyt's melodic voice splashes over me like a cool wave as she comes through the water barrier, her tail splitting into two legs. Four men and four women flank her. Their colorful fins split at the touch of the stone floor and become feet. They stand before us in kilts of the same color as their tails, and the women have shells to cover their tops. Extremely revealing. I notice Lazlo is among them. He smiles at no one.

I lock eyes with Assim, who tries not to widen his eyes. Marja'ni elbows me.

Goddess Hatmehyt glides over, snapping her fingers. A woman to her side hands her a horn.

"Take this, my dearest Neenho. Blow into it, and I will receive the call. We will come." She places it into my hand. For being so big, it's not heavy at all and feels like soft sand in my ...

Hey! It dissolved into sand, seeping into my hand.

"I ... I'm sorry I broke it!"

She and her people laugh, except Lazlo.

"You have taken it, and it is an oath between us. You accepted it. When you need me, it will reappear, and you can call me."

The twins look jealous. I raise my eyebrows at them. Bet they read all about that horn.

"Where is Kade? I want him to stay here and clean the water walls. He's not needed on anyone's journey," I say with finality.

With great timing, he comes struggling down the water tunnel ahead of us. His father bound and gagged, struggling behind him.

"I am ready, Queen Hatmehyt," he says, huffing. He then slings his father down and joins our circle.

"Yeah, Kade, you will stay here and—"

He rounds on me and steps close. Too close.

I will blast that perfect face with a purple fire ball, don't he know it.

"I am going back to my land to plead with my people. Shiza is a big part of Egypt, and we need them, Neenho. Izzi is their queen now. She is my wife. I must expose my father and get my land on our side."

Through the water walls, I see something big floating toward us—a giant shell with a glass dome on top. What the ...?

I look around, but no one else is shocked by this.

"That is how we got to the island, Neenho," Adallah says, seeing my confusion. This is what they came to shore in as well. I forgot about that. I want to ride in that!

A small hole begins to circle in the middle of the water wall and opens up. The dome around the canoe opens slightly, and then a water staircase snakes out. Dark shadows loom over the canoe, and we look up. The huge men that me and Izzi faced earlier are there.

"They will accompany you through the waters, King Kade," the goddess informs him. "It is a dangerous journey from here to Shiza. We have some lost family of our own who broke off and started their own islands. They will try to kill you. There are Murri out there not as pleasant. Dangerous songs that lure men to death."

I'm mad as Kade bows to her and kisses her hand. All the females start swooning. Then he picks up his wiggling father, who has been trying to speak through the gag around his mouth.

"Well, bye, Kade," I say, turning away from him and all his glory. "Let's get back to saving our world."

Adallah throws me a look.

Before Kade walks up the stairs, I have a thought. "Wait." I go to him and pull off his father's gag.

"What is the pharaoh planning?"

"I'll not speak against my god. You all will suffer. Just like the Pakhet tribe—burned to the ground. Whoever did not perish is

174

captured and enslaved to the kingdom. My son will be enslaved, you traitor. You traitor to the throne."

Kade grabs him by the neck, but the water goddess materializes his gag back over his mouth. Kade then ushers him into the canoe.

I look back at my aunt, at Chike and her twins. That is our home. That is where we grew up. Is it true? How did we let this happen?

26

NEPHTHILA

Nephi sits in the garden, watching as Amun pulls the sun across the sky to set for the night. She imagines she can see him, picturing him in his human form, that boyish grin he always had when they saw each other. She remembers the way his eyes twinkled like the stars, because they are one in the same.

As the sun drops lower, leveling with her, it warms her entire body. She closes her eyes, letting the bright, orange light caress her. A tear escapes. "My Amun, my light."

She knows. He knows. They have never stopped knowing. And yet, she knows that his truest of loves is her mother. She got him by default, because she is a replica of that human who gave birth to her.

The sun finally sets, and Nephi stands in the darkness. Warmth, love, and comfort gone for the night as a chill creeps upon her, but it is not from the cool night air.

"Nightmares are real," Nephi whispers as hands wrap around her from behind. She stiffens, smelling the familiar scent. Feeling herself in the person behind her, she closes her eyes, takes a deep breath, and when she opens them, she stares back into herself, the red dress floating around them both.

"You used his love for me. Izzi-Ra did not take the bait."

"The girl was too difficult to control, but the love was there. It freed me. You have it all, which I am grateful for."

"Where is she?"

"Her body was never found, but I know she is in the Underworld."

"We will get her back. We will be one, and then there will only be one. Because there is no space for us all to breathe, Nephthila. It hurts. To miss parts of you *hurts*. How do you breathe when she has the shadow? I have just a *Ba*, and you the *Ka*. We need to be whole again."

"So, kill me then, Nephidema. Kill me and take what you need. I will not fight you."

"You know I cannot just take it."

Nephthila reaches out to touch Kawaad, who slaps her hands away quickly. Nephi does it again, quicker, with both hands, and pulls Kawaad's face to hers, holding her still, nose to nose.

"My child smells just like you," Nephi says.

The red threads of light begin to snake out from Kawaad and lash at Nephi, but Nephi's white light meets them quicker. They are surrounded in a ball of red and white light, but Nephi still has a grip on Kawaad's face.

"Let me see, Kawaad, let me see."

Kawaad is visibly shaking, trying to break free of the grasp, but Nephi's light is stronger, overpowering her. They are both sucked into where Nephi wanted to go—the mountain where they were buried; a woman becoming Pharaoh; Nephi in the palace, being adored by young Drahzil and Zarhmel; Kawaad being locked away.

Then she slows down to where Kawaad fights the children and gets away. She looks down as Izzi-Ra lies on the shore, water and blood flowing all around her.

Nephi breaks the connection, both gasping hard. Nephi is angry. Kawaad is gloating.

"She is alive for now. I would know if she were dead, just like you would. They are both safe ... for now. But make no mistake, I will take them into me. Maybe just the one who is not mine." Kawaad continues, "Oh, and you are no longer needed to be queen. Stay out of sight." With that, Kawaad walks away.

Nephi walks out of her garden and reaches the Nile that passes by.

Kawaad does not know where Nephthys is, but Nephi does. She and her sisters were promised a lot by the goddesses, and it is time they act on those promises.

27

THE GODS

I sis and Horus step from their beam of lights, now standing in the dead city of Jaquel.

"This way," Isis whispers to Horus.

They walk through the ruined city. Isis shows no emotion, whereas Horus looks around in great sadness.

"What happened here? What has happened to Anpu himself?"

They come to a ruined statue of the jackal-headed god.

"Answers that have been buried with its people. We will unearth it all, my son."

They move along, the trail of serpents appearing. They seem to scatter at the sight of the goddess. They weave through the dense path and reach the moss-filled area where the Nile flows through. They stop at the edge. The water below ripples, the beast's shadow looming below.

"Open it now, Tuhetuta," Isis demands.

A silver tentacle creeps out of the water and near Isis's legs.

"Why did we not just go there directly? Why take the human route?" Horus questions.

Isis bends down and touches the beast's tentacle. One silver eye becomes visible under the murky water.

"I want to remind Tuhetuta where her true allegiance lies. And if she ever wants to get out of this punishment, she will do well to remember who put her here, and who alone can take her out. Now, open up."

A tentacle stretches across and turns solid, as the vines on the entryway part to reveal the door.

"We will not emerge until we have Osiris, the Underworld, and Jaquel back." Isis kicks the tentacle into the water then heads into the Underworld.

28

NEENHOKANO

Abdallah, Chike, Assim, and I stand around Izzi. No change. She looks dead.

At the entry, I see the two dolphins bobbing there again. Where is the rest of their family? Why is it only those two? One makes a noise, and the other does the same. They start to play.

Shaking my head, I look back at Izzi. I wish life was that easy, to just swim and play all day.

"Neenho, the princess looks very much like she has descended to the Underworld. Maybe we should let the murfolk perform their ritual. She needs to be wrapped. We should preserve her. Her skin is already drying out," Chike says.

"Amun-Ra will show up the day one of us dies. Trust me on that one. Izzi-Ra is broken. She has gone somewhere to hide because her Akh was wounded. She can heal if she comes back to her body," I say with certainty.

When did I become so ... so ...? I'm starting to sound like I'm ... I don't even know.

Assim is expressionless, as usual. I invade his privacy with my light. Then I snap my light back immediately, embarrassed for intruding. He doesn't know. He continues to look at her, emotionless. I shudder, wishing I could un-feel what I just felt from him.

Chike and Adallah are in that silent-eye talk they do.

"I believe you, NeenhoKano. What do we do to save her? Where would Izzi-Ra hide?" Adallah asks. Her and Chike go into deep thought.

The wrapped wound around Izzi's middle seeps blood. Chike grabs something fast and dabs at it.

I can't take this—her in pain. I feel it. I feel ...

I turn away, back to the dolphins playing. I never really played. Only with Ishiva, if I can call messing with a big cat playing. Izzi-Ra probably grew up playing with lots of royal children, out in the gardens. Her mother's garden. I hear her laugh.

"Izzi!" I kneel at her side, her laughter echoing all around us.

"Did you hear that?" I ask them.

Chike nods. "I heard her laughter."

"I even smell fresh dirt." Adallah sniffs the air. "Neenho, do it again."

"I didn't do anything. I was watching them playing and thinking of Izzi growing up, and then I heard her.

"The gardens," Assim whispers.

There! Again!

I'm staring at the dolphins as they play, as Izzi's laughter rings around us. We are all staring at the dolphins play now. Izzi's voice comes from where they are.

"How can that be?" Adallah whispers.

I feel my power nudging me and allow it to take over. Two purple threads snake out to the playing dolphins. They go near it with no hesitation and start playing with them. We all laugh. I grip them both and bring them near, making sure I can look into both their beady eyes.

"Do you know where she is?"

They both make noises and nod their heads.

"Take us to her, please," I whisper to them.

The dolphins make their talking noises again. I don't know what that means, but I take it as a yes.

"Aunt Adallah, Chike, Assim, grab me and link up. Now."

Adallah grabs my hand, Chike hers, and Assim has Chike. I'm yanked out the doorway and into the water. My purple threads seem to be stuck to the dolphins. Water wooshes past us. I'm too scared to scream for fear of water getting into my mouth. My eyes burn from the water that we whip through. I just hold my breath, hoping wherever they are taking us is close.

A cave is ahead. I want to scream as we enter the dark cavern, ducking and barely missing the jagged edges of rock that gleam with that yellow jewel. The dolphin's swim on.

Izzi's voice grows louder. She sounds like she is telling a story. Excitement rises through me. She is near. I feel her even more. I smell her. Izzi is in this underground cave, but where?

Ahead is just a wall. Nothing else ahead and no turn. The dolphins head for it. I hear Adallah try to yell, "Stop," I think. Her grip on my arm tightens. I want to yell stop, as well, as the dead end gets closer.

Inches from it, I summon my power and throw it at the wall. A hole opens. The dolphins sling us inside, and we fall. Forgetting we are in water, I scream.

Water rushes in as we circle around in an underwater storm. There is lightning and wind as the water circles faster. I have Adallah's hand, and she has Chike's. We circle even faster, trying not to let go of one another. Below is nothing but darkness. I don't want to know what's down there, but down there we go.

I land with a hard thud. Grass, dirt, and blood fill my mouth. Not the first time this has happened.

I do my usual routine, rolling over, feeling for broken bones and blood. I'm good.

I sit up, shake myself off, my locks slapping my face. Everything is bright. The sun is shining, people are going on about their day, no one concerned with me.

"Asir marketplace? What?" Adallah clutches her chest.

Before us is a huge marketplace. Nothing like the one we had back in Pakhet, neither the people nor the goods. Royals trade without a care in the world of how much the items sell for. They float around from vendor to cart, buying their expensive silks and collecting the best-looking fruit. Above the marketplace and on a hilltop sits the palace. I see the statues of the pharaoh, the queen, and Izzi-Ra.

"Adallah, are you okay?" Chike asks.

Adallah nods, but she is not okay.

"Calm, my friend. Peace. Find it now," Chike coaches Adallah, who is breathing heavily, clutching her chest. I have never seen such fear on her face. I have never seen Adallah scared of anything.

"They cannot ever harm you again, Adallah. They cannot. *Etu sa etium'a.* Say it."

"*Etu ... Etu ... sa. Etu sa etium'a.* In Maat," Adallah says.

"In Maat," Chike repeats.

She looks at me and Assim. "She will be fine. The past has a way of hunting you like no other."

Chike holds Adallah's trembling hand tightly. "Lead us, Neenho."

I forget Adallah is from here. I just learned of this. I don't know what to do, but Chike does, so I will not try to press it.

We walk through the marketplace. No one notices we are here.

"The energy here feels like a dream state, like when my people go into the *Kyst*," Chike says. She stops in front of a fruit cart and waves her hand in a man's face. He does not see her. He smiles beyond her and waves to a family walking by. This helps Adallah's anxiety.

"So, we are inside of a memory?" I wonder.

"No, not a memory. Izzi-Ra has retreated to a parallel universe where she never met you, any of us, Neenho."

"What makes you so sure, Chike?" I ask. I look to Assim, but he has no opinion, it seems. This is where he comes from, as well. Must be strange to be here right now.

Chike points into a shop where two young girls, dressed in palace service robes, are admiring a dress that the salesperson is handing them.

"Izzi's wedding dress," Assim says. "Those are her handmaids, Beni and Jita. Jita is related to the pharaoh's right hand, Jabari. We are back to the day of the wedding. The day their powers came in," Assim tells us, watching the girls head off with the dress.

"That means Kade is here." I frown.

"Neenho, really? This is not the time. We must find Izzi-Ra and wake her. The longer she and her other part live in this parallel together, the more she could be stuck. We will be put back into a world where there is no Izzi, or we may have all died on the shore. We have to wake her."

"I met Izzi the day before the wedding. She will have known me," I tell them.

They don't look so sure.

Chike leads the way through the crowd, toward the palace.

29

IZZI-RA

The sun shines through the curtains of my bed. I do not want to get up, but I know I must. Today is a big day.

I roll over on my back and stretch, seeing a pair of emerald eyes looking at me. Before I can really focus, they are gone. I have seen those before. I think ... I think ... I cannot remember. Oh well.

I get up and walk to my deck.

The obelisk is at half past the sixth hour to the closing of the day. Amun-Ra is setting the sun, and when it has set, I will be a married woman. Then my birthday is tomorrow. I feel great. Prince Kade has come all the way from Shiza to make me his wife, and I could not have asked for more.

There is a heavy knock on the door, and then someone enters. Probably Assim, my most noble guard, coming to wake me.

"My little *zahara*, may I enter?"

"Father." I turn toward my father, and I am hit in the gut by the feelings of utmost hate, fear, sadness, and confusion. Then, in an instant, it all goes away.

"What was that? For a moment, I felt ... I saw ..." I shake my head.

I cannot remember. "I must have been reading tall tales again before I drifted into a nap."

"What have I told you about that, my *zahara*? I came to check on you before the ceremony tonight. I wanted to make sure you felt you were doing the right thing. You do not have to marry so soon, my little flower. One day, all of Egypt will be yours, and there is plenty of time to start taking over other lands." He hugs me so gently, and I close my eyes, going limp in his strong arms. I take in his scent of coconut oil mixed with the gold-plated smell of the pendants that he wears and his armor.

"It is time, my dear father, Pharaoh. You know it is time. And Kade is a perfect match for me. I am ready to start building my empire, just like you taught me. Once I get to Shiza, the first thing I will do is train those men to wield their weapons better."

We laugh.

Father taught me how to fight. I hold a long pole fight better than his commanders.

"You are such a strong girl ... I mean, woman. You are growing into a wise, beautiful woman, and I could not be any prouder." He kisses the top of my head and continues to hold me.

I love this moment, this space we are in. My father is the best man.

Another small knock on the door, and then someone enters. My heart drops, and I gasp.

The red dress enters before her, her mane of hair blowing around her, but then she is not there. My mother stands in the doorway, smiling, her crown standing tall on her head, her makeup as beautiful as any painting in the temples.

"What are you two in here doing? Saat, you must get ready. Saat?"

I am gripping my father's hand and breathing heavily.

"Izzi-Ra," my father says, shaking me a little. "Are you okay?"

My mother bends down and checks my face.

"I do not feel a fever."

I saw the red lady. My mother is dead. She was dead. Wasn't she? What is going on?

"Sorry, sorry, sorry. I had a strange dream, and pieces of it keeps coming and going. Sorry. I am fine, you two. Stop fretting over me."

Neither of them are convinced.

My mother sits on the other side of me, and my father wraps his arms around both of us. We both slump and allow his strong arms to hold us.

I close my eyes and take a deep breath, taking in the scent of my mother and father mixed together. The earth and the air, they make my world whole. And tonight, I will marry a prince. Prince Kade.

I sigh giddily, and then a flash crosses my eyes, one of Kade in battle at a mountain. Flying, fiery horses are coming at him as he weakly wields his weapon. I gasp sharply.

"Izzi-Ra, did you say something?"

I snap my eyes open. My mother is laying her head peacefully on father's shoulder, humming, and my father is looking at me so lovingly.

I shake the fuzz away from my head, forgetting what just startled me.

"I need to get ready for my big night, you two."

There is another knock on the door, and then my maidens come in.

"Your bath is ready, Princess Izzi-Ra." Jita beams.

My father stands and helps my mother up. They both smile at me.

I look at them both. I love them so much.

"Our little princess. You mean the world to us, *saat*. Can you do something for me?"

"Anything, Mother." I smile back at her.

"Wake up," she says.

"Mother?"

"Try to remember what you felt when you and Kade meditated in the temple this morning—all love. There is nothing greater than love. We will be with you every step of the way—your father and I."

"We will see you at the ceremony, my delicate flower."

They head for the door.

"Mother, Father ... we will always be a family, right?"

188

"Of course not, Izzi-Ra. I am going to kill you," my father says.

My breath catches as I watch them leave the room. Then I look at Jita, who is still smiling. What is going on? Did she not hear that? Did *I* hear him correctly?

All in an instant, those words and feelings disappear and is replaced by pure joy.

The happiness I feel can have only come from the goddess of love herself. Hathor must be upon me. Wedding bells and love in the air.

I spin around in my dress. I feel like I could cross over into the heavens right now and be with the gods. Kade will be my life, my king.

"You look beautiful. I am so jealous of you, Izzi," Jundi says. My best friends stand before me, such love and joy in their eyes.

Heleka and Geosha are filled with happiness as I stand with my friends, giggling about the cute boys who are here, at my wedding, from Shiza with Prince Kade.

"Excuse me, ladies," I say to them.

I step outside onto the patio deck and take a deep breath. How did I get so lucky? Two of the most wonderful parents, great friends who love me, and a prince who will make me a queen. All that I have ever wanted, I have it all right now.

I look at the sky as it turns purple and pink, the darkness following it. Ra finishes the final touches on what will be a night to remember.

"Thank you, gods and goddesses, for blessing me. Nothing can ruin this moment."

I feel a chill go up my back, like someone is watching me. I feel like something—no, someone—is saying my name. I sniff the air and smell honey. Honey and dirt fill my nose. I step down into the grass, feeling even colder, although there is no wind.

"Hello? Anyone there?" I ask the empty air.

30

NEENHOKANO

She walks around me, in a circle, never walking through me or even close to bumping me. She senses me. She knows I'm here, but she can't see me. I doubt if she even remembers me. But she should. We met last night. We got our powers this night. How can I wake her?

"Izzi," I whisper.

She whirls around. She heard me, but she didn't. She sniffs the air around me. Her nose scrunches. I smell my armpits but smell nothing out of the ordinary.

"Honey and dirt?" she says to herself. "Mother." She laughs.

She walks back up the steps, taking one last look right at where I stand, before she heads inside. I follow.

She walks down torch-lit corridors, holding up her dress. She rounds a corner, happily humming, and then she stops. She inches closer to a wall and rubs her hand over the art. I stand back to get a better look. It's her birth. Has to be. The queen, the gods above her, the baby, the way the sun shines.

"It doesn't feel right," she whispers.

I stare at the story with her. The happiness of her birth, the queen, the way the pharaoh is positioned ... this does not feel right.

I smell grass. I hear the Nile flowing. We are both being carried away, but then it all shuts down.

Izzi shakes her head then continues to skip on. She is seeing flashes of her past, I realize, but she's blocking it out.

I run down the corridor after her.

The music, the decorations, and the energy in the air almost sucks me in and makes me forget this is not real. I'm taken in by the way the royals celebrate. The foods, the females, the food ... I have to keep pinching myself because this is not real. Well, it is, but not right now.

On a raised platform I see the pharaoh. I catch myself as I start to kneel. I have never seen the pharaoh up close and in person like this. Well, except for at the island, when he stabbed Izzi. Still, I'm in awe.

Below him is the Lord of Shiza and next to him sits Kade. I frown. He looks like nothing but himself in the flesh. I'll have to remind him to use more oil on his elbows. They look dry. And so does his lips.

The pharaoh stands and raises his arms. The room silences at once.

"Neenho," I hear a whisper from behind me. Chike and Adallah are crouched in a corner.

The pharaoh starts speaking as I dart over to where they hide.

"Where is Assim?" I ask.

"With Izzi. She can see him. Once she saw him, he became visible to them all," Chike whispers.

"No one can see us, though, right?" Adallah stares at the pharaoh, breathing hard.

"Aunt Adallah, he can't see you," I try to reassure her.

"I know, I know. I just ... This room, this place, him, these people. It has been many moons for me, and yet it feels like yesterday."

"Did you figure out how to wake her?" Chike asks.

I shake my head as dancers come from the ceiling and move in ways I have dreamed about. I remember Izzi telling me—well, showing me—all of this, but she was sitting with Kade, and this time she is not. Because she knows about the wedding. She is accepting the wedding.

I see her peeking through the curtains, smiling. That crazy girl!

Assim comes from behind the curtain and stands at attention off to the side. At first, nothing, and then he looks right at me and winks before turning his attention to the dancers. The dance ends, and the dancers disappear in smoke. Kade and his father clap loudly, clearly impressed. The pharaoh stands and speaks again.

"Neenho, we have to stop this," Adallah whispers to me.

We watch as Izzi is introduced, and then she walks out to sighs and gasps. She looks stunning, as usual. She smiles lovingly at Kade as he takes her hand. The queen and pharaoh stand near them, pulling out a silk blue cloth.

A man walks toward the families. He would look like an average man with a welcoming face, if he did not have glowing marks all over his body. The priest of Egypt. The walking scribe. I've heard about people like him but never thought they were real. Does he shine like this all the time?

The priest stands before them and begins speaking words.

"Neenho, they are being married. If they tie that around their hands, that is it. Neenho, you are glowing!" Adallah says, panicked.

I look down at myself and I'm indeed a bright purple.

"You guys are fading!" I tell them.

No one notices us standing there in a panic.

"Neenho, you have to stop it," Adallah says, her voice sounding far off.

"Think, Neenho, how can you wake her?" Chike asks.

"Should I kiss her?" I ask.

I see Assim trying to keep his cool.

"Neenho, when you and Izzi hold hands, your lights! They shine. That's it. Go grab her hand!" Adallah yells at me.

I turn from them to dash toward Izzi and Kade, but my path is blocked by two stunningly beautiful, out of this world goddesses.

"Nekhbet! Wadjet!" Chike jumps in front of me in a protective stance.

"What business have you here?" Wadjet hisses.

"Drahzil," Adallah says.

Behind us, yep, there he is. The wedding is still going on. If only these people knew.

"I'm really getting tired of you," I tell him, pulling the amulets from under the white top I wear.

He narrows his eyes.

"You will never have these," I tell him.

"But I will."

Her voice sends chills through me.

I want to crawl into a ball and cry as that feeling sweeps over me again. That love and that hate all in one. She comes from behind Drahzil.

"The queen was to die tonight. I will possess her body and open us back into the real world, after I kill everyone in this room and take control of Izzi. Only you will be alive in the new world we will create this instant, boy. Me and you, as planned."

Everyone around us is still intrigued by the ceremony. I have to touch Izzi. I have to wake her.

"Neenho," Adallah presses.

"I know," I say back.

Adallah throws something into the air, encasing us in a cloud of smoke. I see white light and know Adallah is going into action, but her and Chike will not do much damage. They are fading fast.

I dash through the crowd, heading for Izzi. I feel his nasty, clawed hand as he grabs my shoulder and throws me across the room. I slam into the wall hard. I can't keep doing this.

I see Chike and Adallah holding their own against the sisters, maneuvering through the crowd. Kawaad stands back and watches in delight.

I gather my light and throw the biggest energy ball that I can muster at Drahzil. It hits, sending him flying across the room, but not before one of his whips catches me by the leg and flings me onto the platform. I land at the queen's feet. She does not see me. She looks lovingly at Izzi.

"Wake me," I hear a faint whisper.

I look back up at the queen, who is still looking at Izzi, but I swear I ...

Another red whip lashes at me and hits me in my back. I yell in pain and, without thinking, I let warm, purple light flow into my hand as I grab the queen's hand.

"No!" Kawaad screams.

The queen steps out of herself and snatches my hand and flings me behind her as another one of Drahzil's whips heads my way. She catches it in her hand. I stare at her wide eyed. She has managed to make herself stay in Izzi's dream state but be with us. Why hasn't Assim did that!

Assim wants to help so badly, but he is in both realities. One move, and Izzi and the pharaoh will know something is wrong.

The queen has a grip on the red light, white light shining through and seeming to burn him. Drahzil whips it back.

She looks back at me and, again, love floods me. No hatred, no anguish, no pain, just love. She breathes heavily, her eyes watering. I don't know why I'm holding her gaze, but her eyes, all that love in them, I feel swallowed by it.

I lean in closer to her, and I hear a ticking, right in her chest.

"*He'th mi'et*," she says in an old tongue, yet I know exactly what she said.

We both hear the whip of light, and she throws me down then rushes at Kawaad. I duck another red whip and get to Izzi. I elbow Kade, which he does not feel, and snatch her hands, letting my power fully fly. It surges through her like a bolt of lightning, hitting us both. I scream. She screams. Gold light pushes forth, and we are blasted apart.

I sit up, my locks slapping my face. The room is empty.

The queen wraps white tendrils around Kawaad and holds her still, Nekhbet and Wadjet have Chike and Adallah locked, and Assim has a knopesh drawn toward Drahzil.

"Welcome back to reality, Princessss. Now come out and talk to Uncle, and we can fix thisss," Drahzil hisses.

"I will kill you." Her voice echoes throughout the room, giving me chills. My princess.

"Izzi?" I whisper, looking around. I don't see her.

"I will let the goddessesss kill my sister and your warrior," Drahzil spits.

"They're ready to die," Izzi echoes.

Adallah snorts.

"Nephthila, you know you cannot kill her, or you risk your own life in the processss," Drahzil taunts the queen.

"We need to die," Nephi responds.

This time, Kawaad snorts.

"Mother." Izzi's voice rings out.

"*Saat*," the queen whispers back.

"Don't call her that! You don't get to do that!" Kawaad screams. She is trembling but can't get free.

"I am going to kill you," Izzi whispers again.

Then Izzi starts screaming. She screams so loud that we all have to cover our ears. The room fills with gold light as she continues to scream. The gold light becomes blinding.

I drop to my knees, my eyes watering from how bright her light is. I can't even try to throw a thought her way. Her scream is inside and around us.

I am plunged into water. Cold water. I look around and find I'm floating outside the doorway to where Izzi lies. I swim and fall inside, gasping for air. I hear splashes behind me before Chike and Adallah fall through. Assim falls inside next, gasping for air. The two dolphins bob there for a moment then swim away.

"Are you all okay?" I ask, but they just look ahead.

Standing at the fire is Izzi, still in her wedding dress.

I rush over to her. almost slipping. I stand before her, dripping wet, happy to see her.

"I rode on a dolphin," I tell her.

She doesn't move.

"You don't always have to be brave, Princess. You don't always have to save face."

"I heard everything you said to me. I felt your dirty hands on mine. I felt you. You were looking so hard."

"I'm gonna always find my princess."

She looks up at me. Her pretty eyes swim with tears. One escapes but is engulfed by a gold puff of smoke. She pushes my locks out my face then rests one hand on my shoulder and uses the other to cup my chin. Is she about to do what I think she is about to do?

Do not take them from me again, she says in my mind as she takes the amulets from around my neck and places them around hers.

A small gust from nowhere blows, and in this moment, I notice how much she looks like her mother.

31

THE GODS

Nekhbet, Wadjet, Drahzil, and Kawaad fall hard on the black stone. The Red Nile is bright around them.

"The Underworld?" Drahzil is furious. How did they get down here?

"You were tricked," Wadjet hisses.

"Isis," Nekhbet spits.

Drahzil rounds on Kawaad. "You said if Nephthila is in another space, there you could kill her and absorb the child!"

Kawaad is not moved. "I underestimated her. I will not again. The child can shatter. She is *heka*."

Drahzil looks confused, but Wadjet and Nekhbet look alarmed.

"Impossible," Wadjet says.

"When Zarhmel stabbed the girl, she called her *Ba* and *Ka* to safety until her shell was healed. Gods cannot do that. They need a goddess to heal them. Some get lost and never find their way back." Kawaad points to the Red Nile that splits into five pathways. One shimmers a silver and leads into a vortex that they cannot see beyond. Another path flows gold, another a bright white, a black path, and then the red one.

"The girl is immensely powerful to have not broken. She has a connection to the Underworld. And the boy, he entered, as well, and took three Ka's with him on the journey. He is ..." Wadjet trails off in thought.

"Why are we here?" Drahzil asks Kawaad impatiently. He does not care about these semantics.

"Nephthila is here to get her before I do."

Nekhbet sniffs. "Isis is here."

"Horus is with her. They will try to free Osiris. We are on no side without our god," Wadjet says.

"We are with you, but if Osiris is released, we will fight and protect our brother," Nekhbet says.

Kawaad knows this and does not care.

"Upper and Lower, I would not expect anything less from the snake of Osiris and the wings on his back," Kawaad says as a thought.

"Why are we here? Where isss the doomed deity that ferriesss the boat?" Drahzil asks.

They look around with the same confused looks. She should be there. She always shows up.

Drahzil feels different, he notices. He does not want to be here with them. He would rather be helping someone else. But who?

Kawaad looks from Drahzil to the sisters then back at Drahzil. "Look at your arms," she says to him.

Drahzil looks at his arms and notices the dry, green skin that he has had for countless sunrises is slowly being replaced by smooth, golden-brown skin. He feels his face. Although he cannot see it, he feels it has changed.

Kawaad grins. "We are in the future," she whispers. "We must have gotten the amulets. Isis is here to try to get Osiris. It is her last hope! Nephi is here. She was not strong enough to throw us back into the present. She is her strongest in the Underworld. If her and Nephthys connect ..." She glares at the goddesses. "You two knew. We will be back at this very moment, but you two will not be on our side. But, for now, you are. Take us back."

Drahzil only catches bits of the meaningless conversation. What is happening to him?

Wadjet and Nekhbet exchange looks. Wadjet begins to hiss loudly, her bones cracking, her neck extending. She curls into a ball and emerges as a cobra. She lunges at Drahzil and wraps her body around him. He struggles to get free, but Wadjet is stronger and faster.

Nekhbet's bones extend and teeth grind. The top she wears bursts into nothing as black and gold wings extend from her shoulder blades, and her feet extend into claws. She takes flight in the air, soaring around the Red Nile.

Kawaad watches, ready for the attack. She knows the Underworld. She has been there before. She has also been to the future, and it is painful to get back.

Poor Drahzil, is her final thought as Nekhbet digs her talons into Kawaad's shoulder blades and pulls her up.

Nekhbet flies over the Red Nile, heading toward the vortex, but she does not go in. She flies above, soars around, and then dives right into the Red Nile.

Drahzil watches in terror.

Wadjet's golden eyes meets his. She hisses loudly in his face. He tries to move, but she has him in a locked grip. She slams them both to the floor and, with a motion that no human could ever do, she slithers them both into the Red Nile.

Immediately upon impact, Drahzil feels heat, pain, and fear like nothing he has ever felt. He only sees red.

She still has a grip on him as she drags him farther down. He opens his mouth to scream and lets the heat in. His throat, tongue, and lungs are on fire.

32

IZZI-RA

I stand at the water window that surrounds the entire room. An indoor observatory. I stare out at this water world that we have come upon.

We have been here for two nights, but I slept one away down in the temple. I have not ventured off or went with Neenho in his *clou* underwater. I do not care to. My mother is alive. I saw her. She needs my help. I need to get to Asir, but they keep telling me to wait.

I look at the beautiful homes and temples littered below. Small pyramids here and there. So, Nu'el is not a place. It is the deserts that hide Murku.

I watch the inhabitants of this world swim in and out of structures, their tails whipping past in blurs of colors. Some stop to wave at me, their little children swimming along under their bellies, staying close to their mamas.

Behind me, at a table, Assim, Neenho, Adallah, and Chike brainstorm with this Queen Hatmehyt. They said Kade left to Shiza to win his people over. I miss him, though he would be standing here, holding my hand, and constantly asking me if I was all right. The twins left to find the trio sisters. I do not know where that is. Getrea said summon the beetle. Maybe they forgot. The Kemetians are gone. Sho'te stayed. I kind of miss them all.

"We will wait for word from the twins and Kade. We will not make a move on the kingdom until we know anything further," Adallah tells the group.

"How are your sleeping quarters? I had some of my people try to make them as comfortable as possible. It has been many Shemu since we had guests," Hatmehyt says.

"Question, Queen," I hear Neenho say.

"Yes, King," she replies. I am glad I cannot see the stupid smile he must be giving her.

"Why did the men in blue scamper away like they did at the sight of you, Queen Hatmehyt?" Neenho asks.

"Their queen, Qui'l, is my human form. We were split by the curse that Kawaad brought. It seems she has taken on a life of her own. I must travel south soon and deal with that."

"That's kinda cool." Neenho laughs.

I roll my eyes, glad he cannot see me.

"That makes sense. The flood comes from the south each Ahket," Adallah says.

"How were they able to get through Nu'el is what I want to know?" Chike asks.

I have been wondering that as well.

"I have my suspicions," the goddess responds. I look over at her and she is looking at me. I look away.

"Well, shall we all turn in for some sleep?" Adallah says.

"Thank you for your hospitality," Chike kindly thanks the water goddess. Then I hear the chairs being pushed back from the table.

I keep my back to them all. The room goes quiet.

"How can you tell when it is nighttime around here?" I ask. I know she stands behind me, watching me.

"That is my favorite time." She comes into my side view. I side-glance at her. She holds her staff before her, the yellow stone atop alights. With a small wave, the clear blue water dims.

Although darker, I can still make out the world below.

"Look up, Izzi-Ra." She smiles at me.

I press my face closer to the water and look up.

I am in awe. The waters above reflect that of the night's sky. Hundreds of tiny fish are alight above, creating an illuminous glow below.

"Wow," I say. "Neenho would love to live here forever."

"He has already asked. Twice." She glides away then stops and turns back to me. "You do not remember, do you?"

Confused by her question, I ask, "What should I remember?"

"Me." She then leaves the room without another word.

An odd response from a goddess. I will take it at face value. That riddle will be answered some other time.

I look out at the world below for a few more moments. Must be nice to just swim all day. They look like they do not have a care in the world. Well, they did, but now they are at peace again. I am jealous of the families, wishing I had one. I sigh. I forgot to ask where my room was.

I head for the door. As I exit, I see him standing there. Assim is waiting for me, as usual.

I say nothing. He says nothing. He just leads the way. The corridors glow a wet blue. The rocks glisten as if they were hit by a wave. I notice that, even though we are underwater, this place is oddly warm.

We stop at double doors, and Assim pushes them open then steps aside. I half-expect more water walls and a magnificent view of the salt water, but the room is like something back at the palace—an overly large bed, a plush chair, and some garments in a corner. A fire is going.

Assim is about to close the doors when I say, "Stay with me," surprising myself.

"I will be right outside your doors, like always."

"No. Stay. In here. With me," I tell him.

The fire crackles as I lie down, looking at the ceiling. No cosmos of stars like at home. Assim slumps in the chair, staring at the flames.

"Assim, who are you?" I ask.

"Princess?"

"You and Mother were whispering to one another when I was in pain. You are not shocked by any of this. It is almost as if you are, and were, expecting this horrible journey. Who are you, Assim?"

"Just a guy who swore to protect the Princess of Egypt."

"Do you have light?"

"No."

"Did you know about me?"

"Not everything."

"Did you know about Kawaad?"

"Not the full story."

"Did you know about the amulets?"

"A little, Izzi ..."

"No, Assim, I want to know. *Who are you?*" I shout.

He comes to the side of the bed, getting in my face. "Nephi found me. She explained a little to me throughout the years. She said she needed someone she could trust to watch over her child, and her secrets. I will not tell you everything tonight."

"Do you love me?" I whisper. I can feel his breath on my face, our noses almost touching.

"Izzi, don't—"

"Do you love me, Assim?"

"Izzi," he sighs out, and I kiss him. I grab Assim by the face and kiss him. He does not back away but pushes himself onto me. I have always felt this heat between us, but I thought it was annoyance from being around each other all day. Everything that has happened, all the pain, all the excitement, all the anxiety we have experienced is being put into this kiss.

I start to pull him into the bed with me when he pulls away and holds my hands away from him. I look at him angrily, breathing hard.

"I will be outside your door, like always." He releases my wrists then leaves without looking back.

I have no idea what to think. Why did I do that? Assim ... I do not think of him that way ... I ...

I throw myself back on the pillows and pull the quilt over my head.

I do not remember falling asleep. I am not sure if I am asleep. I hear the crackling of the fire. I hear calm waves washing on a shoreline. I smell honey and dirt.

"Mother." I sit up abruptly, eyes snaping open.

I am sitting in grass. Thick, plush, green grass. The sky is a mesh of purple, pinks, and a star-stained midnight. How?

I slowly stand then walk up the small hill and stop. I see the Nile. A tree is off to the side bearing all kinds of fruits. I see her, sitting on the bank, little gold butterflies fly around her then take flight altogether.

"Why am I here?" I ask Isis.

"How are you allowed here is the question." She stands and turns to me.

"Because you summoned me," I tell her. "What do you want, Isis?"

She looks at me with no emotion. I sense she did not think it would work, that I would not be standing here before her.

"We do not fear you."

"I never said you did. Aloud. There is something about me that throws you off. What is it? I did not ask for this. I do not want this. None of it," I say to her.

"What will you do once you have all the amulets?" she asks.

I have no idea, I think. I have not thought about that yet. It will be up to Neenho and I, I assume.

"You fear those, as well. Why?"

"They are made of the skin of Amun. They possess his makers ... Amun should not have made them. They are yours; that much is clear. But, what I want to know is: what will you do when you have them complete?" This time, I do see some fear behind those emerald eyes.

"You have been there, my whole life. We all say our gods and goddesses are watching us, but you have literally been following me my whole life, watching me intently. How does that make you feel, Iziz? Us stupid humans, using the *S*'s all this time?" I smile at her.

"We are on the same side, Izzi. I promise you that."

"No, we are not," I tell her. Then I wave my hand, and I am gone. First, I am in darkness, and then I feel the bed beneath my back. I hear the crackling fire and still smell Mother. I sit up, and on the end of my bed is Neenho.

"Assim let you slip past him? He is fired."

"I came in on a beam of light. He has no idea. I could have been Kawaad or one of the goddesses who hate you. He should be fired, anyway. How are you feeling, Princess?" He looks at me with worry in those big, brown eyes.

I can never be mad at Neenho. He has this way of making me feel calm. Like Mother.

"I am not broken, Neenho. I will be fine. We will be fine. What about this place, huh?" I must change the subject and block my thoughts. If Neenho sees the kiss, it may hurt his little heart.

He perks up, light blinking in his eyes. "When all this is over, I'm building my own house here. I already asked Hatmehyt. She said it's cool."

I laugh, imagining Neenho underwater, trying to build a house that keeps the water out. Silly male.

"I thought you wanted to live in Kemet?"

"Aw ... I did say that, too, huh?"

"Yes, yes, you did. And you want Ptah's floating rock?"

"No way. He can keep that thing! Where is it going? What does he do all day?" Neenho asks.

I giggle into my hands.

Only Neenho can make me feel like all is normal and well.

"Lay with me." I pat the bed beside me.

Like an excited kid, he jumps over and lies next to me. I lie back down, and we stare at the ceiling.

"Neenho, Isis summoned me while I was sleeping. She said we are on the same side. The way she said it was as if suggesting me and you are not the good ones. It irritated me."

Neenho is silent for a moment, thinking.

"I can see how they could think that. We have lights that matches their power. We are the possessors of these amulets, I guess. They call to us. There is a deep secret here, and they fear us. Izzi, we are a threat to the gods."

He is right. No matter what, we may be like them, but we are not them.

"That's because they do not understand."

"Understand what, Izzi?"

"I did not say that," I speak.

We look at one another then sit up quickly.

In the plush chair sits a goddess. She is small, wearing a blue wraparound dress, and a ringlet crown on her head that bears two feathers. Between those feathers is a small scale. A small ball continues to roll between the scale, tipping it from one side to another. Her eye makeup is sky blue, her lips a saltwater blue, and her skin a dark, starry night.

"Maat," I whisper.

"I had to see you for myself. You two have caused quit the uproar. The scales are tipping, no balance. Justice will and won't be served. It is true what you think. We must all choose a side." She smiles at us.

"And whose side have you chosen?" I ask.

"Pleasure to meet you both. The goddess of water and I are awfully close. I must go see her now that the curse has been lifted."

She stands to go.

"Whose side are you on?" I ask again as she summons her light.

"I will choose once the two of you have chosen to be on the same side or not." She steps into her white light that is flecked with blue lights then is gone.

"Another one," Neenho says, lying back down.

"Neenho, she just said we are not on the same side."

"Riddles, Princess. I will never betray you, and if you betray me, I will still fight for you."

"Isis asked me what I was going to do once the amulets were complete," I tell him.

"We will get rid of Drahzil, and then I will live everywhere, and you will rule Asir. That's it. Can we wipe Shiza off the map, as well? Is that place needed?"

I jump out of bed and put on the sandals on the floor. I never changed into night garments, so I am still wearing the flowy, white dress they changed me into.

"Izzi, are you going for a nighttime swim?"

"I am going to the palace. I must go there tonight. These goddesses visiting me and ... Neenho, I must go there tonight. We cannot tell anyone. We just need to go."

Neenho gets out of bed. "What will we do? Kill the pharaoh, free the new beings, and then take the queen? Just us two?"

"Yes. And I have a feeling she knows where the amulet is. I know she knows, Neenho.'"

He sighs. "I wasn't sleepy, anyway. Can we stop by my room and get my shoes please?"

I point at his feet, and when my light disappears, he is wearing gold sandals.

"I can't do that yet!" he says excitedly.

I summon a beam of light. It is pure gold.

"Hey! How do you know how to do this?"

"I saw how you did it."

We step into it then head to my home.

My feet touch the cold stone floor as the beam of light surrounding us fades away. We are in my old room. The sheets are tossed, just the way they were when I last left my bed on my wedding night. How long ago was that? My schoolbooks are messy in a corner. School ... when was the last time I sat in the gardens and told tales to the younger ones?

"I would have expected the Princess of Egypt's room to look better than the murfolk's underwater world."

A small laugh escapes me. I appreciate him trying to make light of this situation. However, I cannot hide the emotions that flood through me right now. This is my room. This was my home. Many days and nights, my mother sat here, comforting me; my father scolded me; and Assim sat outside the door, protecting me.

"I cannot even remember, Neenho ..." I trail off in thought.

"Same," he replies. "Lets finish this, Izzi. I want to end this nightmare, and sleep in that bed."

"You are not sleeping in my bed."

"After you rid our lands of the pharaoh, both of them, you won't need this room anymore. I will take it. You can have any other room in the palace."

I ignore him.

With one last sweeping glance, I exit the room. Neenho tiptoes out and closes the door.

"We need to go to the east end; that is my mother's quarters."

We start off, but then I say, "Hold on," and run back to my room, swinging the doors open.

Neenho raises his eyebrows.

"I am home to take the crown, and I want him to know it."

Neenho shrugs as we head down the corridor. He mumbles about how, if we live through this, he better get my room.

We meet no one as we enter the third-floor main hall. It is strangely quiet around here. I do not even smell food, and there is no one in the lift. What has happened to Abu?

Neenho is in awe of the small statues that guard each entrance.

We take the stairs down a floor. It breaks off into three sections. West, east and north. Mother and Father's wings. My lower wing is sealed off. Strange.

Neenho looks at the statues of Wadjet and Nekhbet that stand near the lift. He then goes over to the two Bastet statues that lead to Mother's chambers.

"If I had my own wing, it would be Thoth," Neenho says. "Thoth and Osiris."

"Why Osiris?" I ask.

Neenho shrugs. I hear him in his mind, wondering why he thought of that god.

We reach the east wing atrium. Neenho is in awe, as usual. He cranes his neck to look at the monumental stone figures that sit in thrones in a circle.

"I see you, Izzi, darting in and out of here, playing hide and seek." His locks hang as he cranes his neck to investigate the stone faces of the goddesses.

I take in a deep breath then breathe out, hearing the faint memories of my laughter as I run from Mother in here.

"Let us move on, Neenho," I tell him sternly, closing memory lane. I am here to kill a family member, something Set did.

"You take it all for granted," Neenho throws my way.

I frown at him. "This is the life I grew up in, draped in gold and jewels, and told I was a part of what made the sun, the moon, and the stars rise and fall each day. This, all of this, is what I was handed, Neenho. You do not take what life was gifted to you as a blessing, either. You grew up in a home full of light and love. It may have been a lie, but the love there, from Adallah, is so real. I would give you this, NeenhoKano. I will trade with you and let you be that child's laughter that echoes through these halls. I may not show it, because I do not know how, but if you want to carry the pain I have inside, please, take it."

Neenho grabs a hold of my hands and puts them over his heart. I feel it beating steadily, a steady thump in his chest, our light intertwining.

"I feel it all, Princess. And, if I could take it into me, I would. For you. I would do anything."

"I know," I whisper.

Our light is bright all around us, as it tends to be when we touch, but it's soft, caressing us. I let it take me as I lean in closer and closer to Neenho's face. I close my eyes and tilt in closer. The warmth I feel is doused immediately, and my hands fall to my side as Neenho lets them go. I am about to go classic Izzi on him when I hear it—the drumming.

We both look frantically around. It is here, in the center of the statues, but where?

Neenho circles around the statues then stops at Bastet. He shimmies up her leg and pulls himself onto her lap. I stand as far back as I can to watch him.

"It's coming from in here—her heart," he says.

I tuck what was about to happen away and climb up the statue. Neenho looks impressed.

"This is my childhood."

The drumming is still faint. I thought it would get louder near the chest, but it's in her, for sure. We both knock and tug away at the stone Bastet, but it is no use.

"*Heka*?" I suggest.

We shrug. Then, giving it all we have, we throw our light at her, trying not to slip and fall.

Nothing, of course.

"Think, Izzi, think."

"I am thinking! It would be inside a goddess statue the size of a baby pyramid."

Neenho sits down, wiping sweat from his forehead. I feel disgusting now, as well.

"Leave it to whoever to put something inside a stone goddess. Just another riddle."

Ugh. Gods and goddesses and their riddles.

I slouch down in Bastet's lap. I have not been up here in so long. Bastet's hand is outstretched upward, facing Isis. Isis's hand is outstretched, facing Hathor, and Hathor's hand is outstretched to Sekret, and hers to Maat.

"Riddles! Neenho, I got it. Ever heard of the tale Dare to Do?"

Neenho's eyes widen. "Of course not, Izzi. Do I look like I would sit through that story?"

"Follow me."

I carefully walk the length of Bastet's arm until I get into her hand. Neenho gets there quicker.

"I will not tell you the whole story, but five goddesses used to play games in a secret lair. They would give each other a task, and if they did not complete it, they had to go into the lair and face a challenge, in their human forms."

I jump from Bastet's hand and into Isis's.

A small scream escapes Neenho.

"You are not the only person agile on your feet, Neenho. Come on."

Neenho dives over in a flip and lands on his feet. Show off.

"Anyhoo, one night, the goddesses were playing their game, and when they went into the lair, a human girl was there. She heard and saw it all."

I jump into Hathor's hand then into Sekret's. Neenho following.

"What happened?" Neenho asks as we look at the final hand.

"She asked for protection. That was all she wanted."

"And ...?" Neenho presses.

"Nothing. That is all she wanted."

"If I had five goddesses at my mercy, why would I only want protection?"

"Do you believe that story?" I ask.

We look at Maat as we ponder this question. I feel my legs tighten as I slightly bend to make the jump. Together, we jump, half-expecting her hand to come alive and snatch us.

Nothing happens. Then we hear clicks.

The stone hand shifts from up to down. We jump from Maat's hand in time and back to Bastet's. Then we run to her lap as her hand goes from up to down. We look up, expecting, waiting for the stars in the painting to align or something and for the third piece to fall from Nun, but nothing happens. Instead, we hear clicking and feel a rumble below us.

"You believe the story."

"So did you." Neenho laughs.

A shaft opens and we all, statues included, start descending like a lift.

We land at the bottom, the statues still intact and in their circle. Torches flare up around us. There is only one corridor. The flames dance off the white stone around us.

"Did you play down here as a child, as well?"

"The lair. It is real. I never knew it was here."

After all that has happened lately, I should not be shocked, yet I am. My mother knows about this place. I know she does. Why did she never share this with me? Maybe she does not know. Maybe this is where Kawaad hid all those Ahkets.

The drumming is louder down here. I feel as anxious as I did that day in Meretseger Mountain, chasing that sound. The pieces around my neck begin to glow. I feel a tug down the corridor.

We enter a room. It is like a small home, with a bed, a chair, a table, and a fireplace. The wall is full of glyphs in the first language. There is no room to add anything else. Neenho examines the wall, while I am drawn to the bed that is neatly made. The quilt is black with a green ankh sewn into it. I bend and sniff it.

"I see you," Neenho whispers. "Come out. We won't hurt you."

I spin around to see who Neenho is talking to, but I only see the wall. What is he talking about? I step near him and immediately feel dizzy for a second, and then it clears.

"What—"

"Shh ..." he says gently. "Please, come out. I know you are not the queen, and you are not Kawaad. We will keep you protected. I promise," Neenho says, holding his sweaty hand out.

I watch in anticipation. I feel her. I can hear her breathing. I know her.

A small hand is there, in his, nails perfectly shaped. The arm becomes visible, followed by a shoulder, a body, and legs. We watch as she materializes before us.

She wears a pink dress, something like Kawaad's red one. It flows around her. Her hair is a bushy mane. Her almond-shaped eyes crinkle into a smile. Her smile makes me feel like all is okay, that nothing bad could ever happen. I want to hug her, but she is not Mother. And, like Neenho said, she is not Kawaad, either. But she *is* them.

"Nice to meet you, Nephthys. I am Neenho. This is Izzi."

They shake hands.

"You two believed," she says.

I cannot speak. How many of them are there? Who is my mother?

"That was the first I ever heard of it," Neenho says shyly.

I am lost. How does Neenho know her name and what does that

mean because we believed? She looks exactly like Mother. Unlike Kawaad, she has the same *ka*. I feel it.

She holds out her hand to me. "Would you like to see what I showed Neenho?" she asks.

I step back.

She does not take offense; she smiles at me knowingly.

"You ... You are the one Drahzil loves. Why are you down here, hiding? Does Mother know? Has she been hiding you here this whole time?" I want answers.

"No. Nephthila nor Nephidema know I am here. I can pass between here and the Underworld, because my *Ka* and *Ba* are here."

"Who is Nephidema?" I ask.

"You call her Kawaad. That is what she wants to be called. That is what the dark man called her. *Kawaad* means powerful red one in the language of Amun."

Nephthys is about to say something when she sees the two amulets around my neck and she steps back.

"So much trouble those have caused."

"You have seen them before?" I ask.

"The beetle was mine. The eye belonged to Nephidema. The ankh kills Nephthila every Ahket. It was hers. But it no longer belongs to her."

She holds her hand out to me. "Please, Izzi-Ra, let me show you. Showing is better than telling." She stretches her finger to me.

Neenho urges me to take her hand.

33

DRAHZIL

Drahzil climbs out of the Nile, gasping for air. He was burning alive. Every ounce of him was on fire, and he begged for death with every thought he could think as the snake-headed goddess dragged him to the bottom of the Red Nile. Just when he thought that was the end, he was plunged into cool water.

He went into shock and floated there for a moment, unable to move. One spark in his brain helped him feel for his light and push some life into him. He swam and swam until he broke the surface.

Now, lying flat on his back, he stares into the night sky. Several stars shine luminously. He remembers, as a boy, laying in the gardens with his sisters and mapping out stars. Adiah was always the smartest. She knew their names and knew exactly which burning light was the god's kingdom. He and Adallah would tease her about being so smart, and she would reply, "You will both need me when you are lost."

Drahzil lies there, thinking of her words. *You will need me when you are lost.* Did she know he was lost? Did she know they would all be lost one day? Could the stars lead them all back to a much simpler time in life? Could the stars bring Drahzil back?

His throat is dry and hot from swallowing much of the Red Nile. He sits up and looks at his arms and hands. The scaly green skin is back. No fresh flesh. He fumes, breathing heavy.

Enough! He is tired of losing. He knows what he wants, and he is going to go get it.

He stands and looks around. It is pitch black, but the silhouette of the mountains in the north tells him where he is. He is on the outskirts of Pakhet. He will have a hike, but he will reach his men's campsite first before he gets to the palace.

Tonight, he will tear down the kingdom. He will rip the crown and head off his brother. When he sees those children, there will be no more negotiating. Drahzil will fight to the death and take the amulets. Then he will kill Kawaad and anyone else who gets in his way.

He stomps off into the night.

34

IZZI-RA

I storm through the corridors. Neenho must jog to keep up with me.

"Izzi, what are you gonna do?"

"Find Zarhmel, kill him, and then rescue my mother," I say matter-of-factly.

I did not take her hand. I do not want to know what she knows. I need my mother. I need my mother to tell me everything.

I know where we are and what part of the palace we are in. After a few corridors, they all look the same, but the art tells the stories. I see wars on the walls, and I know where I am heading. I smell him.

I run down stone steps and into a narrow hall, pushing open a wooden door that leads outside.

"Izzi, where are we ...?" Neenho pauses.

A deep dirt pit encircles the area. The fighting pit. Surrounding the entire area are the palace guards. The pharaoh stands in the center, flanked by a few of his men. I see Obissi next to him, his arms, shoulders, and chest gleaming with symbols that Neenho is dying to touch.

"Izzi," Neenho starts again.

"Neenho, say my name one more time."

"Welcome home, Izzi-Ra," Father says.

"Good to be home, Father. Is this another unwelcomed party for me?" I taunt.

"More like a home going. Obissi will wrap you nice and tight and send you with deserving gifts."

I smile at him.

Neenho is looking at me as if I am insane and, for once, he is right. I am about to lose my mind.

I step into the pit. Father's men go for their weapons, but he holds up his hand to stop them.

"I did not give you a fair chance last time, my child." He snaps his hand, and Jabari hands him a smaller, gold staff. It is mine. He tosses it at my feet.

"You trust me to not use my light?" I ask with a snort.

"For their sake, yes." Father snaps his fingers again.

The men part and more of them come forward with Chike, Adal-lah, Assim, and Rahada.

Rahada?

She stands calmly, as if she is quite enjoying this.

How did they end up with her?

"Aunt Adallah!" Neenho yells. He tries to run for them, but I snatch his arm. Neenho's light puffs around him, dark and dangerous purple.

"Calm down, Neenho," I whisper.

"I will fight you. No light. Once I kill you, I will kill every single man who stands here, except Obissi."

They all laugh, except Obissi.

I pick up my weapon. The dark red rubies gleam on the hilt. It's pure gold and as heavy as can be.

Neenho pulls me into a little huddle. "Izzi, what are you doing? He will wound you. You may shatter again."

"I have watched this man fight in this arena all my life. Keep open our connection. I will let you know when to attack."

Neenho stands back.

I look at the others, who seem fine. Not hurt. Assim looks like he has been roughed up, but that is expected. He was supposed to be one of them, and he betrayed them. He shows no emotion. Nothing with his eyes. He just watches me, as he has always done.

I feel our kiss lingering on my lips.

Father's men have backed off, so it is just he and I. Finally.

I know what he is going to do, because I saw him do it to Kade. With no warning, he charges at me, weapon raised high, ready to come down on me, but he meets mine, and a loud crack sounds throughout the stadium.

Shock covers his face. He weighs at least eight times my size, yet here I am, holding him off.

I kick his shin, and he back off. We circle each other.

"You taught me, Father."

"I know, *zahara*. Just like you think you know my moves, I know yours."

We grin at one another and, this time, I charge with no notice. Usually, I would hit right, left, up, and then try to disarm, but I hear every thought of his. He is aiming to kill me. His only thought is straight to my chest and side, so I block every attempt to wound me. Our staffs create thundering sounds with every clash. He is sweating. His arms are tiring.

I should be, as well, but I have newfound stamina. His stance is off, and yes, I cut down and get his thigh. His men groan. Rahada claps.

He charges at me full force and head butts me.

"Izzi!" Neenho shouts.

I stagger back, a little blood coming from my nose. I let it drip and hit my lip. I like the odd taste of my blood. I feel my power inside of me growing rapidly, like a lioness ready to rear her ugly head.

"You really hate me, huh?" I ask him.

"Loathe."

That kind of stings.

We charge at one another. Sticks clanking, he tries hitting me with his free hand but misses every time. I kick him repeatedly in his shins. This may seem crazy to the onlookers, but there is nothing like bumping your shin into an object repeatedly. It hurts, and it is annoying him, and I like doing it.

When I go to kick him again, he trips me. I drop my weapon, and he kicks me hard in my side. He brings his weapon down repeatedly, and I roll away, dodging each attempt he tries to penetrate. I get a good kick to his shin again then scramble for my weapon. I grab it and, without waiting, turn around quickly and put all my force into it. The sharp tip on the end goes in. My father drops his weapon as we both fall to our knees.

I shove further into his side, hearing the flesh splinter inside him. Blood pours like a small fountain from his mouth, his eyes bulging red.

I ignore the crowd as I pull my weapon out and let it fall.

He slouches there, holding his wound.

I ignite one hand in gold light.

"Do it. My men will kill as many of you and the slaves as possible," he manages to say.

"You are evil, Zarhmel," I tell him.

He manages a laugh. "You knew I was the day I had those slave girls tortured and murdered. The ones you gave your clothes to. I let the guards whip them before they starved them for days then tossed them into a lowly stream of water not connected to the Nile."

I say nothing, but he can tell he has hit a nerve. I have never gotten over that. It was my fault. I …

I take my light and place it near his wound.

"Izzi! What are you doing?" Neenho yells.

I do not heal him, but I slow the blood and the pain.

He looks at me, alarmed. He is weak and can barely move, but he is conscious and will not black out.

"Why did you do that?" he chokes out.

"You are not my father, but I know I have your evil in me. I want you to feel what I felt that day. I need you to feel it."

That lioness that reared her head at the taste of my blood is coming out, and I will not stop it. My power fully takes over.

"Izzi," I hear Neenho's whine as a wind begins to blow around me.

I form a ball of gold light in my hands. I see everyone watching in anticipation. I let it fly toward my captured people. They better duck, or they will be seriously injured. Assim elbows the one who holds him. Adallah sends white light every which way. Her and Chike start fighting the guards. Rahada is on her knees, praying. *Odd girl.*

Neenho is on his *clou*, flying around and knocking weapons out of hands and knocking men down.

I look down at my father, who looks up at me. Bloody teeth show through his smile.

"Smack my men around." He laughs.

My white dress flutters around me from the wind. My hair blows around my face as I feel something in the pit of me that needs to be released. The lioness.

35

NEENHOKANO

I try to keep Adallah and Chike's way clear so they can run for it. Assim is in combat with several men. Not sure if he will make it.

I throw a ball of purple light his way to help him out. Then I snatch as many weapons away as I can and throw them to a far end of the pit. The men are scrambling to get out the pit, whereas some are advancing toward Izzi. The priest stands in the shadows, just watching.

Izzi. She stands in the center. Her eyes closed, her dress flowing around her, her hair in a wild mess. She looks exactly like Kawaad. When she opens her eyes, she locks eyes with me. The veins in her neck are protruding, a grin on her face ...

Izzi, I say in her mind.

She slams the connection closed as she turns toward the men and charges at them. They charge at her. They are piled around her. I can't see anything, and then I hear yells and shouts. Blood is seeping from under the pile, soaking into the dirt.

Izzi is ripping the men apart with her bare hands. She throws a whip around her. It's not disarming, but slicing through them. It's a bloodbath!

Adallah and Chike watch in horror. I see Rahada on her knees, praying? She is so weird.

I turn back to Izzi as she connects with a beam of light before it hits the ground. She reappears on the stands. I watch as Izzi goes through the crowd, killing every man she meets.

One of the pharaoh's men makes it over to help him.

"No, Jabari!" Izzi screams. She jumps from the top level and connects with a beam of light, coming out of the light and at the two men. She smacks the pharaoh and advances on the man. The man, Jabari, drops to his knees and begins praying.

There is a crack of lightning, and then beams of light form near him. Out steps Wadjet, Nekhbet, and Montu, protectors of the pharaoh.

Chike and Adallah make it to the pit as I jump off my *clou* and land next to Izzi.

"I never worshipped any of you," Izzi says before she screams and a blast of gold light hits them all.

They recover and throw light at her. Montu takes flight, and I guess I have no choice. *What is Izzi doing?*

"I worshipped you," I tell the extremely enormous bird god.

He stares at me curiously. He looks so amazing as he tosses a reddish-gold ball of light my way, and I duck just as it's met by several colorful gold ones. Above me is Meretseger and Sekret.

"Montu, enough!" Meretseger's voice booms around us. She claps her hands, and a shimmering, greenish-gold ball catches his wings in a glorious green fire.

Sekret whips her tail and knocks him out the air.

"Neenho, what happened, my boy?" Meretseger asks.

"It's Izzi. She's slaughtering everyone. How did you know to come?"

"Rahada is my earthly eyes and ears. When she prays, I get them fast. Same as that guard there. He is tethered to Montu for some reason. We must get Izzi to stop."

Izzi is sending blast after blast at the goddesses.

Meretseger lands and throws a ball of light at Izzi and the

goddesses she fights. Izzi puts a hand up to halt the light thrown at her. The sister goddesses go to Montu, and they are engulfed in a beam of light and disappear.

Izzi stands away from us, breathing heavily. I see the battle raging inside of her. The hems of her gown are soaked in the blood of the men whom she just sent to the Underworld.

"I could force your light back at you, and it will wound you," Izzi says, looking at the greenish-gold ball of light with curiosity. Then it dissolves.

"Izzi-Ra, please, let me help you." Meretseger steps forward.

Izzi steps backward. A beam of gold light is forming. Before it hits the ground, though, Izzi jumps in the air, connects with it, and is swept away. Not wanting to lose her, I whistle, and my *clou* comes. I jump right on.

I see gold speckles in the air and follow it. It goes around the east end of the palace. I follow the gold specks and spot Izzi. She stands on a staircase that leads into the Nile that passes through the grounds. She dives in and swims across to the other end. Strange girl. She could have just flown over.

She emerges from the water and runs through the grassy field and through some golden gates.

I land and stand at the gates. I've been here before. I know it. I feel it. I know when I go inside, I won't come out the same.

A sweet, honey smell fills my senses and makes me feel warm and at home. I feel lots of love here. The past few days and hours no longer matter. I go inside.

I reach a clearing where lots of beautiful flowers litter the grounds. An archway leads to a glamorous tree.

Recognition hits me. This looks exactly like the underground garden on Murku. Just like Izzi had said, it looked like her mother's place. And there, under the tree, is the queen. She sits there without a care in the world. She is not even alarmed at the sight of us, at how murderous Izzi looks, and is.

The drumming starts. It's loud and intense, going on for several seconds. The amulets around Izzi burn intensely, and then their light dies down and the drumming becomes a hum.

"Mother," Izzi whispers.

The queen watches Izzi, her breathing steady. She is filled with no worries. How can she be like this when there is a war on the other side of the grounds?

"What have I told you, *saat*?"

"A princess is never weak. A female is never weak. She never wavers. She never lets those below her see a fault."

"*Saat*?"

"Not to ever worry about you." Izzi's voice has a quiver to it.

I don't need to try to feel her because the entire air here is all Izzi. It's on the verge of breaking, if that's even possible. I feel like the grass is being sucked into the ground, afraid of what may happen where she stands.

I notice I'm shaking. I feel that aching, that longing I felt back in Nu'el.

She places her hand on Izzi-Ra's shoulder, her red gown flowing behind her. The queen does not look surprised, and neither does Izzi. I guess I'm the only person here freaking out.

"*Saat*," Kawaad whispers to Izzi, "that was the first word I could think of when I held you. A pretty flower was all that came to mind."

Izzi is a dripping wet statue. She makes no movement. I can't even tell if she is even breathing as she keeps her eyes on the queen.

I feel a tug at me, and I lock eyes with the queen. A loud scream in my ears. I can't see anything, but I hear a lot of things. I close my eyes, my hands over my ears, and then I can see it all.

Osiris is in the Underworld. He sits in a black, high-backed chair. He wears only a white wraparound bottom and no top. His arms are wrapped in gold bangles. A gold chest plate with red rings adorns his neck. A statue of Amun-Ra is off to the side.

Next to him stands the jackal-headed god himself, but he is not gray and scary-looking. He is a slender man, with flawless, black marble skin. He has a long, black goatee and wears a tall, black crown with gold threading.

A sekmi soars in. It goes into Osiris.

The other god looks alarmed, but Osiris tells Anubis not to worry. Then Osiris stands at once and whistles. A *clou* forms, and he is off.

A young Nephthila is in her chambers when Osiris appears to her.

"What have you got there, young priestess?" Osiris asks.

Nephthila pulls out the amulet from around her neck. They are together, in one piece. The beetle rests in the center of the ankh's loop, with the beetle's wings wrapped around the eye.

"Those must be destroyed," Osiris tells her.

"I know," Nephthila replies. "I have tried. My inner self has tried. Nephthys, she is now stuck in the Underworld for trying. You have her."

Osiris reaches for them. They burn blazingly, and he quickly pulls his hands away, as if it burned him.

"If you do not get rid of them soon, they will kill you, as it has done her. The power in them is too great for you to bear."

"Without my *Ba*, *Ka*, *Akh*, and shadow together, I cannot possess them."

Osiris appears to be in deep thought before he says, "Together, we will make a pure soul who can harness their power. He will be good, but he cannot live up here. But he can elsewhere. You understand this?"

When she nods, Osiris extends his hand to her. She takes it, and Osiris pulls her into an embrace.

Nephthila lies under the tree. She's in agony. The sky is a faint pink in the east. It's dawn; the sun is about to rise.

Adallah is there, at her side, dabbing her face. Adallah tells her that she will go for help, but the queen insists she stays. Another young girl comes running over. Adiah, identical to Adallah. They bicker and argue about what they should do, but the baby is coming.

"The queen needs help. We have no supplies. No priest to bless the child with a Ka! We must find help," Adallah says.

Adiah looks to the queen and nods in agreement. "Hold on,

Nephi. We will find Obissi." Adiah kisses the queen's forehead, and then the girls take off.

Nephi screams in agony. She spreads her legs wide and takes a deep breath. The sun's rays alight her face as she pushes with all her might. She gasps for air then takes another deep breath. Her scream fills the garden, and then a baby cries. She reaches for what she cannot yet see and pulls the baby to her chest. Joy fills her sweaty, tear-stained face.

"Kano. NeenhoKano." The queen's voice pulls me back.

Although we stand here, I still hear her faint cries and her whispers in my ear. I feel her many kisses on my face.

Izzi has not moved. Did we all just see that?

There is another tug, and I can't see again. I close my eyes and allow myself to be pulled away.

I see the chambers again. Young Nephthila lies in her bed, fast asleep. Osiris leaves her there. He disappears into a beam of light.

Kawaad sneaks into the room. She sees Nephthila fast asleep, but what has her attention is the small mound under the covers. She pulls back the blankets and gasps in shock.

Nephthila's belly is glowing purple and growing before Kawaad's eyes. The amulet lays in three pieces on the stand next to the bed. She snatches them.

Suddenly, Kawaad is running fast through trees. She comes out, and the area turns to desert. She travels all day, it seems. Nothing in sight. She finally stops at a small sand dune.

"I got them," she says to no one. "They are killing me. I know how to harness their power now."

The sand around her begins to stir. A small wind picks up, and the sand around her blows upward, blinding her. When it settles, she is on a mountaintop. She can see the sun setting.

"We must make a child. One who will give it to us. We cannot take it."

She turns around to face the tall, masculine figure in a heavy, black robe. He pulls off the hood, and his locks fall freely around his round, beautiful face. He lets the robe fall.

His eyes are like the setting sun, and Kawaad is mesmerized.

"Set, please, before the sun sets," she cries.

"She will not survive if you take the amulets from her," Set says.

"I do not want it to survive. I want the *He'ka*. With me in power, I can help you overthrow them all. I can help you kill Amun once and for all."

Set looks toward the dying sun as he advances on her.

I hear a scream and waves. I see the Isle of Murku.

The palace that was underwater is above ground. The garden is not enclosed. Kawaad is in the garden. It is not dead like it was when we were there. It is as beautiful as the queen's.

Kawaad is in pain. Blood seeps down her legs, staining her dress. She drops at the base of the tree. The amulets around her neck glow. Hatmehyt is there to help her.

The sun's rays illuminate her face as it sets for the night. She takes a deep breath and pushes. She pushes, screams, and grits her teeth. She takes another deep breath before her scream fills the entire island, and then a baby cries.

She slumps back, breathing heavily. She does not care. She does not want to look. She does not want the baby. Hatmehyt encourages her to hold the baby. She grabs it to quiet it, and then Kawaad is lost.

"*Saat*," she whispers.

The baby glows pure gold.

Kawaad and the baby sleep in the garden.

Osiris is there in an instant. He grabs the sleeping baby girl and takes the amulets.

We swirl into another garden, but this one never seen by man. The sky is light and dark at the same time, the Nile here flows with golden waves. Isis sits on the bank, cross-legged, butterflies above her head. One breaks away and is level at her eyes. Isis snaps open her eyes, and summons her light at once.

Kawaad is on Murku, wreaking havoc. She is fighting the beautiful Murri people. Hatmehyt is there, directing her people to get to safety and clear the waters. Kawaad is furious, throwing a red whip at the water goddess, who meets it with a blue and gold one.

"We allowed you to be here. Why are you harming us?" Hatmehyt pleads.

"Give me my *saat*!" Kawaad screams.

A blast of light surrounds them all. Isis, Shu, and Hathor each have tendrils of their lights around Kawaad. They glide her through the waters and into the underground tomb while she struggles to get free.

"I will kill you all for this. I promise you. If she is hurt, I will kill you all for this. *Saat*!" she cries.

They do not answer her as Isis fashions a sarcophagus. She says an incantation, and the sarcophagus becomes engulfed in red.

"You will never be free again, Kawaad. Only a love for you like none other can free you. No one loves you. You will never hurt anyone again," Isis tells her.

Isis puts the screaming Kawaad into the sarcophagus. Hathor and Shu help push the sarcophagus closed.

"*Saat*! My *saat*! My baby! I want my baby!" Kawaad pounds away.

"You sense it, too, Iziz?" Hathor asks.

"Yes. Osiris was here. But, why?"

I see the island begin to die, and the beautiful Murri people turn to dark creatures.

I am surrounded by the Red Nile now. A marvelous black marble palace is off in the distance. On a hill is Osiris, who has both babies in his hands and the amulets. They are engulfed in light.

Isis and Hathor see him. Isis throws a ball of gold light at the god. The amulet's light goes out.

"Iziz, my love, wait! You do not understand!" Osiris pleads.

Isis and Hathor wound him.

Isis is in a temple. The babies are at her feet in a basket. The boy is fast asleep, but the girl stares wide-eyed at Isis, maybe entranced by the emerald eyes.

Adiah enters the temple. Isis tells her a lot of things, thigs she cannot repeat. She performs a ritual on Adiah then gives the babies to her, and inside the basket are the amulets.

"Take care of them, Adiah. You are now my eyes and earth ears.

Keep these amulets safe and out of tales. No sight of them is to be seen."

Adiah accepts. Unbeknownst to them, Drahzil is listening in a corner.

Adiah is then in combat with many palace men and Drahzil. She is swinging white light everywhere, but she is losing. The baby boy is fast asleep, but the baby girl watches the battle. One of the baby girl's hands is gripping all three amulets. She moves the other around until she grips the sleeping boy's hand. Purple and gold light come from the basket and hit all in the area.

The men fighting begin to transform. Drahzil screams in agony as his skin turns from brown to green, his hands drying up and claws form before his eyes.

Adiah grabs the basket and runs away.

I open my eyes and stagger back. I look everywhere but at Izzi, too scared.

"*Saat* is what Nut called her many children. Precious flowers that she earthed and loved. *Saat* means love of life, and you are my life. Even if you do not believe it now." Kawaad is in Izzi's ear.

"Izzi, Neenho, those thoughts must cease now," the queen says, "because I have, and I do love you both so much. I have your entire life, and your life after this life."

I let the tears fall. This is my mother, and I know that smell, and I know that heartbeat, and I know she loves me, too. I want to hug her, but I'm still afraid of Izzi-Ra's reaction right now. Osiris is my ... He is my ... And Izzi ... Her father is ...

If anything else could have broken the silence, it should have been anything else. Instead, the drumming sounds loudly, and Izzi's neck glows.

Kawaad's face lights up with delight. "Ah, yes. The reason we are all here."

The drumming dies down to that humming sound again.

"All your life, she has lied to you. She has told you nothing about her, about me, about him, about who and what we are. Our fight is not with one another, my child."

Izzi finally comes alive, though there is no emotion on her face. "Queen Nephthila is not my mother?"

The queen has a look of sadness on her face. "You are every bit as much mine as she is a part of me."

"*I don't want a riddle!*" Izzi yells. She sends a blast of wind around us so hard that a nearby tree tumbles over.

I don't know why I do it, but I dart over to the queen, who shoves me behind her, a protective arm across me. My thoughts are all over the place. The queen is my mother. I should have grown up in the palace. Izzi-Ra is ... I don't know what she is, and by the look on her face, she doesn't know what or who she is anymore, as well.

"My daughter, do you not see? You are a goddess. Above all. You come from Set. You, boy, are the only earth god. Osiris created you from the only mortal born child of Amun himself. Do you two not see what you are? Together, we are more powerful than Amun-Ra. With the amulets, we can open up the path to the gods' kingdom and rule the many kingdoms above and below."

"Sister, why must you always try to take and not just enjoy life?" The queen, Nephthila, my mother—I don't know what I should call her—asks.

"I want what was taken from me! I want to rule by my god's side as he promised me!" Kawaad yells.

Another blast of wind, and one of the Bastet statues falls over.

I can't help but see how Izzi has Kawaad's temper, while I'm more like the queen.

Scared but calm, I dare a look at Izzi to see if she heard me, but her eyes have never left the queen's.

"It has been here ... the whole time. It is why you get sick every season. With me near, I heal you. I keep it from destroying you," Izzi says.

"Yes," the queen responds.

Izzi turns to face Kawaad. "I remember. I feel every kiss on my face. The sun was setting. You were alone."

"Hey! Me ..."

I cower back as Izzi throws a look at me. I just wanted to share that I felt the kisses, too. Not a good time, I guess.

"If I possess all three amulets and give them to you, I will die. If he has them, he can destroy them. Because that was the purpose of our births? But he will die."

"Let us rule together, *saat*. You feel my love. You know I do not lie. Let us take over together. Take it from her."

Izzi looks over at us, that murderous look in her eyes, in the air around her.

Kawaad smiles.

What is Izzi thinking? She wouldn't try to kill us, would she? Her face says something else.

"Izzi ..." I start.

"Did you and Set ever consider what she would be like, born of two people filled with hatred and malice?" the queen asks.

Izzi's light snakes out of her from all over. She is a burning ball of gold light with tendrils everywhere.

Come on, Izzi, I think to her mind. *Don't do this.*

When She doesn't respond, I ignite with my purple light.

"I was born with hate in mind, but grew up with all the love in the world. You shamed me at Murku. Do not do it again," Izzi says.

Her lights all whip back and snatch Kawaad, who did not anticipate that, and so she is whipped off her feet. Then I throw my light at her and, together, Izzi and I hold her.

"Weak! You are not as powerful as the seed you were sown from. You cannot kill me. What are you going to do? Throw me back to Murku in a sarcophagus?" Kawaad laughs.

I feel my princess. She is distraught. Her heart is heavy. Then she replaces it with anger and kicks me out.

I feel her light around mine, and I feel the anger pulsating through it. It's too much. I can't hold on. My light sucks back into me and recedes.

"You will join Nephthys until I know what to do with you!" Izzi shouts.

I run and hold onto my mother. She holds me tightly, too, as we watch Izzi.

Kawaad's face is twisted in pain as Izzi sends more hot tendrils around her. Kawaad gets a hand free and sends a red tendril at Izzi, lashing her hard across the face. Izzi screams in anger as she sends more power at Kawaad. She has her in a tight grip. They both scream.

"*Saat*, no!"

There is a burst of blinding light. My mother and I look away.

All is quiet. I hear the Nile in the distance, flowing. Then Izzi's heavy gasps. She is on her knees, looking at a burned spot on the ground. A single piece of red silk lays there.

I make to walk over to her, but my mother grabs my arm.

My mother. She is my mother, and I love her.

She goes to Izzi. I follow but keep my distance.

36

IZZI-RA

I do not want her to touch me, and she knows it. She kneels next to me as I look at the space where I just destroyed my mother. Nephidema is my mother. The evilest god is my father.

Neenho was born of Osiris. No wonder Isis seems to melt when she sees Neenho. I wondered why, all the places we went, they called him a king. He is. The Prince of the Underworld. Earth god.

My eyes burn, my heart is gone, and my power silently fuels me, but not in a good way.

"She will be back. He will help her get back," she says.

"I know."

I do not even know what to say. I do not even know how to address her. Your Majesty?

I hear the drumming.

Neenho is there, kneeling next to her. We both stare at her chest, where her heart drums away.

"You must take it out," she whispers. "It belongs to the princess of Amun-Ra."

"We will find another way," Neenho says. "If we take it, you will die."

I finally look at Neenho. My Neenho. The boy who just wanted to run through trees. The boy who an entire village thought was nothing is their god.

"I knew. I knew the whole time. When we bumped into each other, you smelled like her. You look like her. You calm me like her," I tell him.

"You are still my daughter, *saat*—"

"Stop," I cut her off. I do not want to hear it. My life is a lie, which I always knew.

"You are very stubborn. I will let you have your space while I am away," she says.

Neenho looks confused, as always. "Away? Away where? You just came into my life. We are not taking it out!"

She caresses Neenho's face—a move I know all too well—calming him, slowing his growing emotions.

"I will make this right, Izzi-Ra. I will make this right for you. I promise," she says.

I want to hug her. I want to curl into her lap like I have done so many times in my life. But she is not my mother anymore.

Her eyes glaze over with tears, and she lets them fall freely.

Neenho looks at me angrily. "You're not taking it out, Izzi," he says with authority.

She turns to him and smiles through her tears. "She is not going to take it out. You are, my son."

Neenho looks disturbed. He shakes his head hard, his locks slapping his face, as they often do.

"I made you because of these. It will kill me permanently. You must take it out. Then help me collect my elements to be whole again. The only person who loves Nephidema could free her, and Izzi did. You must free me. Only someone with the truest of love for me can remove it. It hurts, Kano."

The drumming sounds loudly. The amulets around my neck glow.

Neenho is scared. His fear fills the air. He never had a mother, and he just got one, and now he must take her life force away. I wish Adallah was here to comfort him. I wish she were here for both of us.

Mother lies between us, her arms at her sides. This is how Kawaad looked when we opened the sarcophagus. Neenho on one side, me on the other, looking down and wondering who she was.

She looks from both of us, her tears falling from her eyes and behind her ears.

Neenho wipes away her tears, sniffling himself.

"Mother," I whimper.

"Yes, *saat*, I am your mother. I love you. I love you so much. You, too, NeenhoKano. You are my flowers. Look for the blue *kano* flower in my garden."

I let my tears fall, and my heart melt.

She grabs my hand and Neenho's, pulling them together and kissing them. "The fate of Egypt is in your hands. My heart will beat on for you. Take it. We will be reunited."

"I can't. I ... No! There has to be another way. I will call Thoth. He will know." Neenho is beside himself with grief.

I ache for him.

"Shh ..." Mother tells him.

As we cry, I bend down and kiss her head, taking in that scent. That honey and dirt.

"Take it out, Kano. Please, my son."

Neenho and I lock eyes, staring at one another. I let him in, and I go into him. Unseen by her eyes, we swim in a storm of gold and purple light. We see the night we met, the mountain, the Murri people, he and I talking on the cliff on our birthday ... We see her kissing Neenho's baby face countless times, and then her hugging me the night of the wedding.

I look away, breaking the connection.

Neenho ignites one of his hands and allows himself to do the hardest thing he has ever had to do. He punches into her chest, and I slump further into my despair as I listen to her gurgle and gasp for air, her hand tightening around mine, and then ... nothing.

Her delicate, soft hand goes limp.

The amulets around my neck burn brighter as I behold mother, her eyes closed, her last tear escaping.

Dangling over her chest is the ankh, burning purple.

Neenho has his eyes closed, breathing deeply.

I lay her hand down by her side then take off the amulets.

"Neenho, look."

The amulets are erected in the air, each one burning its color radiantly. They circle one another then begin clicking together. The green beetle's wings clasp onto the eye as the beetle rests in the center of the ankh.

The red, green, and purple lights intertwine then turn gold. The light engulfs Mother. Her body is wrapped in gold, and then ... she dissolves. Her imprint in the grass where she just lay all that remains.

The chains of the amulet have connected and become one. They remain floating in the air. I reach out, and they land gently in my hand. The lights die out. The humming and drumming are gone. Forever.

Neenho opens his eyes as he stands. He does not even look at the spot where she was.

"The Princess of Amun-Ra. You were born on Murku. No wonder the place scared you so much," Neenho says, his voice different.

"Excuse me?" I ask.

"Set is Amun's dark side. You were born of Set. Amun made those for his human love, who bore her own child to Amun's dark side. Her daughter became the princess. The amulets stories have been about you this whole time."

"Neenho, you were born of them, too," I point out.

"Prince of the Underworld. Not to mention Pharaoh. I was born to destroy them. And you."

Neenho is standing here, changing before my eyes. His eyes, the twinkle in them has dimmed out. The softness of his voice has hardened.

"We both lost her tonight, Neenho."

"If you say so, Izzi."

I see an argument brewing. I will not get in a screaming match, because he may say something that he will regret later.

She was my mother.

We are facing off, both fuming, when a cloud of fire gets our attention.

We both watch, and we see him, Drahzil, leading his people. He picked the wrong time to come here.

Neenho whistles and is on his *clou* in an instant. I summon my light and think of the north tower.

37

DRAHZIL

Drahzil and his men fly the Venji over Asir and into the palace. The army spreads out, but Drahzil sees exactly who he is after. He hones in on them as the boy floats on his *clou*, and the girl transports to the north tower. Unmistakably, around her neck, is the amulet. Complete.

Ebon hovers near Drahzil.

"Around the west gate, we've spotted foot traffic. Looks like Nubians escaping. Shall I send some men?"

Drahzil keeps his eyes on the children on the tower. He does not want to lose them. He saw the Pakhtians and the Nubians being smuggled out by his sister. He will deal with them all later.

"Drahzil, half the army has been slaughtered. Word is the girl killed them, including Zarhmel," Ebon goes on to tell him.

That gets his attention. *His brother? Dead? At the hands of his own child?* Drahzil has mixed emotions. This makes him Pharaoh again. But Zarhmel has perished.

His hands ball into an involuntary fist, and he feels ... something. His little brother ... He will avenge him.

"We need all men on these two. Nothing elssse is a priority," he tells Ebon.

The snake and the vulture goddesses will show up for him, and so will Montu. They will be able to defeat these two once and for all. He has waited too long, and he will not wait a minute longer.

"Kill them!" Drahzil shouts to the sky.

A wave of fire heads for the north tower and upon the children.

Drahzil sees a flurry of purple and gold light everywhere. He soars higher above it all to watch for the goddesses coming to help the children. Once Isis, or Horus, or whoever shows up, his allies will then appear.

His men fly from the sky in waves. The boy is flying around, throwing massive amounts of purple light at the Venji whose fire is extinguished immediately. His men fall to the ground and do not get back up. Any minute now, the gods will show.

His army is reduced to more than half of what he had. He must go down and do this himself.

Where is Anubis and Montu? Where are the goddesses?

Drahzil dodges a ball of purple light as he dives right for the girl, the amulet gleaming brilliantly against her chest. The only thing he needs. He will rip her head off to get it.

38

NEENHOKANO

I 'm numb. I feel nothing and care for nothing. I throw the hottest balls of purple fire that I can create at these deformed creature men. I hate them. I hate them all! I hate everyone.

I zip around the area. The fire that floated in the sky is being reduced to nothing. Below, Izzi feels the same rage. She throws deadly gold balls and whips all around, screaming her frustrations, making sure they know she will spare no one.

A crack of thunder sounds, and a dark cloud moves in fast. Rain. It starts to rain. The handful of Venji left in the sky, their fire burns out as they dive to the ground. Drahzil's horse is trying to stay alight, but the rain has doused her. They dive toward the tower where Izzi tosses her last victim over the edge.

Drahzil lands, quickly dismounting the horse that scurries away to the other side of the tower. I dive and dismount my *clou* as it dissolves.

"Just us now," I say.

"How it ssstarted. Except Adiah is already dead. You will join her," he spits.

"I am sending you to join your brother," Izzi tells him, throwing a gold ball at him. He dodges it and rushes at us.

With both arms open wide, he tries to slam us, but we both get out the way in time. He releases two red whips, and it meets our lights. We continue to throw more his way, and he blocks them all. His light is so weak; I can feel it in mine.

Why are we entertaining him? I feel his saddened rage, and I even see his life in his light. He overwhelms me with emotions.

I pull my light back and put my hands in the air. The rain has made my locks heavy. I'm done fighting.

"Wait! Wait, Izzi, wait." I hold up my hands between them.

"Get out of my way, Neenho." Izzi looks past me and at him.

"We can kill you. Izzi is playing with you. We can feel your strength in your light. Keep going with just her if you don't believe me." I keep eye contact with him, seeing the battle in his eyes.

"I need those amulets," he snarls.

"For what? To be human again? I can make you human again. Look at your arms," Izzi points out.

Right before mine and his eyes, his flesh goes from that green tinge to golden brown. We both look at her in shock.

"This rain, *I* brought the rain. I can make it do whatever I want!" Izzi raises her arms, and the rain drops freeze in the air. Before our eyes, they turn into white specks and begin to fall. "I am everything. I am the morning sun and the evening stars. If I say night, so it be. If I say die, you will drop dead," Izzi continues.

At those words, Drahzil grabs his neck, unable to breathe.

"Izzi ..." I plead.

She releases her invisible grip on his neck, and his skin flushes back to green, his hand turning back into a claw.

"You will never have these amulets." She advances on him.

He doesn't try to run or do anything. He felt her power. And so do I.

She is glowing a dangerous gold.

In the distance, the statue of the queen is visible. She looks right at us. I feel her calm love wash over me.

"Izzi-Ra, no."

She rounds on me, yelling. "He has been trying to kill us all our lives, and you want to let him live, Neenho?"

"We know the truth now. We have answers. He can't beat us. He can help us. Turn his allegiance." I look beyond to the statue. That is what she would have wanted. That is what she wants.

"We will never know what she wanted because you killed her, Neenho," she throws at me.

We stare at one another, the snow she created piling on her head. From behind her, I can see two red tendrils about to strike. I push her to the side and throw a purple fire ball right at his chest. He is blasted backward and crumples in a heap. He is not dead. I will deal with him later.

We hear a slam then running feet. Assim rounds the corner, followed by Chike and Adallah.

"What has happened?" Chike asks, rushing to Drahzil's side to check his pulse.

"Aunt Adallah!" I run to her and hug her. I need her so much.

She holds me tightly, breathing heavily. Her arms are badly bruised.

Assim goes to Izzi. He reaches for her, but she slaps his hand away.

"I do not want a hug. I do not want your sympathy. I do not want anything!" she yells.

The snow stops falling midair. It's like everything has stopped.

Assim grabs his neck and scratches at it. Adallah and Chike do the same.

"Aunt Adallah?"

One hand on her throat, the other clawing at me.

"Izzi! Stop! You are sucking the air away. They are choking, Izzi!" I scream, but she just stands and watches.

"Izzi! Stop!"

"I am sorry, Neenho," she whispers.

Wind from nowhere picks up. Adallah gasps for air, and so does Assim and Chike.

"Neenho, I cannot—"

"Izzi, we will do this together. We have each other," I plead with her, but I can't reach her anymore. She's distraught, broken. I have never felt this amount of heartache.

"Young male," she whispers.

"Izzi, no!" I yell.

Izzi is shaking her head, mumbling something. The amulets glow on her chest. Izzi looks at the statue in the distance, and then she starts screaming. She screams a high-pitched, groundbreaking scream. The palace even rumbles from her screams. I hear crashing below. In the distance, the queen's statue falls.

Adallah grabs me, and we crouch down as the tower behind us crashes. Chike and Assim rush to our side.

Izzi continues to scream. I want to call my *clou*, but I cannot think. She screams, her gold light beginning to surround us all. I drop to my knees, my eyes watering from the increasing wind. I put my hands over my ears, trying to block her out, but it's all around and inside me. Izzi's scream turns into an echo, and then she bursts into gold pieces.

39

THE GODS

Above the grey clouds, in the clear, starry night sky, past the universe, sits the kingdom. Sekmi fly around the ever-changing structure that sits in half-day and half-night. The structure is in the shape of an ibis.

The sekmi flies into the mouth and through the golden, torchlit corridors. It flies into an indoor natural habitat. Beautiful full fruit trees, plush grass and, around the perimeter, the main Nile that sources the one below. Maat is there, floating cross-legged in the air.

Small birds with human-like faces fly around her. Below her is a lioness and Adallah's cat, Bastet. The small blue birds are speaking. As they fly around the room, whispers come from them. Prayers. Prayers from their worshipers.

Maat opens her eyes, and the lioness below lets out a small roar. Bastet meows.

"Ishiva, Bastet, your people call," Maat tells them.

Bastet meows, and the lioness lets out another small roar.

"The girl is going to be difficult. The boy, we can handle, as you two well know since you have been around him all his life."

Ishiva and Bastet look at one another then back to Maat.

"Thoth has already written what is to come. The only way to

change it is to find the book of Toth and rewrite it. They must never find the book. Now go. Help your people."

Bastet meows loudly as a beam of white light takes her away. Ishiva roars as her white light engulfs her, and then she is gone, too.

Maat continues to stare straight ahead. Her eyes orb over into a grey mist, and then there is fire. Flames flicker inside her eyes.

Below the fiery cloud of the Venji, through mud and into an abyss that leads into the Underworld, flows the Red Nile. A lost army of *Ka* scream in agony as they pass on to their final resting place. No guidance, no proper burial, no journey with the jackal-headed god who is in the Underworld palace.

Wadjet, Anubis, Nekhbet, and Montu are gathered in a circle. They sit with their eyes closed, heads raised to the ceiling. Black birds fly around them with human-like faces as whispers surround them.

"Anpu, what say you to all of this?" Wadjet hisses.

"This game is over. The children won this one. I have no interests in how this end. I am done. Correct, Father?" Anubis looks over his shoulders at the tall, robed figure.

Set drops his robes, flexing his muscles.

Wadjet and Nekhbet are stunned to see him.

"A deal is a deal, son. You bound yourself to my secret. Your word was bond. You are free."

At these words, a small, golden wind surrounds Anubis. When it settles, he is the god depicted in all artwork across Egi. He flexes his muscles and looks over his skin.

Set summons a beam of light. "You all better pick the right side." With those words, he vanishes.

"Now, since that is over, what do you all know about the Book of Thoth?" Anubis asks.

Through the red-flamed, lit corridors and through another part of the Underworld is Isis and Horus.

"Before we free Osiris, we must find Meretseger's daughter. I owe her and must make her whole," Isis tells Horus.

"And then what?" he asks.

"We free my love, and then we find the Book of Thoth."

☙☙☙

Above the Underworld, flowing through the Nile and into the sea, plunged deep below where a human Ka will never reach, is Murku Isle. Inside the temple of Hatmehyt is Meretseger, Sekret, Hathor, and Shu.

"They are gods. More powerful than us," Hathor says.

"They do not know this. What will we do?" Sekret asks the circle.

"We wait. We see what they want to do. They do not seem like they want to dominate us," Hatmehyt tells them.

"You did not see the death in her eyes. She was beyond Sekhmet. My grandchild, she is my blood. I must try to reach her. They are both of me," Meretseger says.

"They wounded me. They almost killed me," Shu mocks. "Who needs a kiss?"

The goddesses frown.

"We wait. Now, what is more important is the Book of Thoth," Hathor says.

☙☙☙

Above the clear, blue waters and past the clouds, into a part of the universe, on his mound, is Ptah. Amun and Thoth are with him as they float nowhere, surrounded by everything that makes the universe what it is.

"I do not have words," Ptah says.

"Neither do I," Thoth adds.

"What a mess," Amun says.

Ptah and Thoth raise eyebrows at Amun.

"Will we save humanity?" Ptah asks.

"What is written cannot be undone. The next two million seasons have been foreseen," Amun adds.

Thoth grunts.

Now the other two gods raise an eyebrow at him.

"True, it is all written ... but it can be changed. It is all written in my book. Safely in my book," Thoth says, bouncing on his toes.

"Good," Amun says.

"Where is this Book of Thoth?" Ptah asks.

Thoth darts his eyes here and there, as if he is lost in thought. "Well... I have no idea," he finally tells them.

The gods stare off into Nun.

40

A MESSAGE FROM NEENHO

I'm not in the mood for this right now. My princess is gone. My mother is... I had to... we just got each other back! I will bring her back. I will find my princess and bring her back. No more secrets surrounding my birth. I know all now. I am Prince of the Underworld. We all know who the Princess of Amun-Ra is. We know who the amulets belonged to and who controls them now. We know who our parents are. Sucks for Izzi though. Don't tell her I said that. Please do actually.

I want to say this nightmare is over, but it's just the beginning. I'm having dreams. Weird dreams. The past is a dangerous place to go, and I am about to be introduced to more of it. Should I tell you what will happen in The Book of Thoth? I am the Pharoah now so...

Quick, while Obissi is not around...

First *asu'te et su fuh naj jupt eh sah* happened right. And then, you know the guys I hate? They ban together with none other than the infamous *Cuh'et, na'ju ye'ey sah eh wu'ey suut no't kah*. And you won't believe this, The Book of Thoth is real! Been right by Izzi her whole life! It sits right *ku'ni eyh gi'en nuk'tah mu'ney et 'tu*. Whole time. And guess who gets it and rewinds time, throwing us all into an alternate reality? *Ju'it tuu sah fuh sak'et et'tuhn.* Sigh. I just want to take long hot palace baths and build my empire.

Well, I think that's enough spoilers for you. I pretty much told you everything. Assim and Kade are soon to arrive. Adallah is probably somewhere in the east wing with that dang cat. Chike and the twins have already arrived. I must go down to the Nile and blow the shell horn. I miss my water goddess. She is coming to Asir. And so are the Kemetian guard.

We are all here, gathered together. No war. No fight. Games are set to start.

My 16th Ahket is tomorrow so, let's see what happens at the celebration.

Oh, you're probably wondering why I haven't mentioned the Gods.

Let me tell you on the next page.

ABOUT THE AUTHOR

Veranice was born in Chicago, IL and raised in Las Vegas, NV. She is the oldest of 5 children. Writing has always been a way to navigate through the world. She started writing short stories about her friends when she was in 6th grade. By 10th grade, she was writing her class-mates creative writing assignments for fun. She holds two degrees in business management, works in the medical field, and has taken many creative writing courses, screenwriting workshops, and traveled abroad taking theater classes. When she is not writing (while listening to N'sync) she is with her two daughters at Disneyland or enjoying the beaches of San Diego, where she now resides. An Egyptian Tale is her debut novel.

Made in the USA
Las Vegas, NV
08 October 2023